CHRONICLES OF SIN:

An Erotic Tale

Act I

Written By: Chari La'Mone & Maritza P. Brown

Editor: Maritza P. Brown
Illustrator: Chari La,Mone

INTRODUCTION

I love sex, wouldn't say I am addicted, but I love it all the same. I have a treasure chest of toys, and a mental rolodex of positions and fantasies that would make a porn star blush. You name it, I have more than likely tried it; at least once, minus gang bangs or trains that's just tacky. Since my breakup with Tyreek, I guess you can say I have been feeling restless and deprived. The dating scene here in the city is like gambling; you spend all fucking night getting fly, catching a cab, and you end up in a spot where the pickings are slim to none. Hell, with the economy jacked up and the price of living sky rocketing, I refuse to waste my good, hard-earned money on possible bad sex.

By the way, my name is Sinclair Hatorri. I am 26 years old, 5"5' in height, athletically built, and I have long, black bone-straight hair that falls right above my firm round ass. My perfectly round supple breasts accentuate my thick, honey-hued thighs, and my slanted hazel brown eyes help identify my Japanese and African American ethnicity. That alone lures men in like a moth to a flame. I am the youngest person to hold the Vice President of AR position at the record label, *Centry Music*. I could date someone else in the business, but I know how artists get down, and since everyone and their mama knew that Tyreek and I were once an item, I would never play myself so they could talk about me. Too many females have had their business secretly spread around after dealing with one of our artists. Whether a break up, or especially after a bad sexual encounter, men around here talk like women. One thing I have learned is if a man will talk about the bad, they will brag on the good, and go psycho over the great. I don't need any drama or on-the-job stalkers. Which brings me back to the dating scene, or, should I say, the club and bar scene. The bars are only good for happy hour, and the clubs are full of the same people every time the doors are opened. Yeah, both places have a variety to choose from, and don't get me wrong, it's not that some of the men aren't good looking, but there's just a certain swag I look for. I need a man who can last more than five minutes, not be intimidated easily, and takes full control. And, since I have yet to find him, I am beginning to think totally out of the box and hit the internet. The one dating avenue I promised myself I would never travel down, but my assistant Samara swears by it, so I just allowed her crazy ass to create my profile. My bestie Rain is going to think I have totally lost my mind but, hey – a girl's got needs, and more importantly, a fire burning that needs to be extinguished. Who, what, where, when and how; well, let's just say are five questions I can't wait to answer.

Scene One

"Sinclair, you ready to roll? I am starving," Samara impatiently asked.

"Just about," Sinclair replied, still typing away on her computer.

She glanced down at the time and realized how late they were running for their weekly lunch with Ever and Rain. Sinclair and Rain were roommates at Howard University and instantly became friends from the moment they met. They met Ever while on a girls' day out shopping spree in a shoe store on 5th Avenue called *Shoeuphoria*. The name captured their eye, but it was Ever's flamboyant attitude and fashion sense that captured their attention – they immediately became fast friends. And Samara, well, she grew on Sinclair after being hired as her assistant at *Centry Music* about a year ago. Samara was rough around the edges with her outrageous weaves, outfits to match, and an around-the-way girl attitude. It took some time to smooth her out, but once Sinclair got to know her she realized just how smart and creative Samara really was, and she took Samara under her wing. To see Samara now, you would never know this was the same girl. She even enrolled at Hunter College with Ever and will begin taking business management courses soon. Sinclair felt like a proud mom watching Samara grow before her eyes.

"Girl, why didn't you come and get me sooner it's almost one o'clock." Sinclair quickly saved her document, reached down to the bottom draw of her desk, pulled out her purse and headed out the door. "Did you call for the car to meet us out front?" Sinclair asked, scrolling through her text messages as they made their way to the elevator.

"It's been out there waiting for about thirty minutes already."

"I just hope Rain and Ever haven't been there all this time waiting. You know how Ever can get when he has to wait too long."

They both laughed knowing Ever is not one with the best patience and has no problems with letting it be known. They exited the elevator and made their way to the black Lincoln town car.

"Driver we're going to our usual Wednesday spot – quickly. We're running late," Sinclair immediately said before the door closed.

"Right away Ms. Hatorri."

******

Across town, Ever stared down at Rain's perfectly manicured toes as she slid her feet into a sleek pair of seven-inch heeled sling backs.

"Girl, your feet look fierce in them," Ever cooed as Rain smiled and stood to her feet.

"You think?" she said while trying to maintain balance before walking over to the floor length mirror.

"Absolutely! And they match perfectly with that dress you bought the other day."

"They do," Rain agreed as she spun around in front of the mirror, making sure she could stay vertical in the heels.

"Take them off and wrap those babies to go," Ever snapped. "Shit, you can wear them tonight for that cutie Geoffrey," he teased with a slick grin.

Rain sat back down in the chair and slipped her feet out of the shoes and placed them back in the box. "I didn't come in here to buy no damn shoes Ever. I came to pick you up so we can meet the girls for lunch, remember?" Rain said, putting her own pumps back on.

"Yes, yes I remember, girl. Let me grab my jacket and clock out. I know you want these shoes though, so I will just put them on your tab," he said, smiling and handing Rain the box. "Take them up to the counter and tell Alisha to put them in a bag for you. I will meet you at the car."

Ever disappeared behind the storefront and Rain followed his instructions. As she stood waiting for Alisha to bag the shoes she didn't need, Rain's cell chimed. She grabbed it out of her *Michael Kors* bag only to find a picture of stiff dick plastered on her iphone screen.

She smiled as she read the text, where are you? We miss you.

Rain pounced her finger tips across the phone keypad and replied, going to lunch with the crew. Miss you too. Will suck that for you later. Her face fell flush as she stared at Geoffrey's nine and half inch dick. Oh, how she loved him and it.

******

Their favorite little deli, *Berg's Kosher House*, was unusually packed, and Rain and Ever had to wait for their usual table.

"They are so lucky that Sinclair and Samara aren't here yet, or they'd have hell to pay," Ever huffed, pouting his large, smooth pink lips.

He hated waiting, especially when it was time to eat. For such a little man, 5'3" and weighing 105lbs wet, one would not believe he eats like a horse. Rain ignored his antics as she usually does and, instead, perused around the crowded deli to see if there was anyone who she knew. After all, this place was definitely one of courthouses' hubs where prosecutors, judges, clerks and attorneys lunched. At the onset she didn't notice anyone right away, but then she felt a presence standing closely behind her and she slightly turned to see who was invading her personal space. And there he was; Dexter Manning, her at work crush. She convinced herself a long time ago that everyone had at least one person at their workplace that they fantasize about – Dexter was hers. Standing six feet tall – easy, with deep sea blue eyes, coiffed strawberry blonde hair, chiseled facial features with a body to match, he reminded her of a taller, more handsome, more intelligent, younger Brad Pitt. Rain figured Dexter had to be her age, give or take a year or two. She never really dipped in vanilla – just that one time in college when she epically failed pledging Delta because one of the hazes was to bed a white boy in Georgetown and she couldn't go through with it. She was quickly dismissed from the line. Back then, she often wondered if she would have told her sorors that she was still a virgin would it had made a difference.

She looked up at him and smiled and he smiled back. Dexter did something to her innards; he stirred them like Geoffrey does.

"Attorney Preston, right?" he asked, not sure of himself.

"Please, call me Rain," she replied as she held her hand out for a formal greeting.

Her panties moistened as his smooth hand clasped onto hers and shook it firmly. Rain could tell his hands never handled hard work, just pens and pencils. A real well-bred white boy. Her smile widened as they released their grasp simultaneously.

"You come here often?" he asked, making small talk to make the wait go by faster.

"Often enough to not have to wait for my damn table," Ever interjected.

"Ever!" Rain spun around. "Excuse him," she giggled, "hunger makes men angry."

"Totally understood," Dexter said as the front door flung open.

"What's going on in here?" Sinclair asked with Samara closely on her heels. "You'd think they were giving pastrami sandwiches away today."

They all laughed in unison, even Dexter and then the hostess approached them and asked them to follow her.

"Perfect timing," Ever quipped as he hugged the girls and trailed behind the hostess.

"Looks like it's time to eat," Rain said, looking into Dexter's dreamy blue eyes. "Have a nice lunch. See you back at the office," she joked. They both knew the courthouse was too big and too busy to ever see anyone on a regular basis. Not to mention, they worked in different departments; she, for the Public Defender's Office; and he, for the State's Attorney's Office. They still have yet to try a case against each other and Rain's been there for two years now.

"I look forward to it," he smiled, showing off his perfect smile with his perfect set of white teeth.

Rain couldn't decipher if his reply was flirtatious or just him being kind, but she was feeling him: Bad.

"Who's that? Damn, he's fine for a white boy. Is someone trying to put some cream in their coffee?" Samara teased while staring Dexter down like he was a piece of prime rib.

"Now that's what you call cheesecake Baby! Eat it," Ever chimed in, high fiving Samara.

After they were all seated, Sinclair's cell interrupted them before they could get started. She looked at the name and instantly started pulsating begin between her legs.

"Samara, can you order a Cuban and a lemonade ice tea for me, please," she asked while answering her Face Time call and excusing herself to the rest room.

"Give me a sec," Sinclair spoke into the screen as she waited for someone to come out of the bathroom. She was glad that the deli only had bathrooms for one person at a time. She tapped her foot anxiously as the petite little Jewish woman brushed passed her as she exited the bathroom. Sinclair rushed in and locked the bathroom door. She knew she was running the risk of someone knocking and interrupting her, but she didn't care. She propped the phone up on the sink so Trevor could get a good view of her.

"Hello handsome," Sinclair cooed.

"Hey sexy, you ready for me?" Trevor asked licking his full lips. The visual of his chiseled chest and neatly twisted shoulder length dreadlocks, mixed with the seductive sexiness in his voice sent her arousal into over drive.

"Aren't I always, Master?"

The sound of her voice calling him Master turned him on. "Good, now take off your panties," Trevor commanded.

Trevor was Sinclair's new weakness with his take charge and control demeanor. He always gave Sinclair the release she was looking for because she enjoyed being told what, how and when to do things. Sinclair slowly stepped backwards as she began to play R. Kelly's *Sex Me* as quietly as she could to avoid bringing any attention to the other deli customers on the other side of the door. She seductively swayed her hips to the hypnotizing rhythm as she turned around with her back facing him then ran her hands up her thighs lifting her skirt. Teasingly, she bent over easing her panties down, giving Trevor a full rear view of her soft wetness.

Trevor's eyes danced as he watched her preform a mini striptease for him. "Now, unbutton your blouse."

Once again Sinclair obliged, licking her ruby red lips and slowly releasing each breast out of her bra.

Trevor stepped back exposing his thick, hard erection.

Sinclair lifted her left breast nipple to her lips and kissed and licked it while staring deeply into Trevor's eyes.

"Now make me cum," Trevor demanded.

Sinclair repositioned the iPhone, turned down the volume and then lifted one leg up on the sink countertop. Trevor let out a loud sigh at the sight of her hair-less honeypot. Sinclair licked her index and middle fingers, making them nice and wet then slowly stroked her clit in a circular motion. Trevor hissed and moaned as Sinclair pumped her fingers in and out of her wetness. She stroked fast and hard as Trevor continued to pleasure himself at the sight of her. Sinclair slid her fingers inside and began bouncing on them imagining they were Trevor's satisfying penis. As Sinclair became wetter, her juices trickled down her thigh and Trevor watched in delight as he stroked himself faster and harder.

"Sin, are you about to cum?" he asked in between his moans.

"Yes, Master its right there," she managed to gasp, feeling pleasure on the horizon.

"Stop!" he demanded.

As hard as it was to do so, she did as she was told and with much anticipation, waited for her next command.

"Now, slowly stroke your clit."

Sinclair once again did as she was told.

"You feel it?" he asked, coming closer to ejaculation.

"Yes, Master, I feel it," she moaned softly trying not to make too much noise in case someone was on the other side of the door.

"Cum with me," he commanded, repeating those words over and over until they came in unison.

Sinclair squealed as quietly as she could as Trevor growled in delight.

"Shit!" Trevor cried out, "You always do this to me," he said, referring to the rush he was now feeling.

"Glad you're pleased, Sir," Sinclair slyly replied while trying to gather her thoughts.

"We still on for Saturday night, right?" Trevor asked, cleaning up his mess.

"Saturday it is," Sinclair replied before blowing Trevor a kiss and gaining her composure.

"Don't be late, and you know what to wear," he stated as a matter of fact and hung up without saying good-bye.

Sinclair's honey hued skin was flushed red with pleasure and pure delight. "Thank you Trevor," she said to the reflection looking back at her in the mirror above the sink as she reapplied her lipstick. She needed that release.

Trevor was just one of several gentleman callers that Sinclair met online since cutting Tyreek off fully and allowing Samara to create a profile for her on a few dating sites; and she liked Trevor best. She wasn't sure if it was his manly good looks or his dominating sexual prowess, but she found herself giving into allowing someone else to have full control and it was becoming alarmingly pleasurable to her. And, although their sexual play was just shy of a couple of months old, Sinclair found herself falling deeper into his dark fantasies, and she likes it.

"Everything alright?" Rain asked noticing the flushed look on Sinclair's face.

"I am fine," Sinclair said, trying to conceal the pleasure of her trip to the bathroom.

"Alright now, I thought we were going to have to call the dogs to come look for you," Ever said, smacking on his sandwich.

"I thought it may have been that damn Tyreek again," Samara spanned in disgust. "You would think after four months he would get the hint," Samara continued taking a sip of her cherry Coke.

"He's still trying to plead his case? Boy, bye! The whole damn world saw that mess. Even Shaggy couldn't get away with "It wasn't me." Okay!" Ever smacked his full lips, making a popping sound.

"He's been sending all kinds of gifts to the office, which by the way, thanks for the tennis bracelet and diamond hoops, girl," Samara said, flashing her new trinkets.

"Now, those are fierce," Ever said, grabbing Samara's arm and examining the sparkle.

"You're more than welcome, and you can keep any other jewelry that comes in too." The anger and frustration spewed from Sinclair's lips.

"If he's sending gifts like that I got dibs on the next piece that comes in Mara," Rain giggled. "Hell, we all need compensation for that public debacle he put *us* through."

"Okay!" Ever chimed in, "Hell, if Wayne would've sent me gifts like this, I just may have forgiven his trifling ass."

Sinclair sat quiet as she fell into a mental trance and the voices of her friends faded into the background.

Sinclair lay across her plush, king size bed, sinking into the pillow top. She reached for her iPad and scrolled through her FaceChat timeline until she stumbled onto a link. The headline read, RAPPER ARSENAL TY BUSTS HIS LOAD IN FREAKY THREESOME!

"BUSTS LOAD! Freaky threesome? This has to be some bullshit. Look at the source; MediaSpill. That's the biggest gossip site for misinformation," she mumbled to herself while clicking on the link. Sinclair sat and watched as nervousness took hold of her stomach. The hotel room was dimly lit and the camera poorly angled, however, the faces and sound were crystal clear. Two woman stood in the center of the room kissing one another while Tyreek looked on.

"You spit fire on that mic, les' see what that mouth can really do, Papi," a Latina girl teased as she sauntered over to the massive bed.

"Yeah Ty, come put in this work Daddy," an ebony girl said, while spreading eagle on the bed for the Spanish girl to taste her forbidden fruit.

Tyreek sat in the big, lazy boy style chair, sipping out of a Hennessey bottle while watching the two women pleasure one another. His eyes hung low as his partially naked body relaxed, seeming to enjoy every man's fantasy unfold before his eyes. The ebony girl sat up as the Latina one unhooked her white bra, exposing the ebony one's huge areolas and hard nipples. The ebony one licked and kissed down the side of the Latina one's neck, palming and rubbing between the Latina one's legs.

"Umm Papi, this feel so good, come join us," the Latina one said, giving him the come hither finger.

The ebony one shifted her eyes, staring him down then continued to go down the Latina one's body, flicking her tongue seductively, beckoning him to join them. Tyreek staggered to his feet, dropping his boxers and exposing his erect, massive penis. He stood there rubbing and stroking his manhood so that it could grow harder. The two women flocked to swallow his goodness and devour him at the same time; one on the dick - one on the nuts. Tyreek tossed his head back, taking another swig of his Hennessey bottle then pushed the Latina's head further down on his girth.

Sinclair's eyes filled with tears as her heart felt as if it were being torn out of her chest. In pure disbelief, her blood ran hot with each tear that escaped her eyes.

"This mothafucka!" she yelled at the top of her lungs. "He's gonna fuck some bum bitches with synthetic hair, saggy titties and busted open pussies. Is he fucking serious right now. I've busted my ass to help him get to where he is and this is the thanks I get. Low budget, fake-ass wanna be 50 Cent! Mothafucka!" Sinclair threw her iPad across the room sending the audio device into the wall.

"Sinclair…Sinclair!" Rain called out, bringing Sinclair back to the present.

"Microwave ass bitches," Sinclair said with anger filling her eyes.

"What the hell," Rain asked as Ever and Samara looked on with puzzled expressions.

"Um, what are microwave ass bitches?" Samara asked.

"Yeah because ah, I have heard'em all, but Baby that is a new one," Ever said, putting his hand on his hip.

"A microwave ass bitch is a bitch you fuck and "bing" you're done with them. They serve no other purpose than to be a release as they are nothing but low class, no couth having hood rats in designer knock offs and plastic hair," Sinclair said ever so eloquently while sipping on her lemonade iced tea.

Samara and Rain sat with blank stares consuming their faces.

"Well, Honey there must be microwave ass niggas too because I gotta few on speed dial. I call them to come warm the fudgsicle here and "bing" be gone!" Ever quipped, breaking the tension and causing everyone to bust out into laughter in unison.

Scene Three

Buzz me in. Ever's iPhone read as it pinged to alert him that he had a message.

He knew it was Wayne. Who the fuck else would be so damn demanding. Not to mention, only his girls and Wayne knew where he lived.

What do you want Wayne? Ever typed.

Stop playing and buzz me in.

Ever knew he'd lose the text war, so he walked over to the intercom system and pressed the buzzer. His stomach turned as his finger released the button and his body tensed up. He hadn't seen his lover of the past two years in over a month. Their break-up was bitter, and Ever tried to avoid him like the plague. But, the more Ever ignored Wayne, the more Wayne became obsessed with him. Ever scooted over to the oversized floor length mirror that sat perfectly in the corner of his loft apartment to make sure he had it together. With hard wood floors throughout, a California king-sized bed positioned almost in the middle of the huge room, a modern sleek kitchen with granite countertops and stainless steel appliances, and a spacious bathroom, Ever felt as though he had arrived. He examined himself in the mirror from head to toe to make sure he looked delicious. He wanted Wayne to see what he was missing and regret every minute of it. His tight jeans hugged his butt just right as he twirled like a princess before the mirror. The hard knock on the door startled him and Ever stopped mid-spin as his heart started to race. His emotions started to unravel as he approached the door to open it.

He was welcomed with a bouquet of roses, his favorite and he started to melt. Ever thanked him and grabbed the flowers from Wayne's hands. Ever moved to the side and allowed Wayne to come in.

Before walking pass him, Wayne leaned over and kissed Ever lightly on the lips. "I've missed you, Baby. I even came by your job today to take you to lunch, but you weren't there," he whispered.

His cologne permeated through Evers nostrils and he hated Wayne for wearing it. *Polo Black,* his favorite.

"I went out with the girls for lunch. What are you doing here, Wayne? You look like you should be at work." Ever tried to ignore the advances and the way Wayne was looking in his police uniform. Ever was a true sucker for men in uniform.

"Actually I just got off a double shift, plus I just told you. I miss you. You don't miss me?" he asked, sitting down on the sofa in the living area of the loft.

"That doesn't matter. What matters is that you wouldn't miss me if you just accepted the truth," Ever said, becoming annoyed. He didn't feel like rehashing the same argument over again.

"I have accepted the truth," Wayne said, defending himself and leaning back on soft cushion. "The plain truth is I am in love with two people, and I don't want to let either one of them go."

"Oh, but you have, hate to remind you. We're done Wayne. I refuse to be your part time fuck buddy. It's not okay," Ever huffed and walked over to the refrigerator to grab a cold beer for Wayne. Wayne always had to have a beer after work. It calmed his nerves after surviving another day.

"You were never my fuck buddy and we will never be over," Wayne said, taking the beer from Ever and putting the bottle to his lips.

Ever watched Wayne take a long swig and started to yearn to have those lips wrapped around his dick. He turned to walk away but Wayne grabbed his hand and pulled him down to sit next to him.

"Why can't we just go back to how we started?" Wayne asked with pleading eyes.

"Because when we started, I didn't love you." Ever stared back at him. "When you walked into my store two years ago to buy her a gift I just thought you were some down low nigga that wanted to get his rocks off. Hell, truth be told, I thought we'd suck and fuck each other a few times and then part ways. You didn't look like the stick around type, and you certainly shouldn't be since you're married with a damn set of twins," Ever said, feeling his anger awakening.

"And, it would be a totally different scenario if she knew about me like I know about her ass."

Wayne shot Ever a glare that told him to shut up about her knowing anything about their relationship. "Look E, you know this shit we got is our thing."

"That doesn't make it right," Ever leaned back and took the beer out of Wayne's hand to take a sip. "And, it's not fair to Toy. She should know the truth about you, about your bi-sexuality. I mean really Wayne, just because her name is Toy doesn't mean you have to treat her like one."

Wayne sat up, put his elbows on his knees and his head in his hands. He hated when Ever called him bi-sexual or gay. "How many times do I have to tell you that I am not bi-sexual, or on the down-low," Wayne tried to convince both Ever and himself.

Fact was, Wayne always secretly found himself attracted to some men, he had a type: They had to show feminine tendencies, but he somehow was able to suppress those thoughts all the way through community college. It wasn't until he was at the police academy where he had a few same sex encounters with his roommate, who like Wayne, struggled with his secret desires. Neither, ever having had intercourse with the same sex, their encounters only consisted of mutual masturbation and oral sex. It wasn't until Wayne laid his eyes on Ever's tight ass and pretty face that he became intrigued on what it would feel like to have anal sex with a man. "You are the only man I have had a relationship with," Wayne confirmed, "and, if this was to ever end, I wouldn't want anyone else. So no, I won't tell Toy about us. And, you knew from the jump that I never would and you told me you were cool with it. Now, you got me all fucked up and want to skip out on a nigga."

"That's because I'm all fucked up Wayne." Ever sat up and put his arm around Wayne's broad shoulders. "Shit, two years ago I didn't know we'd still be here. And, now that we are, I want more and I think you need to come to terms that you'd rather be here."

Wayne lifted his head and looked over at Ever. Ever was right, he would love to spend all of his time with Ever, every waking moment, but being married made it impossible. Almost five years now to his high school sweetheart Toy; and, just a year ago, they gave birth to a beautiful set of twin girls, Kendall and Kennedy. Being raised by devout Christian parents with a father who is a Pastor, Wayne knew divorcing Toy was not an option, nor was coming out. Not to mention, Wayne would never leave his children. He was truly conflicted. He stared into Ever's eyes and silently called him closer.

Ever, hypnotized by his charm, leaned into Wayne and kissed his soft lips and ignored Wayne's neatly shaven mustache and goatee. Their tongues wrestled as they both struggled while seated to disrobe until they both were naked from the waist down.

Both fully erected, their lips never parted and they took each other in their hands and stroked each other's hard-ons. Ever caressed the tip of Wayne's dick with his thumb and index finger causing Wayne to pull back and moan out loud. "Damn, I miss the way you handle my dick."

Ever smiled and kept up his hand-job as he licked and kissed Wayne's neck before sliding down and wrapping his lips around Wayne's pulsating tip. Ever licked the precum from the opening of Wayne's penis as his hand continued to stroke the shaft. "Don't you cum yet Wayne. I want this dick inside of me," Ever managed to say in between licks.

The mere thought of being inside of Ever's warm ass caused Wayne to pull Ever off his stiff dick by Ever's hair and told Ever to get on the bed.

Ever obeyed and slowly walked over to the massive bed with Wayne trailing so closely behind, Ever could feel Wayne's stiffness hitting his butt. Ever leaned over quickly, anxious to feel Wayne's hardness push through his anus, which Wayne did with ease and let out a loud sigh.

"I've been thinking about this ass for weeks now," he confessed as he eased himself in and out of Ever's open cavity.

Ever smiled and moaned at Wayne's confession and his fucking, and allowed himself to become totally relaxed to take all of Wayne in, just the way Wayne liked it. Ever gripped the sheets and planted his knees firmly into the mattress and allowed Wayne to fuck him like this would be the last time because Ever silently prayed it really was – it had to be.

Scene Four

Sinclair slipped into a tight fitting leather thong underwear and bra set. The leather string to the thong rubbed up against the folds of her lips causing both her hips and the Ben-wa balls inside her to twitch back and forth. She had already came on herself three times and she cursed Trevor for making her wear them tonight. She couldn't imagine what he had in store. They only met on Saturdays, and Sinclair had to admit, every Monday she looked forward to the end of the week. This Saturday marked their two month anniversary and Trevor had already warned her that she would be in for a treat. He scared and excited her at the same time and she loved it.

When they first met online on one of the many dating sites Samara had Sinclair posted on, Trevor didn't come off so domineering, and he acted like a true gentleman. So much so, that Sinclair accepted his dinner invitation within a week of Face Timing him. Something inside her told her that he would be able to satisfy her most sensual, darkest cravings just by the way he would smile at her – like he was the devil in disguise. His charm sucked Sinclair right into his freaky web on that very first dinner date: where he seduced her into giving him a hand-job right in the middle of dinner while sitting in a private booth. Sinclair suspected the waiter knew because he kept coming over to the table until Trevor slid him a fifty dollar bill and told him to fuck off for a few minutes. Sinclair couldn't believe what she was doing but at the same time it turned her on like nothing had ever before and she found herself cumming right along with him. The excitement of jacking him off in public and him cumming all over her hand intrigued Sinclair to the point that every day after that she beckoned to Trevor's every call or text.

Tonight was no different, her innards did somersaults as she finished getting dressed. Part of her felt like a kid who skipped school and was about to face her angry dad, and the other part of her felt like a kid who made the honor roll and was going to be able to eat as much chocolate cake as she wanted. Sinclair grabbed her car keys and wallet, and headed for the front door of her brownstone. As she turned the knob, she heard a knock and nearly jumped out of her skin.

"What the fuck! Who is it?" she asked through the door, annoyed.

"It's me, open the fuckin' door!"

Sinclair shook her head back and forth as she grabbed the knob and opened the door. "Look Tyreek, I don't have time for your bullshit tonight. I'm on my way out, so move!" she stammered, trying to push pass him.

He picked her up by the waist as if she was a feather and carried her back into the house and shut the door behind him.

"What the fuck is wrong with you?" he asked putting her down but not releasing his grasp.

"What is wrong with me? You sound crazy right now. It certainly wasn't me caught on camera fucking two bitches," Sinclair said, trying to stand still so the balls inside of her wouldn't move. "Tyreek just leave me alone. It's over! Stop sending me gifts, stop coming by my office, stop sending me flowers, and stop texting me. I've moved on," Sinclair said, feeling relieved. She really was over him. At least at this moment because the only person on her mind was Trevor.

Feeling rejected and deflated, Tyreek picked Sinclair back up so that they looked each other eye to eye.

"I swear Baby, if I could take back that night, I swear I would. You know how weed and fuckin' with that Hennessey get a nigga. I don't even remember that shit, I swear on my kids. Baby, please don't do this. You my bitch! You been holdin' a nigga down since day one. You can't let some chickens destroy what we've built," Tyreek pleaded and carried her over to the couch. "I love you, girl. You know these fuckin' four months have been torture for a nigga, so stop playin'." He placed his lips over hers before she could speak and devoured her mouth with his.

The passion in his kiss caused Sinclair to melt in his arms and she responded by grabbing the back of his neck with keys and wallet still in hand, giving in to his kiss. "Let me have you," he whispered in her ear as they came up for air.

Sinclair wanted to give in. Hell, she loved Tyreek, but she was done with his lying, cheating ass. Not to mention, she was just starting to have fun. "I can't do this Tyreek. I really have to go. Put me down," she pleaded.

"Not until you agree to go away with me. Just for a few days. You know I gotta go to Jamaica in a few weeks to shoot this video. Come with me."

"Nuh-uh," Sinclair said and tried to escape his embrace. "Put me down!"

"Say you will come with me and I promise I will put you down and not bother you until we board the private jet in a few weeks," he said with a wide grin on his face.

They both knew she'd concede to his demand. As Vice President of A.R., it would be expected of her to want to see what her artist was doing.

"Okay, okay. But I'm not coming alone. My girls are coming, even Ever; to keep me away from your ass. Now put me down! I really am late," she said, playfully slapping his muscular biceps as he released her.

Scene Five

"You're late." The voice startled Sinclair as she entered his front door that was slightly left ajar; she assumed for her and stepped into the foyer.

"There was traffic on the FDR," Sinclair said into the air.

The lights were dim and she could hardly see as she made her way into Trevor's living room, where she found him standing in front of his floor length window that looked out onto a private man-made lake. Only in places like Scarsdale do you find houses with backyards like this. Sinclair loved it here.

"Somehow I don't believe it was the traffic that made you late," Trevor said with his back still facing her.

Sinclair stood still as a surge of guilt invaded her body. She didn't know why because she and Trevor were not exclusive. Hell, they didn't even know each other's full government names, or what each other did for a living, or if either were really single. Yet, she could feel his control enveloping her as she stepped toward him.

"Crawl to me." His voice was calm but demanding.

Sinclair stopped in her tracks, stunned at what she just heard. "Huh?"

"You heard me. Crawl! But first, take off your clothes," he demanded.

Sinclair maneuvered out of her tight skirt and blouse, and slowly got down on her knees. Once on all fours and feeling both ashamed and aroused, she crawled over to Trevor until she was facing and looking up at him.

"So, why are you late?" he asked, trying to stay angry as he admired her round ass engulfing her leather thong.

She could see the anger in his eyes and decided to tell the truth. "I was literally walking out of the door when I found my ex standing on my porch and he bum-rushed me," she said, trying to be still so the Ben-wa balls would stop making her feel so good.

"I see. You were with your ex. Did you fuck him?"

"What?" The question caught Sinclair off guard.

"Late and hard of hearing tonight, are we? Did-you-fuck-him?" he asked again, slowly.

"No, I didn't fuck him."

"No, you didn't fuck him, what?"

"No, I didn't fuck him, Master."

"But you kissed him," he said, looking down at her and grabbing her head by her hair. "Didn't you?"

The combination of the balls stirring inside of her and him tugging on her hair created a sensual sensation to travel from the top of her head to the soles of her feet, leaving her mute. She nodded her head yes.

"You kissed him with that mouth. The mouth that was supposed to be kissing this," he said as he unzipped his pants and pulled out his semi erect shaft.

Without having to say another word or do another thing, Sinclair effortlessly slid his dick into her mouth and sucked it gently to apologize.

Trevor hissed as the warmth of her mouth greeted him. He looked down watching his erection disappear deep in her mouth. He reached down grabbing a fist full of Sinclair's hair then pulled her head back causing his dick to bounce off her chin as it escaped her oral grip on him.

"Surely you couldn't have thought I was going to let you off that easy now do you, Sin?" Trevor snapped, looking down at Sinclair still on all fours. Trevor stroked his delicious tool as he reached on top of the fireplace mantel.

"Close your eyes," he said, looking over his shoulder and hiding what was in his hands.

Sinclair closed them as her mind raced with curiosity as to what the surprise could be.

Trevor seized the moment by clamping a studded collar and leash around her neck.

Sinclair's eyes popped open as she reached up to feel the leather and metal studs of the collar. Sinclair began to speak but before a word could escape her lips she was quickly told to hush.

Trevor grabbed the end of the leash and guided a crawling Sinclair down the dimly lit hallway to a bedroom with a red light illuminating the area.

"Stay right there," Trevor commanded, walking over to the platform bed in the center of the room. Sinclair sat in the doorway, trying to keep her composure as best she could. Her legs trembled as her juices slowly trickled down her thighs. The clicking sound grabbed her attention distracting her from her inner battle. Trevor returned to Sinclair tugging on the leash so that she could stand to her feet.

"Sin, I had something else in mind for you, but seeing how you think it's okay to have me waiting, I have something that will ensure you never make that mistake again," Trevor said, staring Sinclair in her eyes.

The authority in his voice was so commanding, Sinclair coward to him, "I am sorry Master, I - ."

Before she could finish her sentence Trevor pulled her head back and slid his tongue in her mouth. He walked her backwards towards the bed, tongue still intertwined with hers. As she reached the foot of the bed, Trevor pulled away and pushed her onto the bed. Trevor slowly crawled over her, guiding her beneath him to the headboard, then grabbed her right wrist and handcuffed it to the bed. Once both her hands were secured at each end of the bed posts, he stood up to finish disrobing. Sinclair, watched him as his shirt and pants fell to the floor to reveal his masterpiece of a body. Shackled, riding the waves of ecstasy rippling through her body, Sinclair eagerly anticipated his next move.

Trevor locked eyes with her while stroking his hardness then climb back onto the bed to mount her face.

"Oh shit! Damn, Sin, your mouth and throat are truly a blessing," Trevor exclaimed pumping his tool in and out of her mouth with precision.

Muffled moans escaped her mouth as Trevor reached back to massage her clit.

"Take me deeper down your throat," Trevor commanded.

Sinclair opened her passage as wide as she could, allowing Trevor deeper access. He slid his fingers in and out of her, playing with the Ben-Wa balls, sending her beyond ecstasy before pulling them out of her wetness. Sinclair's body shook uncontrollably as she released all over his hand, coating it with her sweet nectar.

Trevor un-cuffed her hands. "Turn around and put your ass in the air," he demanded, releasing her from her present position.

She did as she was told as Trevor reached down in his night stand drawer to retrieve a pair of nipple clamps.

"Full of surprises tonight, I see," Sinclair said, breaking character.

"Did I say you could speak?" an under tone of anger laced his speech, letting Sinclair know he was still upset over her tardiness and the reason for it.

"I am sorry Master," Sin seductively apologized with her back facing Trevor.

He kissed and gently bit the side of her neck while pinching Sinclair's nipples making sure they were fully erect. Sin hissed in delight as the cold clamps were made secure. Trevor pushed her down on the bed, gripping her hips then pushed his massive tool deep inside her warm wetness. Usually his every touch was sensual but tonight he overflowed with aggression and Sinclair loved the mixture of guilt and pleasure she was feeling. Trevor pounded her with steady long strokes causing her ass to ripple as he pulled back to admire her. Trevor loved the way Sin handled his dick and became even more aroused by the way she was taking her punishment. He grabbed a fist full of her hair, bringing her up on her knees then grabbed the chain connecting her breasts gently pulling on them.

Sinclair moaned and screamed from the pleasure and pain.

"Are you going to be late again," Trevor growled in her ear.

"No Master, I promise I won't ever keep you waiting again!" Sinclair cried out, feeling herself about to explode with pleasure.

"Don't ever put those lips, those sexy ass lips on another man unless I tell you to. You understand me Sin?"

"Yes Master, I promise."

"Give me what is mine!" Trevor growled, feeling his orgasm on the horizon.

Sinclair worked her hips to match his movement, harder and faster until they came together, and Trevor collapsed on top of her.

Scene Six

The hot, humid night created a stickiness in the air that had Samara cursing at the moon as she sat in her kitchen chair in front of the wide open window with her feet dangling out of it. *Why didn't I just break down and buy that damn A/C,* she thought as she tugged at her wife-beater that was becoming damper by the minute. Samara looked over at her helmet on the table by her front door. "The better question is, why am I sitting here in this sweltering apartment in the first place?" she said aloud.

What better way to cool off than to jump on her Ducati and take a ride. She jumped up from the chair and threw on a pair of black booty cutters, a new, dry wife beater tank top, knee high biker boots, pulled her hair into a ponytail, and was off. The night air felt good on her moist skin and she instantly felt a relief. This would be her last ride of the summer before fall semester classes begun. Samara always enjoyed jumping on her bike and clearing her mind. The empowerment of controlling a man's piece of machinery between her legs and the adrenaline rush it gave her was the next best thing to having an orgasm.

As she zoned out, racing down the road it began to drizzle; at first, she thought about heading back home but decided to keep riding. She was stopped at a light when the sound of Silk's *Lose Control* was blaring out of the drop top BMW next to her caught her attention. She looked over and the gentlemen behind the wheel had his eyes glued to her ass. Any other time she would have ignored him because she could tell by his wire-framed glasses, clean shaven boyish face, and nerdy smile, and fair skin that he certainly was not her type; she fawned over the rough neck, thug, dark chocolate types. But the combination of the steamy night, it being her last hoorah on her bike before storing it for the winter, and the heat brewing in between her legs that needed some cooling off, she felt like he'd do.

"Nice bike," he said, turning his music down.

"Nice car. You ever ride a piece of work like this before?" Samara flirted, lifting the mask on her helmet.

"I have, but nothing as nice as that," he said through a set of perfect teeth, staring back at her ass.

Samara felt the steam between her legs turn to fire as her alter ego, Sasha began to take over.

"Wanna ride?" Samara heard herself asking, and not referring to the bike.

He looked in her eyes to make sure she was serious and then looked back at her ass. "Wouldn't mind if I do."

She told him to meet her in the park two miles up the road. The light turned green, and she took off. They playfully raced up the road until they reached the park. Sasha arrived first; she hopped off her bike and rested it on the kickstand. Sasha was leaning on her bike, helmet secured on the back when he pulled in and parked beside her.

"About time, for a beamer it sure moves on the slow side," she teased.

"I was just enjoying the view," he said, turning his car off.

"I love that song you were playing by Silk. Can you put that back on and hit repeat?" she asked, stepping closer to the car.

He did and just as he was shutting his car door to turn to face her, Sasha pushed him up against the wet car and began kissing him. The kiss was soft and gentle as their tongues massaged each other. She felt her pussy swell, getting wet. She lowered her hands to his dick, which was already semi hard, and rubbed it through his sweats; he moaned to her touch. Sasha gently bit his bottom lip then slowly worked her way down his neck, over his chest, and past his rock hard abs until she reached her goal. She slid his sweats and boxers down to his knees then placed his hardness in her hands; it was just the way she liked it, long, thick, and slightly curved to the right. She took the head in her mouth tasting his sweet pre-cum. She worked him in her mouth, short and quick at first, then slow and long, while gently squeezing his balls. She could feel him twitching as he started to throb on her tongue. She sucked hard until his hot stickiness coated her throat.

She swallowed, stood up and pulled her shorts completely off. He picked her up, sat her down on the wet, hot hood of his car and placed her legs around his shoulders. Her pussy lips to his lips, he began to devour every inch of her as the misty rain covered their half-naked bodies. His tongue felt so good, sliding around her throbbing clit. He started sucking on it gently, just the way Sasha liked it. She moaned and relaxed into the moment, and soon after, she came hard and long. Her pussy contracted, jumping uncontrollably as her juices covered his mouth and chin. He slid her off the hood of the car and she motioned for him to follow her. At that moment, rain started falling harder as thunder crackled in the distance. She bent over her bike and he entered her from behind; filling her to capacity. The music was still playing in the background, Sasha gripped the side of her seat, pushing her ass back hard to the beat, demanding he pound her harder. His balls slapped against her ass as she slid her hand down in between her legs and started gently rubbing his balls. He moaned wildly and grunted as he pulled out and released his hot shot all over her ass.

After a few moments, Samara quickly composed herself, suppressing her sex addicted, promiscuous alter-ego back into her subconscious. She picked up her shorts, slid back into them and gently kissed him on the lips before hopping back onto her bike and saying, "Thanks for the ride."

"Can I call you sometime?" he tried to yell over the roar of her muffler as she sped away, leaving him standing there.

As she rode home in the night rain she smiled, *what a way to end my summer.*

Scene Seven

"Hell yeah, I am coming!" Rain shouted into her cell phone. "Who would pass up an all-expense paid vacation to Jamaica?"

"Okay, good," Sinclair replied. "I will have Samara email you and Ever the itinerary. But, make sure you clear it with that damn square ass fiancée of yours. You know he hates me."

"Geoffrey's not going to care and he doesn't hate you. He's just uptight," Rain teased but she was right. Attorney Geoffrey Frederick Brooks is a forty year old straight laced, Harvard Law Alumni, whose family lived among the wealthy in the charming tree lined back roads of Greenwich, Connecticut. He's the love of Rain's life. Her everything. Having met only two years ago, their relationship took on a life of its own the very first day they laid eyes on each other while representing co-defendants in one of New York's most infamous drug cases. It was never their intention to fall head over heels for one another, but the sexual chemistry between them was undeniable, which eventually led to Geoffrey leaving his wife.

"I can't wait. Let me get off this phone, so I can tell Geoffrey."

"Tell me what?" Geoffrey asked as he entered the kitchen.

Rain spun around to face him as she ended her call. "Sinclair just booked us an all-expense paid trip to Jamaica in a few weeks. One of her artists is shooting a video."

Geoffrey frowned as he slid his reading glasses off his nose. "I'm not so sure I agree with this," he said as he sat down at the kitchen table. "You know your girl can get wild. Hanging around all of those rappers and gangster wannabes. I'm not feeling it."

He hated acting like the jealous boyfriend, but Rain knew his true feelings for Sinclair. He didn't care for her, but he tolerated her because he realized that in order to be with Rain he had to. Not to mention, he felt that Sinclair lived in another world: The entertainment world, where most anything is likely to, and usually does happen and she was surrounded by the same type of people he represented daily: thugs.

Sensing his hesitation, Rain walked over to Geoffrey and sat on his lap. "Babe, come on. You know you don't have to worry about me. I only have eyes for you. Plus, it's a free trip. What better way to end my summer?" She hugged his neck and began to nibble at his ear. She knew all of his weak spots.

Geoffrey wrapped his arms around her waist and allowed himself to relax into her seduction. Geoffrey held onto Rain's waist a little tighter as their mouths met. He closed his eyes and began to reminisce about their passionate night before. The thought of having Rain bent over the bed with a butt plug in her ass while fucking her from behind started turning him on and he shifted Rain to his other knee as his dick swelled.

"I'm going to go with the girls, okay?" Rain whispered as she pulled back from his kiss.

He looked down at his crotch and then back at Rain. He smiled. "If you really want to go with your girls you can, but you have to make it up to me."

"Right now sound good?" she asked, looking down at his bulging crotch.

"Right now sounds real good," he replied and he lifted her as he stood up, and carried her to the bedroom.

Scene Eight

It had been well over three weeks since Ever's last encounter with Wayne and he was missing him - bad. Not answering Wayne's calls or numerous text messages was killing him, but Ever refused to play number two to anyone and had done so long enough. It was time that Wayne admitted who he really was and stop making Ever his dirty little secret.

Dodging Wayne was like taking on another full time job. Each night after closing the store, Ever would leave out the service entrance, hop in a cab and head home. He felt like a fucking fugitive. Once at his building, he would instruct the driver to go into the parking garage and make his exit. He knew Wayne would never come by his job to cause a scene, but he would damn sure do so at his apartment without any reservations. Lately, Ever's new routine had become going inside his apartment as quickly as possible, and lighting candles to guide his way in the darkness. He hoped that if Wayne was lurking, he wouldn't see any lights on and just go home to play happy little husband.

With every light off in his loft, except for the light illuminating his nightstand, Ever laid his Louis Vuitton suitcase on his bed, humming Bob Marley's *Buffalo Soldier* while placing the neatly folded stack of clothes inside of it. *Jamaica ain't ready for me honey*, Ever thought as he sat down taking a long sip of his Merlot. Sinclair arranging this little Jamaica getaway could not have come at a better time. He had just placed his passport in his matching carry-on when a knock at his door interrupted his pre-vacay celebration. Ever got up to answer it when the knocks turned to pounding. Ever's heart dropped, knowing who it had to be. Only one person would be brazen enough to be at his door with drama. Ever tip-toed to the door and peeked through the peephole. Wayne stood there in his uniform with blood shot eyes, looking disheveled and broken like he'd been to hell and back.

"I know you're in there Ever, open up the God damned door," Wayne demanded, pounding on the door.

Ever jumped back and then quickly pushed his body up against the door to brace it in fear of Wayne busting it open.

"Go away Wayne! And stop bangin' on my damn door causin' a scene. You know I don't do messy. Now take your drunk ass home to your family before you wake up my neighbors!"

"Ever! Ever! Look, I am sorry just open the door! Please, I love you! There, I said it in the open for all your nosey ass neighbors to hear. I LOVE YOU EVER!" Wayne yelled, dropping his head as he leaned up against the door. Wayne's life had been a mess without Ever. Now, wallowing in a drunken stupor, he felt as if the better part of him was gone, leaving him no choice but to come face to face with reality.

Ever sat motionless in shock of Wayne's open admittance, debating if he should break down and give Wayne one more chance.

"I said go away Wayne! There's nothing left for us to discuss. So go back to your lie of a life and just leave me alone," Ever's voice cracked as he held back his tears.

"E, please don't do this. I haven't been the same without you. Just open the door so we can talk, I just want to talk to you. I'm not leaving until you talk to me."

Ever took a deep breath then reluctantly opened the door. Wayne stepped in the dimly lit apartment, reeking of booze. He attempted to hug and kiss Ever, but Ever stopped him in his tracks.

Ever flipped on the light and crossed his arms over his chest. "You can't talk if your lips are covering mine," Ever quipped.

"Almost a month again. You can't keep avoiding me like this. Can I get a kiss or even a hug?" Wayne asked with desperation lacing his speech.

"You have exactly five minutes to say what you have to say Wayne and then make your exit stage left."

Wayne sat on the sofa placing his head in his hands, as Ever stood patting his foot fighting his urge to console Wayne.

"Can I get a beer?"

"I don't have any beer for you; besides you smell like you've had enough. Four minutes and counting," Ever snapped.

"Alright, alright. Ever there's a part of me missing without you. I've realized I need you in my life. I am living a lie; I just don't know how to end things at home without hurting her and the kids. I just need -."

"You need what? More time! I know you're not going to sit here in my face and part your lips to say that bullshit to me, AGAIN!" Ever walked over to the door and opened it. "I knew I shouldn't have opened the damn door. That is exactly why I tried to avoid your fraudulent ass. I'm giving you time Wayne. Go ahead and figure it out; you just won't be fucking me while you do. I shouldn't have let your confused ass in here. GET OUT!" Ever demanded, feeling angry and disappointed hearing more of the same shit from Wayne.

"I am not going anywhere until you hear me out and forgive me," Wayne slurred as he staggered to his feet. He fumbled and grabbed the side of the chair to get his balance when he noticed Ever's suitcase.

"I see, you think you're going away, huh," Wayne growled, walking closer to Ever with jealousy smothering his face. "You going away with some nigga?"

"Yes, I am going away; to get away from your ass. And no, not with someone else. So while I am gone you can think about what you intend to do. Now sashay your drunk, tired ass out my house Wayne!" Ever yelled, glad Wayne was jealous but annoyed by his presence at the same time.

"Like I said, I am not going anywhere." Wayne plopped back down on the sofa and folded his arms.

"Oh no? Okay, stay right there." Ever stormed off into the kitchen.

Wayne placed his hands behind his head, thinking he had won.

Ever returned with a large stainless steel meat cleaver. "You're either leaving in one piece or in pieces. Play with it!"

Wayne's eyes bulged out of his head as Ever came towards him, meat cleaver high in hand.

Wayne jumped up from the sofa and made a quick dash for the door. Ever smiled at his exit and slammed the door with such force it shook his windows.

"And, don't bring your ass back here again unless you come to tell me that Toy knows about me!" Ever screamed as tears filled his eyes.

Scene Nine

"Girl! You out did yourself this time!" Rain exclaimed as she entered her spacious suite at the Shady Palms Resort in Negril.

"Glad you approve, Madam," Sinclair joked. "But seriously, all of the credit goes to Samara. That is her job to coordinate these trips and she did a fabulous job," Sinclair concurred as she followed Rain into the well-dressed room that was donned with cherry wood furniture surrounding a cozy looking king-sized bed.

"Speaking of Samara, where is she? And, Ever?" Rain asked, plopping her suitcase on the sofa in the living area of the suite.

"They had to catch a later flight. They had orientation or something like that going on at school. They will be here for dinner. Now freshen up so you can meet me at the video location. Chop-chop, remember this is work for me!" Sinclair snapped, slipping into boss mode.

"Whatever you say boss, but if I get bored I am heading back here to relax by the pool," Rain replied, trotting off to the bathroom. "Cause this is not work for me!"

*****

The warm sand massaged Rain's toes as she walked along the beach towards the video shoot location. She could see the army of people not even a half a mile ahead and she slowed her pace a bit to enjoy the alone time she was having. Her oversized framed sunglasses shielded her eyes from the blazing sun while the sarong loosely wrapped around her waist flowed in the breeze. She couldn't help thinking about her conversation with Geoffrey before leaving that left her wondering what he had up his sleeve.

"Since I have agreed to you going to Jamaica without me, you have to promise me that you will behave yourself," Geoffrey said, covering her neck with soft wet kisses as they showered together.

"Do you really want me to behave myself?" she moaned, feeling her naughty side awakening. Not that she has had many lovers, but Geoffrey was the only man who could make her do

anything he wanted sexually. She wasn't sure if it was his soft, smooth lips and the way he used them, or his thick, ten-inch dick that he also knew how to use extremely well, or the combination of them both; but Rain was hooked.

Aroused by the mere thought of Rain doing unmentionable sex acts while he watched caused Geoffrey's dick to harden against Rain's tight, wet naked body. "Believe me Baby, there are times when I would love to have you misbehave for me," he growled in her ear.

Rain pulled back from his embrace as the beads of water pounced on their naked bodies and she looked Geoffrey in his eyes. "Oh yeah, like when?" she asked, licking the water beads from her lips.

"You think you ready for that?" he said calmly, looking down at her. His 6'2' frame hovered over her 5'5" frame like a large umbrella.

"Haven't I been ready for everything you've given me so far?"

Her comeback caused him to think. His mind raced to the first time they noticed each other in the courtroom, to them fucking in the law library in the courthouse, to her sucking his dick on numerous occasions in his company's parking garage, to him introducing her to an array of sex toys, to them even sleeping together in his marital bed before his divorce. "Yes, Baby, you have done everything I've asked of you thus far, but I need more, especially now that you are going to be my wife," he whispered as he took her hand and placed it on his growing manhood. "I want you to go have fun with your girls, but when you get back you have to promise to have my kind of fun with me." He kissed her deeply before she could say a word.

Rain returned the kiss while stroking him into full erection, so that he could take full control of her body. "Okay, I promise."

"Hey! Here comes my girl now!" Sinclair shouted as Rain approached the group.

"Hi everyone." Rain waved and spanned the crowd. She noticed Tyreek immediately and winced.

"You didn't tell me he was the artist making the video," she said between gritted teeth into Sinclair's ear.

"If I would have told you, you would not have come. Plus, I need you here to help me keep my legs closed around him," she said, smiling. "You all know Rain; Rain this is Donny, Brian, Coco, Sammy, Trell, and you know Tyreek."

"What up Rain," Tyreek said, making sure he was noticed.

"Hi Tyreek. Listen, I know you all are working, so I will just make myself comfortable over there under that tree out of your way," Rain said dryly, a little upset that she had to share her weekend with Tyreek. She wanted so much better for her best friend, but she also knew what it felt like to love who you love. Hell, she never thought she'd fall in love with a married man over ten years her senior. So, Sinclair being wrapped up in Tyreek's gangsta, thug lovin', cheating ass is totally understandable.

Rain sat under the palm tree and watched Tyreek do what he does best: perform. She also watched her best friend gaze at him loving and helplessly, and realized that it was going to be hard as hell to keep the two of them apart this weekend. "Samara and Ever better get here quick to help me with that mess," Rain said aloud.

"Excuse me?" She heard a male voice say over her shoulder.

"Huh!" she huffed, startled as she turned around. "Oh, sorry. I didn't see you standing there. I was just talking to myself," she chuckled. "How long have you been standing there?"

"Just walked up," Brian said, admiring her beauty. Rain was just his type: chocolate complexion with well-defined facial features and an athletic body to die for. "Enjoying Jamaica so far?"

"Always," she replied, leaning back and digging her fingers in the sand. "How could one not?"

"I agree," Brian said, sitting down next to her.

Rain looked over for a brief moment and wondered what he was doing but then she remembered: this is vacation, enjoy yourself and loosen up. "So, what do you do Brian? How do you fit into this madness they call entertainment?"

"I'm Reek's road manager. I make sure everything goes smoothly while on the road. A glorified baby-sitter, really," he said in a serious tone and looked over at Rain.

They both burst out into laughter. "You are funny," Rain said, pulling herself together. "But I guess you are right." She looked at his clean shaven face and found him quite attractive. His muscular arms and legs to match made him somewhat desirable too, but she kept her composure. *You're an engaged woman now*, she reminded herself.

They made small talk as the sun fell behind the horizon and the director wrapped up for the day. Brian helped Rain stand to her feet and they walked back over to where everyone else was standing. Rain approached Sinclair as she and Tyreek were in their own world.

"You ready?" Rain said, interrupting their canoodling.

"Yo, can you give us a minute," Tyreek snapped.

Rain ignored him and looked at Sinclair with the 'let's go' eyes.

"Tyreek we gotta get to the airport to pick up Samara and Ever. I will call your room later, okay?" Sinclair asked with pleading eyes.

"Naw, fuck that. We had a deal. Go to the airport, get your girls, and y'all meet us at the Rockhouse for dinner. My treat tonight – everyone's welcome!" Tyreek exclaimed, throwing up his arms.

"Let's go Rain." Sinclair pulled Rain by the arm and started to walk off the beach.

"Eight o'clock Sin! Don't fuck around and have a nigga chasin' your ass all over Jamaica!" Tyreek blurted out as he watched the ladies walk away.

"What was that all about?" Rain asked as they hopped into the awaiting cab.

"It's nothing. You know Tyreek is crazy." Sinclair brushed off the incident and pulled out her cell phone to see yet another missed call from Trevor.

Scene Ten

Ever tapped his foot in frustration while he gazed at the long line ahead of him in Customs. The process of going through Customs had been longer than he expected. Samara had worked his nerves further by talking his damn ear off during the entire flight.

"We need to go Honey. I need a drink asap," Ever snapped as he approached the window. He was loud enough for the short brown skinned agent to frown.

"Enjoy your stay on the island," the agent said in her thick Jamaican accent.

"Thank you, we will," Samara replied, turning to face Ever. "What's the problem you've been really bitchy today. This is supposed to be a vacation away from all that," Samara continued, grabbing her bags and heading out the airport.

"Girl, that fucking Wayne worked my nerves over last night. I guess I am just not in the greatest of moods right now because of that. And, the fact that you were just a chatty Cathy on the damn plane. Rare form for you chica, but I get it with this being your first time coordinating a trip like this," Ever said as he looked over at Samara through his dark Oscar De La Renta glasses. Realizing he hurt her feelings with his nasty tone. Ever wrapped his arm around her shoulders. "Girl, no T, no shade, and you know that," Ever said, smiling at Samara.

"I thought you and Wayne were a done deal."

"We are as long as he keeps lying to his wife and to himself."

"Don't tell me you fucked him Ever please, for the love of God, don't say that, or I will punch you in the head."

"No girl. He came beating on my door like he had a warrant for my arrest, yelling and being messy, talking about "I love you Ever, open the door," so I did. Baby, believe me when I tell you his ass was a hot mess; that's an understatement. The man smelled like he had been rolling around in a brewery," Ever said, shaking his head still in disbelief as they sat down on the bench outside of the small airport to wait for Sinclair and Rain.

"So what happened? What did he want?"

"That negro stood in my face after all of the 'I love yous' and 'my life isn't the same without you' and then asked for more damn time. Can you believe that shit? Chile, scandalous," Ever complained, waving his hand to cool off from the heat that permeated the night air.

"Oh, hell no the fuck he didn't," Samara replied in disbelief.

"Oh, yes the fuck he did. Then when I told his ass to get out he refused, so I made him get out with my meat cleaver, Baby."

Ever and Samara burst into laughter as he imitated Wayne's hundred meter dash to the door.

"Well, Sin and Rain need to get here so we can get you a Red Stripe or something because it sounds like a bitch could use a drink!"

Again, the two shared a whole hearted laugh as Sinclair and Rain pulled up.

Scene Eleven

The cobblestone driveway lined with palm trees led to an open lobby of the lavish resort. Samara opened the window to the cab as soon as she got in and inhaled the island air. She was proud of herself. The resort looked exactly like it did on its website. She knew Sinclair as well as the crew had to be pleased.

"Thanks again for the invite Sin. My suite is all that and a bitch could live in that shower." Ever smiled as he made himself comfortable in the back seat of the cab. "Trust me, it is just what a bitch needs right about now. Shit, a bitch is fresh and clean and ready to get shit started!"

"Glad you are loving it," Sinclair replied, smiling from ear to ear. "But I must say, all the thanks and credit should go to Samara. You did an amazing job arranging this weekend."

"Thanks," Samara beamed. "But, really all thanks should go to Google."

They all laughed as the cab raced through the one lane streets, avoiding the stray dogs that popped out of nowhere every now and then.

"Why don't you explain to Ever why we're really here; I am sure Samara already knows," Rain huffed, her nerves still being worked over by what she saw transpiring with Sinclair and Tyreek.

"What is she talking about?" Ever enquired.

"Ok, well the artist who is shooting the video is Tyreek." A nervous Sinclair confessed, preparing herself for an ear full from Ever.

"TYREEK! Oh, hell no!" Ever yelled, throwing his hands in the air. "Girl, you know this is some messy shit right here." Ever shook his head and thought about his dilemma waiting for him back at home and then said, "But you know what, if you like it, I love it Baby. I got my own smelly shit to clean up back in New York, so just do me a favor the next time his trifling ass do something at three a.m. forget my number! I refuse to try and survive another disaster caused from that tornado called Tyreek!" A somewhat disgusted Ever rudely snapped, turning toward the window.

"It's not like that you guys. Y'all seem to forget he's also my artist. I brought y'all here to help keep me away from him."

"Well, Baby if you want that man and he wants you, ain't nothing Jesus and all the angels in heaven would be able to do to keep you two apart, let alone us. If you were really, really over him you wouldn't need anyone to try and keep you from him, you would have the strength to do it on your own," Ever smacked his lips and pouted, angry at himself for not being able to take his own advice.

"Now that's not fair, Ever. Let's not forget about what you told me about Wayne when we got here," Samara interjected, breaking her silence and coming to Sinclair's aide.

Sinclair and Rain both looked over at Ever. "Do tell," Sinclair said devilishly, happy the attention was being drawn to someone else.

"Yes, please Ever, we'd like to know what you've been hiding." Rain added her two cents.

"Nothing to tell except that Wayne is just like Tyreek; a selfish bastard. They want their cake and want to eat it too. That's why I really can't say anything to you Sin, except that we both have to cut their asses loose, or bitches will go insane!"

They all laughed. Ever always had a way with words.

"I agree. Now, I am not passing judgment you know I am the last one to do that; but you two really need to figure out where your hearts are with these men and move on from there. Sin, you know I can't stand Tyreek's ass and hate him for humiliating you the way he did. And, Ever, you know I really like Wayne but hate that he is a down low nigga, playing his wife. But hey, like E said, if you like it, I love it!" Rain confirmed.

"Honey you said a mouth full, enough to last us the rest of the weekend. So, no more talking about these lames. Let's have some fun!" Ever exclaimed, as he noticed the cab pulling into the Rockhouse parking lot. "Driver, hurry-up, a bitch needs a drank now!"

****

The ambiance of the Rockhouse was casual and inviting, and

the fact that Tyreek paid to have the restaurant shut down so he and his entourage could eat in peace, spoke volumes of how he flowed. He certainly was the man, having his moment of glory. Sinclair looked up at him as he stood to toast his crew.

"I just wanna thank you mofos for always sticking with a brotha. I must say the video is the shit and my lady, Sin could not have picked a better location," he said looking down at her as she sat next to him at the head table.

Feeling awkward, Sinclair spanned the room with a phony smile plastered on her face. She wanted to kill Tyreek. Her girls and Ever sat at a table across from hers, and they all stared at Sinclair like she was crazy.

"Let's give Sin a round of applause for always holdin' a brotha and his crew down," Tyreek shouted as he lifted his glass. "Salute!"

Everyone clapped and raised their glasses to honor Tyreek and Sinclair.

"He's an ass," Ever slurred as Rain and Samar blurted out laughing.

"Be nice," Rain chuckled. "You know Tyreek has to play the part."

"He should have been a damn actor. His ass would have won an Oscar for that worthy performance," Ever said, shaking his head.

"You are in rare form tonight," Samara chimed in. "Maybe you should try to eat something on the full plate in front of you to soak up some of that Jamaican Rum punch."

"Shhh Samara. I'm good! A bitch is on vacation and I am going to enjoy it!" Ever slammed his hand on the table, causing a few people to look over at them.

"Okay! Okay, we get it," Rain said, trying to calm Ever down. "Let's wrap this dinner up and head over to Margaritaville."

"I concur; let's blow this joint," Ever said, standing up and straightening his shirt.

The three of them got up to leave as Sinclair approached them. "Hey, hey wait a minute. Where are you guys going?"

"To party!" Ever snapped. "We can't take no more of that

mess of a man of yours."

"He's not my man, so stop playing," Sinclair said, defending herself. "This is business for me, but you know he is going to try to get in any way he can with me. Ignore him. We still have to have desert, at least stay for that," Sinclair pleaded.

"I want desert, but not the kind you eat," Ever quipped. "Meet us at Margaritaville when you are done with his trifling ass." Ever spun around and headed towards the door, trying to keep his balance.

"Maybe you guys should drop him off at the hotel," Sinclair said with some concern.

"Yo Sinclair! We 'bout to be out. Y'all rollin with us right?" Tyreek spat as he approached the ladies.

"Actually, we are on our way to Margaritaville," Rain replied for Sinclair.

"Cool, cause that's where we're going," Tyreek said, wrapping his muscular arms around Sinclair's waist from behind like they were still a couple.

The uncomfortableness showed all over Sinclair's face as she tried to play it off. "See, ladies we all can go together, but we have to drop Ever off first, he done."

"You ridin' wit' me," Tyreek interjected like he was part of the conversation. "Y'all can ride with Brian. He will take your batty-boy back to the hotel first," Tyreek chuckled.

"Be quiet Tyreek!" Sinclair smacked his arm playfully as she relished in the moment she was having in his arms. She couldn't help it. "Is that okay with you guys?" she found herself asking.

Rain and Samara looked at each and then back at Sinclair like she had lost her mind.

"You sure you want us to leave you?" Rain asked. "You remember what you told me earlier, right?"

"Yup, I do, but it's cool. The bar is not too far from here. I should be okay," Sinclair assured her.

"Fuck you mean?" Tyreek interjected again. "Of course you gonna be okay. You wit' me. Fuck this – we out! Yo, Brian scoop up these two and the one outside and meet us at the bar," Tyreek ordered as he pulled Sinclair by the hand.

Rain and Samara stood there shaking their heads as Brian approached them.

"Ready?" he huffed.

"Yeah, let's go," Samara said, "we can't forget we have the drunken princess outside. He's probably raising hell, knowing these Jamaicans don't care for his kind."

They all laughed as they made their way out of the restaurant.

Scene Twelve

"Why you acting like we didn't set this shit up?" Tyreek asked before lighting his blunt as he and Sinclair made themselves comfortable in the back of the black SUV.

"What are you talking about?" Sinclair asked, playing stupid.

"Don't play with me. I said it was cool to bring your girls but the deal was that we – you and me – was supposed to spend this time together. We gotta make shit right again, Sin." He took a long pull from the blunt and held it in for a few seconds.

Within minutes the back of the SUV was filled with smoke and Sinclair was catching a contact.

"They got the best weed in this muthafucka," Tyreek said to no one in particular as he pulled on the blunt again.

Sinclair inhaled the second hand smoke and allowed it to fill her lungs as the euphoric feeling began to make her feel light. She missed this. She wasn't a weed smoker but she enjoyed the smell of it and Tyreek loved to smoke it. Not to mention, it made her extremely horny.

"So you wit' trying to make this shit work or what?" Tyreek asked, looking over at her now with blood shot eyes.

Sinclair allowed her head to fall back onto the headrest and tried not to think about what he was asking her. Instead, her mind floated to thoughts of Trevor and his kinkiness. She twitched in her seat as she felt herself getting wet. No man ever had the ability to make her feel this way, and now she wasn't so sure she was ready to give it up.

"I don't know Tyreek. I think I still need some time."

"Man, I gave you time Sin," he said, pulling on the last of his blunt. "I can't take it no more, Bae. I need you," he said pulling her closer to him so he could nuzzle her neck. "Don't you miss me like I miss the fuck outta you?"

The feeling of his soft wet tongue against her neck sent a shiver up her spine and she moaned yes.

"Then stop playin' and let a nigga love you," Tyreek said, lifting himself off of the seat so his body hovered over hers.

It was clear that they had forgotten they were being driven around in an SUV but the driver paid them no mind. He was used to Tyreek.

"I miss you girl, and I miss this the most," he said, sliding his hand up her sundress.

He could feel she was wet already and grew more excited. "Damn, you want me."

Sinclair couldn't deny that she missed his touch and was loving the way Tyreek was making her feel, but what she wanted was Trevor. She allowed Tyreek to finger her slowly as he unbuckled his jeans to expose what made her cum many times before.

Sinclair immediately became conflicted: her mind was telling him to stop but her body was telling him to go. Sinclair looked into Tyreek's eyes as her eyes began to well up. She needed him to see the pain his reckless behavior had caused her.

He did. He gently kissed her all over her face as he entered her slowly and released a loud sigh. "I'm so sorry Babe. Please let me make it up to you," he whispered in her ear.

The combination of marijuana and hormones had begun to help Sinclair's body win the internal battle it was having with her mind. She let out a muffled moan as he entered her slowly. As he stroked in and out of her, he repeated that he was sorry each time. Lost in the moment, Sinclair began to claw his back with her manicured fingernails as she pushed Tyreek deeper inside of her.

"I love you Baby, I am so sorry. I will never hurt you again," Tyreek moaned softly in her ear, tugging at her heartstrings.

Sinclair looked up and got lost in Tyreek's eyes remembering why she loved him, but as she was about to respond in her moment of weakness and say she loved him, the images of the videotape flashed before her eyes. She blinked hard trying to make them disappear but that only made the images of him betraying her more vivid in her mind.

"Stop! GET OFF OF ME NOW TYREEK! Driver take me back to the resort," Sinclair snapped, pulling down her sundress and fixing her hair.

"What happened? I thought everything was cool," a puzzled

and upset Tyreek questioned.

Sinclair shook her head fighting back the tears that were building up in her eyes.

"Sin, just let me make this right. Please!"

"You call this making it right? Fucking me in the back of an SUV like *I'm* some fucking groupie? Save this bullshit for them microwave ass bitches that seem to be more your speed," Sinclair bitterly snapped.

Tyreek sat quiet, feeling the sting of her words. In that moment, he decided he would have to either step up his game if he was going to win her back, or let her go completely.

Sinclair sat, wiping the uncontrollable tears streaming from her eyes.

Tyreek looked over at her and gently placed his hand on her shoulder. "Sin, please look at me."

"I don't need to see you in order to hear you." Sinclair's voice cracked.

Tyreek reached around grabbing her chin and turning her face towards him. "I am so sorry I ever hurt you. You were the best thing to ever happen to me," Tyreek said as his heart became heavy. He leaned in and kissed Sinclair softly and passionately just like he use to.

Sinclair felt her heart melt, seeing and feeling the sincerity from Tyreek. She let her guard down and gave into his kiss, allowing it to take her away. The car stopped alerting them they had reached Sinclair's requested destination. She pulled herself away from Tyreek and opened the door to exit the vehicle.

"Sin, don't leave like this," Tyreek begged.

"Goodnight Tyreek," she replied. "Just tell the girls, I got sick," she said as the driver helped her out of the SUV.

Tyreek sat and watched as she disappeared into the lobby of the resort. He had to figure out a way to make things right with her. "Let's ride out," he ordered. "And, take the long way to the club." He was in no party mood now.

Scene Thirteen

The early morning Jamaican sun kissed Rain's chocolate skin causing it to glisten. She sat back in the wicker chair and enjoyed some quiet time on the outdoor dining patio. She is and has always been an early riser. She often justified it by saying that if you're not out of bed by nine o'clock, you've already slept half the day away. She'd been up since sunrise, completed an hour workout, showered, slipped into her beach attire, and marked their chaises at poolside, and it was only eight a.m.

"Good morning ladies," Rain greeted Samara and Sinclair as they approached the table. Rain sipped on her coffee as the ladies sat down on each side of her. The morning breeze flowed through the air as the waiters made their way around the outdoor patio catering to the few guests.

"Morning." Sinclair yawned. "This is the life isn't it?"

"It really is," Samara agreed. "I could live here. You sure you don't want to open up an office down here, maybe add some Reggae artists to our roster."

Sinclair chuckled. "Sounds good, but I don't think so. You'd never get anything done with all of this sun and fun."

"I have to agree," Rain added as she waved to the waiter.

"Now he is a cutie," Samara said, sizing up the waiter as he approached their table.

"What can I get for you lovely ladies tis' mornin'?" the waiter asked with a thick Jamaican accent.

"Just two more cups of coffee, please," Sinclair replied with a grin on her face. "He is a looker," she said as she watched him walk away. "He could be something to play with for next couple of days Samara."

"I think Samara is all set with her playmate for this weekend," Rain interjected.

"What! What is she talking about?" Sinclair asked Samara. "Give me the juice 'cause I am thirsty."

"Rain is just stirring the pot," Samara said, trying to brush off the comment.

"Trust me. The way Brian was all over you on the dance floor last night, you'd think they were a full- fledged couple," Rain confirmed.

"Stop it!" Samara blushed. "Brian and I are cool. He just had a baby not too long ago."

"So," Sinclair added. "But he ain't with that crazy baby mama. Brian always did like you Samara. Maybe you should see where it goes."

"Nuh-uh, I refuse to mix pleasure with business. Plus, he's -."

"He's a down-low brotha," Ever completed her sentence as he pulled out the only empty chair from the table.

"Well, look who finally decided to join us," Rain laughed as she watched Ever slowly take his seat and adjust his sunglasses.

"Please, chile stop yellin'. My head feels like it has a hammer inside of it."

They all burst out into laughter as the waiter sat the coffees down on the table.

"I'll take one of those too, if you don't mind," Ever said to the waiter without taking his eyes off the girls. "Okay, what I miss?"

"You missed a damn great time," Rain said, thinking back to the night before. Margaritaville was packed to the rafters and the locals really showed us a good time. "You too, Sin. What happened to you coming with Tyreek?"

"We can come back to that," Samara interrupted. "Let's get back to Brian being on the down-low. Ever what are you talking about? You think every straight brother is a secret bootie buster," she chuckled.

Sinclair and Rain joined in on the laughter, causing Ever to become annoyed.

"I do not!" Ever defended himself. "I just know a secret lover when I see one. And, Brian is one of those dudes. When he dropped me off last night, during the entire ride he kept looking at me in the rearview mirror. Now, I ask you intelligent, beautiful ladies: if a nigga has two fine bitches and one good looking diva like myself in the car with him, would he keep his eye on the diva if he was really straight?"

The three women sat and pondered the question, realizing that Ever had a valid point. No one could give an answer.

"See, he would fuck me before getting with Samara in a heartbeat. Seriously, no shade Samara," Ever said, looking over at Samara.

Sinclair gave the issue some serious thought and came to the conclusion that Ever could very well be right. Brian has been Tyreek's road manager for years and Sinclair has never seen him in a solid relationship with a woman. Hell, his baby's mama was just another groupie who probably was really trying to get with Tyreek and just ended up settling with Brian. "Let's see," Sinclair blurted out.

"Let's see what?" Rain asked.

"We're here for another couple of days, let's see who Brian would really get with: Ever or Samara. Time to prove, or disprove Ever's theory," Sinclair said with a devilish grin.

"You are so bad," Rain smiled, "but I love it. You two with it?"

Samara thought about it for a minute. She wasn't into playing games, especially with peoples' hearts, but Brian did give her the impression last night that he was interested. Hell, he couldn't keep his hands off of her, and the passionate kiss they shared when he walked her to her suite when the night ended made her more than curious. "I'm game."

"You know a bitch like me loves a challenge. Not to mention that I could use a good stiff dick," Ever said as a matter of fact.

They all joined in the laughter as the waiter sat Ever's coffee down in front of him.

"Let the games begin!" Ever said as he lifted his coffee cup in the air.

Scene Fourteen

As the morning hours passed the ladies and Ever lay poolside to work on their tans. Samara and Ever discussed who would approach Brian first and decided that everyone should go out again to keep things on an open playing field.

"Those two are really serious," Rain said to Sinclair as they flipped through their magazines in an effort to ignore the details of the competition.

"I know right," Sinclair chuckled.

"You started it, Sin," Rain said, shaking her head. "If all hell breaks loose, it will be all your fault!"

"Speaking of the devil," Sinclair said slowly as she watched the birds swoon around Brian and Tyreek as they arrived on the scene.

They all stopped talking and looked at the two men relish in the attention that the young groupies were giving them.

"That's why I can't fuck with him," Sinclair whispered as she slid her shades down on the bridge of her nose to stare at Tyreek gripping some girl's butt and posing for the cameras.

"Trifling ass," she mumbled under her breath, sliding the dark shades back in place with her middle finger.

"Good morning ladies and Gentleman," Brian said cheerfully as he approached them. His attention was immediately drawn to Samara's round ass that was in the air as she lay on her stomach tanning.

"Morning Brian," the ladies chimed while Ever waved, taking a sip of his iced tea.

"And, how are you feeling this morning Ever?" Brian questioned, walking over to Ever's chaise.

As Brian looked back to see where Tyreek was, Ever looked over at Samara with the 'told you so' face.

Samara mouthed back to him, *"It ain't over yet,"* before laying her head back down to finish tanning.

"What up ladies," Tyreek said, strolling up to the group. They all greeted him with a dry hi.

"Ayo, Ma let me holla at you for a second," Tyreek said, extending his hand for Sinclair.

"I'll pass. I am good where I am. You sure you don't want to go finish playing grab ass with them microwave ass bitches you were just over there with?" Sin snapped, staring at him through her dark lenses.

Rain let out a long, loud, disapproving sigh then turned her head in the opposite direction, Samara quickly spun her head around and lifted her sunglasses in anticipation of Tyreek's response.

"Com'on Ma, you know that's a part of the game. I gotta please my fans. They come first," Tyreek said, causing everyone to take a double take at his comeback.

"Well, Baby, open mouth and insert foot. You may as well jump in that water and drown," Ever quipped, taking another sip of his tea.

"Damn Tyreek, you sure know how to fuck shit up," Samara barked with disgust filling her speech.

Rain turned her head and just shook it from side to side.

"Yeah, so get the fuck out my face and continue pleasing your fans. That's what you do best, right? I saw how you make them come first. ASSHOLE!" A tearful Sinclair shouted.

A few guests poolside and in the pool looked over at them.

"My bad; that was the wrong choice of words. Just let a nigga talk to you for a minute," Tyreek pleaded, regretting his statement.

Sinclair sucked her teeth as she stood up from her chaise and then wrapped her white sarong around her waist before she stormed off to her suite.

"Way to go Casanova," Rain said sarcastically as she clapped her hands.

Tyreek turned to follow Sinclair, but Ever grabbed his arm. "Don't you think you've done enough to hurt her? Why don't you just leave well enough alone and move the fuck on," Ever demanded with anger in his eyes.

Tyreek snatched his arm back stepping in Ever's face. "I fucked up I can admit that. Shit, I don't even remember that fuckin' night. If it wasn't for the fuckin' video I wouldn't have believed it myself. Now I gotta carry that shit with me. I love her and I am trying to make things right," Tyreek spat. "Shit, haven't y'all ever fucked up before? Haven't y'all done some shit that you will regret for the rest of your lives? Matter fact, none of y'all can come at me for loving her and wanting to make shit right. *All* of you have skeletons in your closets," Tyreek sneered as he pointed at each of them and stared them in the eye. Tyreek crossed his arms and placed his right hand on his chin as if he were in deep thought before continuing. "Yeah that's right: Ever, you were fucking with that married muthafucka at one point, right? And Rain, your fiancée left his wife for you; and, if I remember correctly, you fucked that nigga in his marital bed. Scandalous! Let's not forget about Samara." Tyreek walked over to Samara's chaise. "Yo ass got caught fucking your last man's roommate on the living room floor of his apartment. So none of y'all can tell me that y'all shit don't stink just like mine," Tyreek said, leaving everyone in silence as he turned to go after Sinclair.

They all sat up in their chaises and looked at each other.

"Now that was a read," Ever chuckled, pulling his shades over his eyes. "And, that damn Sin talks too damn much."

They all laughed.

Scene Fifteen

Sinclair laid across her bed with her face buried in the bed spread, drowning in her tears. She didn't hear Tyreek walk through the unlocked sliding patio door.

He dropped his head in disappointment as he approached the bed. He hated himself for inflicting so much pain on her.

Sinclair felt a presence next to the bed and rolled over expecting it to be the girls and Ever. "What do you want?" she asked dryly when she noticed it was him. She sat up in the bed.

Tyreek knelt beside the bed and took her hand and kissed the back of it gently as sheer red, orange and white curtains blew in the breeze.

Sinclair quickly pulled her hand back before she could allow her body to give in to his touch. "What have I done to you to deserve this? I thought we were happy Tyreek. I thought you loved me."

"I do love you Sinclair; more than you can ever understand. Just give me another chance that's all I am asking. I know I could never get the trust between us back the way it was but I am willing to right my wrong no matter what," Tyreek said gently as he got up to sit on the bed next to her.

Sinclair sat there with tears streaming down her cheeks. Tyreek continued to rub her hand with one hand as he gently wiped away the tears from her cheek with the other. Staring in her beautiful hazel eyes, Tyreek maneuvered their bodies so they lay on the bed facing each other.

"I love you so much Sin. I just want to make you happy again," Tyreek said, leaning in and pecking her on the lips softly.

Sinclair felt her heart flutter as she stared him in the eyes.

Tyreek leaned in again, but this time kissed her with a deep passion that allowed his actions to speak for him.

Sinclair gripped the back of his head and sunk into the kiss as her body began to run hot with lust coursing through her veins.

He pulled her body close to his before rolling on top of her. Tyreek brushed her hair away from her face and stared deep into Sinclair's eyes. "I love you Sin," he whispered.

"I love you too, Ty," Sinclair replied before pulling his face to hers and sliding her tongue into his mouth.

Tyreek's heart skipped a beat as those words penetrated his eardrums. He slid his hands down her face, tracing her body then softly palming her breasts. His kissing down the side of her face before licking and nibbling her neck caused her to quiver beneath him as his dick hardened. He slipped her right breast out of her turquoise bikini top and took her erect nipple into his mouth, tickling it with his tongue.

Sinclair moaned low as she gyrated her hips against his groin, feeling her clit stiffen.

Tyreek placed his left hand between her legs and rubbed her clit into eruption. Passionately, he kissed his way down her navel as he slid her bikini bottoms off. *Finally,* he thought to himself as he came face to face with her honeypot oozing its sweet nectar. He had been denied access to this lovely place since that fateful night. Tyreek gently kissed her clit and slowly licked it in a circular motion.

Sinclair gripped her breasts in delight, loving the way Tyreek was pleasing her.

Tyreek sucked and nibbled her pearl then slid his index and middle fingers deep into her wetness, stroking her g spot.

Sinclair felt her body tense up as the warm tingling sensation between her legs grew more intense. Her body soon shook and trembled uncontrollably as Tyreek enjoyed witnessing the incredible orgasm he was causing her to have.

Sinclair looked down at Tyreek with hunger in her eyes as he looked up at her from between her legs with that same lustful glare. Within seconds, they were in opposite positions and she was mounting his waist as he sat up to allow her to slide his shirt over his head. She pushed him back onto the bed and kissed his chest, stopping at each nipple, flicking them one at a time with the tip of her tongue and then biting them gently.

Tyreek hissed. He missed and loved the way she stimulated his body.

Sinclair slid her hands down to his waist, removing his shorts and boxers at the same time to reveal his massive manhood. Her eyes grew as she watched it go from big to enormous as she stroked his shaft. She licked her lips before inhaling him as far down her throat as she could without gagging.

Tyreek moaned her name from the pleasure of watching his girth disappear in and out her mouth.

Sinclair looked up at him with an intense stare as he gripped her long mane around his fist and gently pulled and pushed her head as he pumped her mouth.

Sinclair slurped and slobbered on him as the combination of her saliva and his pre-cum escaped down the sides of her mouth.

Tyreek could feel himself ready to explode but refused to let it go until he was deep inside of her. He reached down and glided her head away from his dick by her chin as he tried to sit up.

Sinclair sat up and looked down at Tyreek. "Stay just as you are," she demanded, assuming the identity of the master instead of slave.

Excited by her forceful attitude, Tyreek lay back down and relaxed as he watched Sinclair take position.

She wrapped her arms around his neck as she squatted down over top of him, slipping him inside of her slowly.

Tyreek shut his eyes tight and bit his bottom lip as the warmth of her wetness welcomed him back home. Slowly, she bounced up and down as he gripped her round ass to maneuver it on his erection.

Sinclair closed her eyes, lost in the moment as beads of sweat rolling down her back caused her to shiver as it made contact with the breeze rolling off the ocean and into her room. Sinclair looked down at Tyreek and kissed him with more passion than she had ever felt before biting his bottom lip.

"Ouch!" he snapped, coming out of the moment and touching his lip.

"Shut up!" Sinclair demanded before smacking his hand down and kissing him again. She was beginning to enjoy inflicting pain on Tyreek. Somehow it eased her own.

Shocked at her dominating behavior, Tyreek looked up at Sinclair wondering who she was, but also found himself intrigued enough to want to find out. He did as he was told and lay back down to allow Sinclair to take full total control.

Scene Sixteen

The sound of the waves rolling ashore and the island birds chirping awakened Sinclair from her coma like sleep. She rolled over, stretched, and looked over at a still sleeping Tyreek.

What the hell are you doing? she thought as she slipped from under the sheets. She reached down and picked up her cellphone then tip-toed into the bathroom. Sinclair tapped the circle button in the middle, awakening the screen to see seven more missed face-time chats and text messages. She opened the messages cringing at the thought of the contents.

Trevor @ 10:26pm: *So you're just going to ignore me Sin? I haven't heard from you all weekend?*

Trevor @ 10:29pm: *This is how you want to play it huh???*

Trevor @ 10:35pm: *Ok Miss Sin – your choice. When you get back your punishment will fit the crime.*

She pressed the top button to put the phone back into hibernation. She started to become anxious at the thought of Trevor having his way, and suddenly felt the need to get away from her current circumstance. She splashed water on her face then stared at herself in the mirror, realizing that by opening the door to her past could bear unwanted consequences on her present.

Sinclair exited the bathroom quietly and quickly slipped back into her swimsuit that was on the floor before creeping out the door, leaving Tyreek still in his slumber. Sinclair scurried across the courtyard as the sun began to rise on the horizon. She headed towards Rain's suite and noticed a shadowy figure off in the distance coming from where Samara and Ever's suites were. Just as she approached the door she could see that it was Brian walking in her direction. Sinclair tapped lightly on the door with urgency, hoping Rain would answer before Brian noticed her. As Rain opened the door Sinclair rushed in and quickly closed the door behind her.

"Damn chica, you almost knocked my coffee out my hand. To what do I owe this urgent early morning visit? And, who in the hell are you running from?" Rain asked with a raised eyebrow.

Sinclair rushed over to the bed and sat down. "I just seen Brian coming from either Ever or Samara's suite and I didn't want him to see me, but more importantly, I think I fucked up, girl," Sinclair replied, dropping her head in her hands.

"You fucked him didn't you," Rain snapped in disgust. "I knew it. I told Ever and Samara that last night when you wouldn't answer your phone. You fucked around and laid up with that nigga all weekend. And, once again you missed another wild night of fun. You let him suck you right back in girlfriend."

"I did. Now I've opened the door for more lies and deception."

"Well, you should've known that would come with that slimy son-of-a-bitch," Rain said, walking back out onto her patio and sitting back down in her lounge chair before taking a long sip of her coffee.

"I'm not talking about Tyreek; I'm talking about me and Trevor," Sinclair reluctantly confessed, walking out onto the patio and sitting in the chair next to Rain. Sinclair had never disclosed any details of her new sexual escapades with Rain; let alone her S&M relationship with Trevor. Now, with Trevor being upset and Tyreek thinking he has another chance; she needed some level-headed, sound advice.

"Wait, what? Trevor? Who's Trevor? Is he the Winston to your Stella?" Rain joked.

"No, he's someone I've been seeing for a couple of months now. I haven't said anything to you or the crew because it started out as nothing serious. Not to mention, you wouldn't like how I met him," Sinclair said, feeling anxiety overcome her body.

"Okay, so I guess it's serious now, so how did you meet this mystery man?" Rain questioned, bracing herself for the answer.

"I had Samara make a couple of profiles for me on a few online dating sites. We met, and instantly, he awakened a side of me I never knew existed," Sinclair said with excitement lacing her tone.

"Girl, I thought you were going to say something crazy like he was Tyreek's half-brother or something. So, you met him online, isn't that the norm now-a-days. He sounds interesting already," Rain said, leaning into the conversation, curious to know more.

"You know I was a mess after the break-up and I needed to get over it fast. One of the sites was an online booty call type site."

"Hold up, you have a profile on an online booty call site? Sin, things aren't that bad in the dating world," Rain interjected.

"No, but I wanted to explore new horizons. Just hear me out before you lecture me, mother Rain," Sinclair jokingly said before continuing, "I went on a few dates, had sex with some new people, but after each encounter I felt worse than before. Then I met Trevor. He excited me just from our few conversations online. After we exchanged numbers, I was expecting it to be another failed, random sex drive-by. But, on our first date the sexual chemistry was off the charts, and in short, he seduced me into giving him a hand job under the table at the restaurant," Sinclair paused, waiting for a disapproving response before continuing. She got nothing but an attentive Rain, hanging onto her every word. She continued, "Since that night we have been having the wildest, most stimulating sex I have ever experienced. We have random video sex sessions any and everywhere. And, in the bedroom, I am totally submissive to him. He takes full control and I obey his every command. I even call him - ."

"You're a sex slave," Rain blurted out before Sinclair could finish.

"Well – yeah, if you want to look at it that way."

"What other way is there to look at it? That's some S&M shit. In the words of Ever, Scandalous! So does he tie you up and whip you? I mean, do y'all use handcuffs and leather masks and shit? How does that work?" Rain's line of questioning and interest caught Sinclair off guard.

"Yes he has tied me up, we've used nipple clamps and dildos. No leather masks or cuffs, yet," Sinclair paused, thinking of the punishment she would soon have to face, "but I love it, Rain."

"So how did you fuck up?" Rain asked, confused.

"Last night while I was caught up in Tyreek, I missed several texts and video chats from Trevor and he's pissed. I know he knows that I slept with Tyreek. I know it. I can feel it. And, the last time he found out I just kissed Tyreek, he wasn't happy," Sinclair said, thinking about the leather studded dog collar and working herself into a panic.

"Are you and Trevor a couple? I mean, did you two agree to be monogamous?

"We've never put a title on anything, but I am ALWAYS available to him. Hell, girl we still don't even know each other's full names. We know very little about each other's lives. It's part of the game. And, for me to miss his texts and face time chats is unacceptable."

"He knows you came here to work right?"

"Well, yeah."

"Does he know that your job is to deal with a famous asshole all weekend and that takes up all of your time?"

"Absolutely not!" Sinclair responded, "We don't know anything about each other's private lives. He doesn't know what I do for a living, nor do I about him. I just know whatever he does, he makes a decent living. I just told him I had to go away on business but he made me promise to make myself available to him. And, I did."

"Okay, just tell him that the combination of the long flight and hot island heat caused you to pass out from exhaustion. Totally realistic excuse. Hell, it's the only one that will make sense at this point. Besides, if you two are not exclusive, you are free to fuck whoever you want, whenever you want. Just do me a favor, and use caution this time with that grease ball ex," Rain said sternly.

"Yeah I know. I left his ass sleeping in my room. I'm glad that Samara booked his and his entourages flight out today and ours tomorrow in the morning. I am going to hang out here until I know he's gone. I am not ready to have the 'so where do we go from here' conversation."

"Well, I have an extra new bikini in my carry-on. You are welcome to borrow it, so go take a shower because you look and smell like you have been well fucked for the day," Rain chuckled as she waved Sinclair away.

"Shut-up Rain, you're just jealous that you didn't get any this weekend!" Sinclair laughed, heading for the bathroom.

******

The restaurant at the resort was small and quaint: Perfect for their last night in paradise. The girls and Ever sat at a private table off in the corner of the room and sipped on their cocktails.

"Thanks again ladies for inviting us," Ever said between sips. "I had a lovely weekend!"

"Yeah, I bet," Samara said sourly.

"Uh-oh, I hear a tinge of hate in your comment, girlfriend," Ever teased. "Don't be mad 'cause I'm right."

"Wait, right about what?" Sinclair interjected, remembering the bet and seeing Brian earlier that morning.

"You know," Ever said with a slick grin. "If your ass would have come out with us last night, instead of letting that nigga take all your cookies from the cookie jar, you would have seen it for yourself."

"You knew all of this time and didn't say anything to me all day?" Sinclair asked, looking over at Rain.

"I didn't know," Rain defended herself. "I left the club early last night to have phone sex with Geoffrey. This is news to me too, so spill it y'all."

"Do you want to tell them about our night?" Ever asked Samara.

"You tell'em. Shit, Brian didn't end up in my room last night," Samara replied with disappointment filling her tone. She really thought Brian was into her.

"Okay then," Ever said, looking back at Rain and Sinclair. "I will start where Rain left. Up until then we were all just drinking and turning it up. So, by the time Rain turned in for the night, Brian was pretty inebriated and very horny. He danced with Samara all night, right Samara?"

"Yup, all fuckin' night," Samara confirmed.

"So, by now I am thinking, Samara won. So, I am at the bar drinking and chatting it up with the bartender. Every now and then, turning to see if Brian's interest in Samara's ass has faded, but his dick was glued to her fat ass for every song. I have to admit, a diva was feeling a little rejected." Ever sighed.

The girls chuckled and in unison said, "Then what happened?"

"Then it was time to go home, and since Brian was drinking, he had one of his boys drive the SUV. So, we climbed in the back seat with him sitting between Samara and me. We are all fucked up, laughing and giggling, and every now then, Brian leaned into Samara to nuzzle her neck with those soft ass lips," Ever said smiling at the thought of those lips.

"Then what," Sinclair snapped.

"Miss Samara doses off," Ever continued. "And before you know it, Brian's hand is squeezing my thigh. At first, I thought nothing of it, you know maybe drunk, nervous energy, but then I felt his hand moving up my thigh right to my package!"

Eyes bulged as the ladies leaned in to hear Ever's every word. They sipped on their drinks and gave him their full attention.

"So you know me, I let him. I was curious to see how far he was willing to go with his boy staring at us through the rearview mirror. He didn't care Honey! At first he rubbed on my dick through my shorts until I was hard as hell, so I looked over at him and asked, "You know what you are getting into, right?" He just looked at me but didn't stop rubbing. I couldn't tell if his boy could see his hand in between my legs because it was dark but it was clear that he didn't care. Almost like his boy might have seen him act like this before," Ever said as matter of fact.

"So, how far did y'all go with my girl sleeping next to him," Sinclair asked, feeling for Samara.

"We didn't get far in the truck. By the time he built up enough courage to put his hand inside my pants, we were pulling up to the resort. He pulled himself together pretty quick once his boy parked and got out to help sleepy head over here. But I got out and stumbled to my room with a half stiff dick. I didn't give Brian or anyone else any indication that I wanted him to follow me, but before I could close my suite door and slip out of my sandals, his ass was tapping on my door. And, well you can imagine the rest right?" he asked them as he gazed over at each of them.

"What?" Rain gasped, "That's how you are leaving it? I am sorry but I think I want details."

"Me too," Sinclair added.

"Not me, but if you are going to tell it, I will listen," Samara said dryly.

"You ladies are nosey as hell," Ever laughed. "Well, you know what grown folks do in the bedroom, so I will give you bitches the short version. Once in my room, we disrobed. I must say he does have a handsome body and a very nice size dick. But then we did what men do: sucked each other off and fucked each other into a slumber. I have to admit, I never figured him to be a bottom, but he enjoyed that more than being a top."

"Wow, I knew it," Sinclair said. "I always thought there was something a little off with Brian. Good dude, but off you know?"

"Well, now you know why," Samara confirmed. "I am just glad we did this little bet before I let his ass have some of this good stuff."

They all chuckled and welcomed their steaming hot meals as the waiter approached their table.

"Let's just say it will be interesting when we get back home tomorrow," Sinclair said, picking up her fork and seeing her cell light up to warn her of another missed text from Trevor. "Interesting, indeed."

Samara entered the large classroom with mixed feelings: a part of her wanted to smack Sinclair for coaxing her into going back to school, and the other part of her was excited like it was her first day of high school ten years ago. "I'm going to kill Sin when I get to work later," she mumbled to herself as she brushed pass the few students already seated in the back row of the classroom. In the back is where Samara always felt most comfortable. It's the place where a teacher paid the least attention to, probably because most interested students sat as close to the teacher as possible. Samara tried to get comfortable in the desk-chair ensemble and then pulled out her text and notebooks from her book bag.

"Here we go," Ever said, sliding into the empty desk-chair next to Samara.

"Where were you? I tried to wait for you but the train came," Samara asked, relieved that Ever made it. She didn't want to start out alone.

"Girl, a damn water pipe burst at the store. Alisha didn't know what the hell to do, so I had to go there first. She just dropped me off. What'd I miss?"

"Nothing. The professor isn't here yet."

"Good," Ever stated as he pulled out his books. "You ready to learn something today Samara," he joked.

"I guess. Hell, Centry's paying for it so I might as well take full advantage, right?"

"Exactly," Ever quipped.

The two of them continued to chat it up about how they both wished they were back in Jamaica and how it didn't seem like two weeks had already passed.

"We had a damn good time, didn't we?" Ever rhetorically asked, thinking of his wild night with Brian.

"That we did. Have you heard from Brian?" Samara asked staring over at his smiling face.

"I did actually. We've talked on the phone a few times but haven't hooked up again, yet," Ever said with a devilish grin.

"You like him!" Samara said with excitement in her voice. "You like him don't you Ever?"

"Well, let's just say he is a breath of fresh air compared to the shit Wayne puts me through."

"Yeah, but isn't Brian just like Wayne when it comes to being comfortable with who they are. I mean, you don't want to latch onto another down-low brother do you?" Samara asked with concern.

"Look Honey, this is different. I have absolutely no expectations with Brian. It is what it is. My heart is under lock and key. My ass, however, is open for business!" Ever stated with two snaps of his fingers.

Samara's laughter caused some of the students to look back at them just as the professor entered the room.

"Good morning class," a baritone voice bounced off the white walls.

The entire classroom immediately quieted down and sat up in their seats like good pupils. Samara adjusted her butt in the seat and looked up at the professor with shock and awe plastered all over her face.

"What's the matter, girl? Your ass look like you just seen a ghost," Ever asked as he noticed the surprised expression on Samara's face.

Samara slid down in her seat and pulled out her baseball cap from her book bag. She slid the cap on so it nearly covered her eyes.

"What are you doing?" Ever asked, "You know him?"

Samara looked over at Ever. "Shh, don't cause a scene," she whispered. "I will tell you about it later."

Samara stared at the handsome professor from head to toe and was immediately taken in by the base in his voice. It commanded attention and the entire class was giving it to him.

"Welcome to Business Management 101. My name is Professor Lawrence Mackey. Most students call me Professor Mack, which is fine. As you all know, this is a once a week class that runs three hours. We will have two breaks and I expect everyone to stay for the entire class period. This semester you will learn the basics of managing a business," Professor Mack said boldly as he peered out into the sea of fresh faces eager to learn. His gaze was caught by a New York Yankees baseball cap pulled down over a young lady's eyes. She looked familiar. He tried to continue his first day of class speech, but couldn't take his eyes off that baseball cap. "What I have here on my desk are my class rules and the syllabus for the semester. Please come down, check your name off the attendance sheet, and pick up these two forms."

Professor Mack watched the students become unglued from their seats and filed into a line to his desk. The Yankee cap didn't move.

"What's wrong girl, get up and come on," Ever snapped, tugging on her sleeve.

"I can't," Samara said. "You go, check my name and grab the stuff for me. I don't want him to see me."

"So you do know him, you sneaky little snake," Ever laughed. "I'll do it for you this time but your ass can't sit back here all semester hiding from that hunk of a man," Ever said as he walked away.

Samara watched Professor Mack as he greeted and shook hands with the students and she hoped he wouldn't look up to see her still sitting there, but he did.

Professor Mack stared at the back row of his classroom and smiled as his memory started to surface. It was her: The freaky, mysterious motorcycle chick.

Scene Eighteen

The files stacked high on either side of Rain started to overwhelm her as she sat at her desk. She tried to stay focused but realized she needed room to breathe. She gulped down the last bit of her now lukewarm coffee and tossed the paper cup in the garbage. After muddling through the stacks of manila folders and pulling out the ones she needed to work on, she skirted off to the law library on the sixth floor.

The library was quiet and comforting. Rain quickly found an empty table in the back corner next to the window. She pulled out the chair and immediately opened the first file. It didn't take her long to become immersed in her work so much so that she didn't hear Dexter approach her.

"Excuse me, anyone sitting here," he whispered as he approached the table and pulled out the empty chair across from Rain.

Before she could look up to say anything, he was already seated and opening his file. "Um, guess not," she whispered and flashed him a phony grin.

"Oh, hi," Dexter said, realizing it was Rain. "Sorry didn't mean to invade but this is usually where I sit when I come in here. I promise not to bother you."

"No, it's okay," Rain replied, suddenly feeling bad that she was being so sarcastic.

She watched Dexter out of the corner of her eye as he skimmed through his file, making notes on his legal pad. She couldn't help it. He stirred her insides. She chewed on the cap of her pen as she watched him lick his lips every now and then.

"You married Dexter?" she blurted out.

"Excuse me?"

"Are you married?"

"No."

"Girlfriend? Steady, I mean." Rain clarified her question.

"No. I date but I don't have time for anything that heavy. Why, are you married?"

"Not yet; engaged," she said, flashing her ring.

"He's a lucky man. A smart one too," he flirted.

Rain felt a wave of heat rush through her body as they stared at one another.

"Glad you think so," Rain said, trying to read him. She couldn't.

"I do think so," Dexter smiled. "Beauty and brains; you're a double threat. Why'd you ask me if I was married? You have a clone you want to introduce me to?"

His questions rolled off his tongue with ease and Rain finally could surmise that he did find her attractive. This revelation scared her and she immediately felt nervous. "Um, no just curious, I can't imagine that someone hasn't hooked you yet," Rain said gathering her files to leave. She could no longer concentrate.

Dexter watched Rain intently as she stacked one file on top of the other and stood up to leave. "Where are you going? We're in a middle of a conversation. Do I make you nervous?" Dexter asked with a devilish grin.

"Who, me?" Rain looked into his deep blue eyes. "Not at all, it's just that I came up here to concentrate and you are throwing me off my game." She smiled.

"Sorry, I didn't mean to. It's just that I've never had the opportunity to sit and talk with you before, so now that I finally have the chance I find myself unable to shut up," Dexter laughed.

"I'm flattered, really I am, but I have a tough case to try tomorrow and I have to get this research done: Maybe next time."

"I really hope there is a next time," Dexter replied almost in deep growl. "You know what they say flattery will get you everywhere."

Rain picked up her stack and held them tightly in her arms. "Are you flirting with me Dexter?"

"Please call me Dex. My friends call me Dex and we're friends right? And, I'm only flirting with you because I can't help it. I hope your fiancée doesn't mess things up, or maybe I do."

Rain could feel her cheeks flush as she turned to leave. She couldn't believe her fantasy work crush was actually crushing on her. It made her feel good, so good that she put an extra sway in her hips as she felt his eyes penetrate through her slacks causing the heat between her legs to rise. Trying to seem unaffected by his advances, she waved to him without turning around. "See you around Dex. It was nice talking to you."

Sinclair sat tapping her pen against her cherry wood desk waiting for a reply from Trevor. She had texted him the moment her plane touched down at JFK two weeks ago and still nothing. Frustrated - she walked over to her window and stared out at the sunlight dancing off the Hudson River. Flashes of her night with Tyreek began to play like snippets before her eyes: she could hear herself moaning, feel Tyreek thrusting in and out of her. She bit her bottom lip as her hormones began to rage out of control. Her mind shifted to instant replays of her and Trevor; causing a small puddle to escape onto her panties.

Sinclair was torn between someone who held her heart and someone who made her feel alive. She didn't want to play games with anyone but why should she have to choose. She wasn't obligated to Trevor nor was he to her. For all she knew, he was probably enjoying the company of another woman at this very moment. As for Tyreek, she felt it was time for a little what goes around comes around for him. He had taken advantage of her trust and love; so why should she give in to him so easily, which would certainly disrupt her good time. She decided in that moment she was going to have her cake and eat it too; and with that, all thoughts and feelings of guilt disappeared instantly.

"Oh - my - God, Sin you will never believe what happened to me in class today," Samara huffed bursting into Sinclair's office, shutting the door, then plopping down on the plush cream couch, trying to catch her breath.

"Samara, it's only the first day! Don't tell me you and Ever went in there and cut up on someone already," Sinclair said, shifting mental gears.

"No-no, this is worst than anything you could ever imagine. You may want to have a seat for this one," Samara advised Sinclair before continuing.

Sinclair frowned in confusion as she sat down, resting her chin on the back of her folded hands.

Samara took a deep breath, "I fucked my professor," she blurted out, taking Sinclair by surprise.

"What! On the first day of class you sneaky slut," Sinclair teased before realizing this was no laughing matter. "So what happened?"

"Before we left for Jamaica I decided to take my bike out for one last spin before classes started, and that night it was fucking hot as hell, and I had to get some air. Truth be told, I was in need of a sexual exchange and so long story short; this guy driving a bangin' BMW pulled up next to me at a stop light. I flirted with him a little than told him to meet me in the park down the road. We never exchanged names, numbers, or anything. Hell, I don't even think we spoke more than three sentences to one another. It was a quickie and adrenaline fix for me. You know how riding my bike gives me a rush. Anyway, my ass is sitting in class this morning and who walks in to teach the fucking class: that stranger! Just so happens he is my business professor," Samara said, pulling her baseball cap down covering her face.

Not knowing exactly how to respond to Samara's unbelievable story, Sinclair sat back in her plush chair to allow it to sink in. "Only you Samara! Did he recognize you?"

"No, yeah, well, I don't know, I hope not. I kept my baseball cap pulled down over my eyes during the entire time. I had to send Ever up to sign me in and get my assignments."

Sinclair chuckled, picturing Samara trying to be incognito. "You don't think pulling that hat down over your face drew even more attention to you? So, what are you going to do, you can't hide the whole semester. This is like Players Club girl," Sinclair laughed remembering the scene where Diamond tries to avoid her teacher.

"Yeah, but the only difference is I fucked him and Diamond just showed a little ass!" They both laughed, lightening up the mood. "And, this ain't the fucking movies," Samara continued, "I don't know what I am going to do, I haven't thought that far yet, but I have to do something."

"Just go in there and act as if nothing happened. If he says something, tell him it wasn't you. Shit, men always run that line to us!" Sinclair laughed out loud.

Samara couldn't contain her amusement from Sinclair's antics and joined in on the laughter. "Thanks Sin," Samara said, gathering her composure and stood up to get to work. "I knew you would shine some light on the situation. I will keep you posted."

Then again, this may work out in my favor after all. Maybe I can get some extra credit, or maybe even an A out of this deal, Samara thought as a smirk spread across her face and she opened Sinclair's office door to leave.

Scene Twenty

Sinclair stepped out of the shower and wiped the steam off the mirror to make sure she removed all the soap from her body. She walked to the back of her walk-in closet where she kept all her kinky clothes -- as she called them. After thumbing through outfits, she decided on a red, latex, corset-mini dress with matching thigh high boots.

After almost three weeks of unreturned texts and calls, her imagination swirled and ran wild with the possibilities of what Trevor had in store for her when he finally reached out. His only instruction was to be ready in an hour and that he was sending a car for her -- something he had never done before. Sinclair pulled her hair into a tight ponytail on top of her head; giving her eyes the extra slant Trevor loved. She gave herself a once over in the mirror. *"You look like walking sex, girl,"* she mumbled aloud just as the phone rang.

"Hello, Miss. Hatorri?" A gentleman's voice asked.

"Yes, this is she. Are you downstairs?" she asked already knowing it had to be the driver Trevor sent for her.

"Yes ma'am, I am," he replied.

"I'll be right down," she said, applying her bright, matte red lipstick before heading for the door.

Sinclair's anxiety filled her body as the driver sped up the Major Deegan Expressway. She began to tap her almond shaped nails against the door as her left leg shook uncontrollably. She felt like she needed a cigarette, but never smoked before. *Easy girl, calm down,* she thought, taking a deep relaxing breath and easing over to the mini bar to pour herself a stiff drink.

The driver pulled into the tuxedo driveway that led to Trevor's house. As the driver exited the car to open the door for her, Sinclair felt her alter ego kick in. She stepped out of the car with a sudden air of confidence. It was as if being on his playing field caused a shift in her character.

"Have a good evening," the driver said, tipping his hat and checking Sinclair out one more time.

"Thank you, I plan to," she replied in a seductive tone.

As she strutted towards the door, Trevor emerged from a path on the side of the house. "We won't be going in there for this evening's exchange." Trevor's commanding tone sent a shiver through Sinclair's body.

"Good evening, Master," Sinclair replied with a slight drop of her head to not make eye contact.

"I have something special in mind," he said, leading her down the dimly lit path. Trevor said nothing else as they continued towards the small guest house; the only sounds were Sinclair's heels clicking on the slate pathway that led to his guest house. Trevor opened the door then stepped aside allowing Sinclair to enter first. Her eyes almost bulged out of her head. From the outside everything looked normal; the inside was a sex dungeon. It was dimly lit with red lights, black painted walls and had been completely stripped of all furniture except for a queen-sized bed in the center of the room with a stockade headboard complete with the holes for the head and hands to go through. Off in the corner was a small platform with shackles bolted to the floor and hanging from the ceiling to the center of it. On the wall to the far right were shelves running from one end of the wall to the other filled with all kinds of sex toys; from dildos to that damn leather mask Rain asked about. There were red gag balls, anal beads and a variety of sexual creams and lotions. Sinclair's mind was on overload: part of her was saying, *"Run, you're in way over your head!"* and the other part was aching to be man handled.

As she stood there soaking up her surroundings, Trevor walked up behind her and began kissing and licking the nape of her neck.

"Do you know why you are in here?" he whispered in her ear. His hot breath caused a shiver to run up her spine.

"Yes, Master," she moaned.

"Tell me why." His voice turned up one octave as he wrapped his arms tightly around her waist.

"Because I didn't answer your texts or calls, but I was working. You have to under–."

"Shut-up!" he snapped, spinning her around to face him. "I don't have to understand shit. I am the Master, remember. You agreed Sin to be there for me always, and you also agreed that if you disobeyed you'd willingly suffer the consequences. I was worried about you that entire weekend. It didn't make me feel good," he said, walking her to the platform and placing her feet in the shackles. "Are you ready for your punishment," he whispered in her ear as he reached for the hanging shackles with one hand and her wrists with the other causing her sex to purr in delight.

"Yes, Master," Sinclair seductively whispered into the air.

"I love it when we do it with the lights on," Geoffrey growled as he rolled over onto his side to face a well-fucked Rain. "It turns me on to see you in ecstasy." He leaned in and gently kissed the tip of her nose.

Rain smiled in delight as she felt his love surge through her body. She could not have asked for a better well-groomed man. He was perfect and she couldn't understand why his first wife couldn't keep him. And, he always assured Rain that their divorce had nothing to do with her and everything to do with his ex-wife not being able to fulfill his salacious sexual appetite. "Do I satisfy your every need," she asked, thinking about his past.

He looked her in the eye and asked why she'd ask him that.

"Because I just want to make sure you are happy. I don't want you to ever think that I am not here to meet all your needs. I want to be the wife to you that you never had," she said softly.

Geoffrey stared deeply into her eyes and wondered if she was ready to take the next step. It was the step where his ex-wife drew the line and caused their relationship to take a nose dive. "I want you to be too, but I just don't want you to leave me," he moaned, pulling her in close to him.

Being the driven, ambitious, hard-working man he is, Geoffrey found in his early twenties that his best stress reliever was watching porn. There was just something about watching a woman's face, especially a pretty woman, as she is being pleasured. It turned him on in a way that nothing else could. Well, that was until he met Tammy his senior year in college. Tammy was bisexual and loved threesomes. So, when she invited him over to her dorm after a few weeks of dating, he never expected to find her and her roommate giving him a show. That first time, he was so turned on that he didn't even join in. The voyeur in him was born. The rest of that year he, Tammy, and her roommate became inseparable. He wasn't surprised either when Tammy finally broke it off before graduating. Years later, he heard that she and the roommate were still together. He would have looked them up after law school but he met his ex-wife at the same time when his mind kept telling him that that wild sex life was just a part of college. But after a few years of dull sex and minimum stimulation, he introduced the idea to his ex and the thought alone disgusted her. He knew then it was over.

"I would never leave you," Rain whispered, reassuring him as she pulled him back into their moment.

"You promise?"

"Pinkie swear," she said, holding up her pinkie finger. They locked fingers and she pulled their hands to her mouth to kiss his. "Now tell me. What's your deepest fantasy?"

Geoffrey hesitated before speaking slowly, "I want to watch you."

"Watch me do what?" Rain asked becoming intrigued.

"I want to watch you make love to someone else."

Rain looked at him to make sure he was serious. She didn't know what he was going to say but she certainly didn't expect him to say this. "You want to share me?" Rain asked with some disappointment in her voice.

"Not your love, Baby, just your body. It's just that you are so beautiful and your body is to die for. It gives me great pleasure to be able to have you every night, but my greatest pleasure would be to watch someone else do things to you that drive you wild," he said, justifying his dark need.

Rain pulled away from him and sat up in the bed. A part of her was offended, yet her inner sex kitten began to purr. She looked down at him as he lay there looking up at her, allowing her to let it all soak in. "I don't like women," she blurted out.

With a furrowed brow, Geoffrey sat up next to her, "Why would you say that?"

"Because most men want to see two women together. That's what you are trying to say right?"

Geoffrey sat and thought for a moment. He was so excited that she didn't smack the shit out him like his ex-wife did, he was caught off guard. "Well, not exactly, I guess."

"You mean you want to watch another man make love to me?" she asked with a girly innocence in her voice.

The thought alone caused a tingly sensation travel throughout Geoffrey's body. He never had the opportunity to watch a woman with a man live. "Would you?"

Rain stared at him. "You're not testing me are you? If I say yes, you won't flip out and start calling me all kinds of whores, will you?"

"Baby, if you say yes then that will only confirm that that ring is truly on the right finger. It would mean that you are willing to love all of me." He kissed her on the cheek softly.

"I'm not saying yes, but I'm not saying no either. Can I think about it?"

"Of course you can."

Scene Twenty-two

"Girl, I am so glad you got your ass here today. I was starting to run out of excuses," Ever said, moving his book bag from the seat next to him so Samara could sit down.

"Yeah, I figured that I can't keep running from this man all semester. Hell, I already missed two classes and your notes suck!" she laughed.

"Whatever!" Ever snapped. "If your ass wasn't so nasty, you would have been here taking your own damn notes."

"Good morning class. Let's begin! Mid-terms are only a few weeks away," Professor Mack stated as he pulled out his book and stood stoically at the podium.

If only everyone else knew how freaky you really are, Samara thought as she watched him gracefully teach his class. He was sexy as hell and having a big cock hiding under those slacks started to awaken Sasha. Samara shifted in her desk-chair for the next three hours as she watched Professor Mack pace back and forth in front of the class.

"OK class, if anyone has any questions, email me and we can set up a one on one meeting. With that said, I expect everyone to get high marks on your mid-terms because I am here for you. Have a good week and remember to study."

The students simultaneously gathered their books and rose from the seats to leave.

"Um, Ms. Washington I would like to see you in my office," Professor Mack said to Samara as she tried to breeze pass him.

"Excuse me?"

"I would like to speak with you for a moment, do you have time?" he asked, staring at her intently.

Ever stood next to Samara, waiting for her to say something. She was frozen. He nudged her. "Girl, go ahead. Our next class doesn't start for another forty-five minutes. I will be in the cafeteria," Ever said, brushing in between them to get to the door.

The two of them stood there looking at one another, both replaying that night in their heads as they waited for the room to empty.

"Follow me," Professor Mack demanded like an angry school teacher.

Turned on by his masculinity, Samara felt herself recoil as Sasha started to emerge. She followed closely behind him as they exited the classroom through a side door that led to a hallway full of small offices. She felt like she shouldn't have been back there, and that turned her on more. They entered his small office and he motioned for her to take a seat as he shut the door behind him. He walked over to his desk and sat on the edge of it in front of her. "What are the odds?" he asked.

"What do you mean?" she asked, trying to be coy.

"You know what I mean," he said, uncrossing his leg so his bulge was in full view of her face. "What are the odds of us two running into each other again; Hell, for a minute I thought that night was just my imagination, but the way you made me feel reminded me it wasn't. Do you do that often?" he asked as he leaned into her.

"Do what often?" she asked, leaning into him so close their noses almost touched. "This?" She grabbed his crotch and rubbed gently.

He didn't move. "Yes, that." He felt himself growing in her hand.

"No, not always. There are times when a certain kind of guy awakens me," Sasha confessed.

"And, I am that type of guy?" Professor Mack moaned.

"What do you think?" she asked, unzipping his pants and releasing his growing manhood. She wanted to suck it.

Caught up in the moment and forgetting where he was, Professor Mack allowed her to free his Johnson and slip it into her awaiting mouth for only a few minutes. "Stop!" he managed to say as he pulled out of her mouth. "We can't do this here. Matter of fact, we can't do this -- period."

"Isn't that why you brought me back here," Sasha said, disappointed.

"Yes, well – no. I wanted you to come to my office to talk to you. You are a beautiful young lady who doesn't need to be having hook ups with strangers. I am just concerned for you. Since that night I have been thinking about you."

"I can tell," Sasha said, staring at his stiff dick. "Stop playing Professor. You know you want me. That's why you can't stop thinking about me. Tell you what: we don't have to tell anyone about our little secret," she said, reaching for his manhood.

"Wait! I am in a relationship," he said, moving from the desk and out of her reach. "I can't do that to her."

"You already did," Sasha said as she stood up to leave. "Listen Professor, you know what this pussy tastes like and feels like, and now you know where to find it. And, you will learn that I don't like my time to be wasted."

Professor Mack watched her leave as he tried to convince himself his lust for her wasn't real.

Scene Twenty-three

"I'm too exhausted to deal with this," Ever complained as he plopped down in his chair, tossing his text book on the counter. Trying to study at *Shoephoria* was proving to be impossible this evening. Ever was in need of a release; he picked up his phone contemplating whether or not to call Brian. Ever's mind quickly replayed their romp in Jamaica, causing his dick to jump as he reminisced. A wide grin spread across Ever's face as his fingers bounced across the screen typing Brian's name in the contact list.

"I was wondering when I was going to hear from you," Brian said without even saying hello.

"You busy tonight?" Ever questioned as his dick began to stiffen and pulsate.

"I'm actually packing for Reek's overseas tour, but for you, I'll make time."

"Good to know. So, why don't you swing by my place around ten for a late dinner? That will give me time to get settled in from work. I will text you my address," Ever purred into the phone. He didn't know what had come over him because Wayne was the only man who knew his address. Yet, there was something about Brian that made Ever feel safe.

"Ten it is. Oh, and Ever, keep this between us," Brian nervously requested.

The request brought Ever to a bad place for a moment, but he brushed if off reminding himself he had no expectations of Brian. *Besides I already outed you to my girls*, Ever thought to himself.

"What grown folks do in the privacy of their own home is their business," Ever said, falsely assuring Brian that his secret was safe. Ever continued just as the chime on the front door alerted Ever that a customer had entered the store.

"Gotta go, someone just came in. See you later," Ever said before hanging up the phone.

"Welcome to Shoeph-." Ever's jaw dropped in disbelief. He couldn't believe his eyes; there stood Wayne and his wife, Toy.

Wayne stood there staring at Ever with a devilish smirk as Toy clung to Wayne's arm like she was the luckiest woman in the world.

Ever tried to keep his composure and remain as professional as possible as he recited his greeting, "Welcome to Shoephoria, how may I help you?"

As she opened her mouth to speak, Ever's mind zoned out. Her words seemed to be escaping her mouth in slow motion. Ever had seen pictures of both she and the kids in Wayne's wallet, but she was even more beautiful in person. He questioned how could she not know about her husband, or did she even care. Ever returned to reality as he realized she was waiting on a reply.

"I am sorry, I was distracted by those ruby and diamond encrusted earrings you are wearing – fierce!" Ever lied, saving face.

"Thank you, they're an anniversary gift from my husband," Toy cooed, causing Ever's stomach to turn. "As I was saying," she continued, "today is our fifth anniversary and he surprised me with these earrings, and an all-day shopping spree. One of my co-workers told me about this place, so I just had to put it on my list!"

The jolly ignorance of this woman was like nails on a chalkboard to Ever, "It must be wonderful to have such a loving and devoted husband," Ever replied through a forced and phony smile. "Alisha, get this man a glass of champagne and make him comfortable while his wife and I max out that credit card," Ever snapped as he rolled his eyes at Wayne and took Toy by the arm and sat her down in a comfy chair on the other side of the room.

"Since this is our fifth anniversary, he said he has a romantic weekend getaway planned for us. I need something special," Toy said to Ever as she welcomed a glass of champagne and leaned back in the chair.

"Do you know where he is taking you?" Ever pried.

"He won't say, but I need something like that," she said, pointing to a fierce pair of red stilettos. "Something sexy for the bedroom. You know, to spice it up."

Ever wanted to gag on his lunch. He knew exactly what she was asking for. "You want some come fuck me pumps."

"Exactly! I am just not sure that will turn him on."

How 'bout something up his ass- got dick? Ever thought as he chuckled to himself. "You look like a size six. Stay right there Honey. I know just the shoes," Ever said as he darted off to the back of the store. He was disgusted by the nerve of Wayne; bringing his wife to his place of business to flaunt her. But Ever was determined to never let Wayne see him sweat. He kept his composure as he helped Toy pick out her fuck me pumps and he even wished them a happy anniversary as he walked them to the door to see them out.

Once they were gone, Ever snatched up his phone and sent Brian his address. Unbeknownst to Brian, Ever would be taking his frustrations out on Brian's ass later – literally.

Sinclair sat in shock as Rain told her about Geoffrey's request to watch her have sex with another man.

"And, you're sure this isn't some kind of test," Sinclair questioned with a raised brow.

"That's the same question I asked. No, he's serious," Rain confirmed, taking a sip of her Cosmopolitan.

"Who would've thought, Geoffrey – a certified freak," Sinclair teased. "So what are you going to do? I guess the better question is what do you want to do?"

"I don't know what to do. A part of me wants to do it to please him, and hell, please myself a little, but the other part just feels that bringing another person into our bed is just a recipe for disaster. But, he's waiting for an answer."

"I say do it! Fuck it. If that's what he wants give it to him."

"I have to think on it some more. What if this backfires in my face and he decides that he does want to see me with another woman? I am not doing that shit," Rain said in disgust as if the question were being asked at that moment.

"You never crossed that threshold?"

"What, being with another woman, hell no. Have you?" Rain curiously asked.

"You know the business I'm in, anything goes so, yeah a couple of times. It's not as bad as you think. You never know, you may like it. But you're jumping the gun on that. First, you need to decide what you're going to do about another man before you go adding another woman to the equation," Sinclair said, causing them both to laugh.

"Yeah, you're right. But, enough about me. I tried to call you that night but someone was obviously too busy," Rain said, shaking her head sure that Sinclair was with Tyreek.

"Yeah, but not with who you think."

"Thank God, leave that in Jamaica girl."

"I did. I haven't seen him since, and thank God he just left to tour overseas and won't be back for another month. But girl, you have no idea what I walked into." A shiver went up Sinclair's spine as she relived her night with Trevor.

"Do tell, girlfriend," Rain said, leaning in to the conversation, knowing it was going to be juicy.

"So, you know Trevor had been ignoring me since we got back from Jamaica. Guess he was giving me a taste of my own medicine. And, I must admit it worked because I was a wreck!" Sinclair confessed, thinking back at how she had been behaving. "Anyway, he finally sends a text that only gave instructions to be ready in an hour. When I got to his house I was expecting something kinky to go down. You know, maybe a whip and some handcuffs, but I never would've guess he had a sex dungeon for a guest house."

"Wait! A what?" Rain's eyes bulged with intrigue.

"You heard correctly. A sex dungeon. It was complete with dark walls and was dimly lit with red lights. He has a stockade bed, shackle platform, there were all kinds of things in there. And, yes he has a leather mask," Sinclair said, chuckling with Rain before continuing. "After he gave me a verbal lashing for not making myself available to him, he walked me over to this platform in the corner of the room. Once he made sure both my wrists and ankles were securely shackled, he walked behind me placing a blindfold over my eyes. I am not even going to lie to you, I was scared, but not the kind of scared you would think. It was the kind of fear I get when he turns me on. I get wet and my hormones rage out of control. It's a rush and a turn on at the same time." Sinclair paused and waited for Rain's reaction.

"What?" Rain snapped. "Continue, this is good!"

Sinclair chuckled. "Anyway, I heard his footsteps go off into the distance, and heard him fumbling about at his wall of sex gadgets and toys before returning to me. He told me to open my mouth wide. I did and he slipped a ball gag in my mouth, snapping it in place behind my head. I became so wet with anticipation I could feel it trickling down my thighs, girl! He spread my legs wide then began to devour both my ass and kitten. His tongue worked wonders slipping in and out of my kitten then round and round my booty hole until they were both nice and wet. I wasn't sure at first what he was putting up my ass, but it seemed to be long and oddly shaped. I later found out they were a long strand of pearl anal beads. He bent me over and plowed into me without warning. I tried to let out a loud cry, but I was muffled by the ball gag. Believe me when I tell you, the shit was AMAZING! Trevor pounded in and out of my pussy at first then he began to pull out slow, and back in hard and fast. Each time he pulled out he would slowly pull on the anal beads allowing them to escape one at a time. Trust me when I say, you haven't had an orgasm until you have experienced one both vaginally and anally. Between the pleasure, the pain, my muffled moans, and being restricted, my ravished thighs were coated with my juices. I just kept cumming harder and harder with each bead he pulled out. By the time he pulled the final bead on the strand out, he erupted so hard, *his* body was shaking and convulsing just as hard as mine," Sinclair fanned herself with her hand as her body ran hot thinking about it.

Rain just sat there stuck for a moment in the visualization, gazing at her best friend and wondering who this Trevor guy really is. "Well, damn girl. You are really slipping into that domination world, huh?" Rain finally questioned. "You just be careful. But you look stress free and happy," Rain teased.

"Yup, I am, which is why I am telling you to do it. You only live once. And, your man is giving you the go ahead. Why not take advantage," Sinclair said, holding her apple martini up to toast Rain.

Scene Twenty-five

Samara couldn't remember how long it had been since she studied so hard for a damn test. Her head began to pound as she sat in the quiet campus library. There were only a few people left in the building and you could hear a pin drop. Samara was in her favorite spot in science and astronomy section on the third floor. She closed her eyes and tried to memorize the meaning of business terms. She hated to admit it, but Professor Mack's class was boring as hell. However, she knew she needed to pass it if she wanted Centry to keep paying her tuition. She also felt the need to prove to Professor Mack that she wasn't just some little slut running around fucking strangers after midnight. Samara wanted him to know that she was smart and had a plan.

"Ok, ok," she whispered as she rubbed her belly as it growled at her. She hadn't eaten since lunch time. Samara opened her eyes and gathered her books to leave.

"Hope your studying for my midterm." She heard a low voice behind her.

Samara stood up and turned around and was greeted by Professor Mack's handsome smile. He reminded her of Edris Elba, maybe a bit taller and a shade or two lighter, but definitely the same swag and sex appeal. "As a matter of fact, I am. And, you just watch me, I am going to ace it."

"I expect nothing less from you Ms. Washington."

"You know you can call me Samara, right? I mean, you and I can certainly move past formalities," she said, smiling at him as she slung her book bag strap over her shoulder.

"Let me walk you to your car, Samara." He smiled.

Samara led the way through the room full of tables and chairs, down the steps to the first floor and out to the walkway. They didn't talk much as they walked along the street lit pathway that led to the campus parking garage. But every now and then one would try to make small talk.

"How are you liking college so far?" Professor Mack asked as they approached the glass door to the garage entrance.

"I'm still getting used to it," Samara sighed as she brushed pass him and pressed the elevator button. "How long have you been teaching?"

"I've been teaching for about fifteen years, but this is my fourth term as a professor," he said proudly. "What level are you parked on?" he asked as they entered the elevator.

"The roof," Samara replied as she stepped in and leaned back on the elevator wall. She looked him up and down and shook her head.

"What's wrong?" Professor Mack asked.

"Nothing, nothing at all. You just do it for me that's all," she said with Sasha's lust in her eyes. "But, I know, I know, you are in a relationship."

Professor Mack chuckled at her flattery and allowed her to step out of the elevator as it opened up onto the roof level. "You are something else Samara. I swear sometimes I think you are two people."

"They say that about all Gemini," Samara said, walking close to his side. "Let me give you a ride back to your car. Where are you parked?"

"Basement level, but that's okay, really," Professor Mack assured her as they approached her car.

"Really, it's the least I can do. I promise to be good and to keep both hands on the wheel." She smiled and tried to look innocent.

"Only because you promise to keep your hands on the wheel, OK." He laughed and slid into the passenger seat of her Honda Accord coupe.

Samara kept her word and delivered Professor Mack to his car safely without harassing or raping him. She pulled into the empty space next to his BMW. "I remember this car," she teased.

"Funny. Well, thank you Ms. Wash -, I mean, Samara. I look forward to seeing you in class this week," he said, looking over at her before pulling the handle to open the door.

She couldn't help herself and before he knew it, she had smothered his lips with hers and they were kissing with a passion beyond their control. Their heavy breathing caused her car windows to fog. She rubbed her manicured fingers up and down his dress shirt until they finally landed on his belt buckle and started to undo it.

"I shouldn't," he whispered as they came up for air. "I mean, I can't."

"Yes, you can," Sasha whispered, nodding her head and easing her hand down his pant. "It's alright, I promise you'll love it," she said in a breathy low tone that caused his entire body to stiffen.

Before he could say another word, Sasha's head was in his lap and his dick was lost on her mouth. She had devoured him.

"Oh shit!" he stammered. "Damn, girl! Suck that dick!" He gripped her by the back of the head to control how fast it moved up and down. The slurp sounds emanating from her full mouth made him want to explode, but at the same time, he wanted to enjoy it for just a few minutes longer. His fiancée rarely gave head and it had become clear on what he was missing. He bobbed Samara's head up and down on his dick until it was a brick. He slowly reached over with his other hand and slid it beneath her pants. The feeling of her moistness made him want to taste her. He slid three fingers inside her and pumped slowly as she adjusted in the seat to give him more access.

"Why don't we just go back to my place," Sasha said, dismissing Samara's rule to never bring men home. "We can really get into each other if we had more space," she said before slipping his hard-on back into her mouth.

Professor Mack removed his hand from her pants and licked his fingers. He would love nothing more than to take her someplace and fuck the living daylights out of her, but knew he couldn't. His fiancée was home waiting up for him. "Sorry Baby, not tonight," he managed to say before exploding in her mouth and watching the aftermath ooze out of it.

She took her time cleaning him up before sitting up to face him. "I'm sorry, I don't know what came over me. I told you, you do something to me," Samara confessed, feeling slightly embarrassed.

Professor Mack tucked his shirt back in, zipped up his slacks and buckled his belt. "No, I'm sorry Samara. I am the teacher and you are the student, so I know better. But, I have to make a confession." He shot her a serious glare. "You do something for me, too. The way you handle your sex game is incredible."

Samara blushed at his compliment and she wanted to tell him all thanks should really go to her alter ego, Sasha, but decided to take all of the shine. "Thank you. Sometimes I lose control." Samara smiled innocently.

"I know," Professor Mack laughed. "But seriously Samara, we can't keep doing this. Agreed?"

Samara looked into his sexy eyes and with much reluctance blurted out, "Agreed."

Scene Twenty-six

"You, okay?" Rain's co-counsel Amber asked as they cleared the defendant's table in the courtroom. "You almost missed that objection. Could have added a few more years to our client's sentence."

"That's why you're here, right? To have my back, catch my misses?" Rain snapped.

Amber looked at her friend and could see the anxiety washed over Rain's face. "Rain, stop," Amber said, putting her hand over Rain's. "What's up?"

"Sorry Am-ster, I just have a lot going on at home and coming in everyday to defend people who are really guilty is wearing on me," Rain said somberly and sat down.

Amber sat down next to her and continued to hold her hand. "Go home, get some rest. Take tomorrow off to pull it together. Everyone needs a mental health day. I'll cover your cases." She smiled.

"You mean, you will make Mark cover my cases," Rain laughed, feeling some relief.

"Hey, I can't help it if he will do anything for me. And, we both know he will kill himself if he knew I am a lesbian."

Their laughter filled the now empty courtroom.

******

Rain stood still in the shower, hoping the beads of water would wash away some of the anxiety that covered her like a blanket. She thanked Amber for covering for her, and for not asking what was really troubling her. Rain would have never been able to find an appropriate way to tell Amber that her fiancée is bringing home a guy he knows from the gym to fuck her brains out while he watches. She allowed the aqua bullets to pierce her skin from head to toe as she thought about what Geoffrey had planned for her later.

You are crazy, she thought. *What if this guy is ugly? What if Geoffrey realizes he doesn't want to watch this? What if his dick is too little? Or, too big? What if you don't like it? What if you do? She silently questioned herself.*

It wasn't until the water started running cold that Rain realized she had been in there too long. She quickly hopped out and dried off. She applied Geoffrey's favorite perfumed lotion from her neck to her toes and then sprayed on the matching perfume. She walked back into her bedroom and stood at the foot of the bed, naked. She glanced back and forth at the two outfits Geoffrey left out for her to choose from and she hated them both. They both looked slutty. But then again, she realized that what she was about to do was probably as slutty as slutty gets. "Here goes nothing," she mumbled as she swiped up the black and red number that had the crotch-less panties.

By the time she squeezed into the corsette, she could hear Geoffrey talking to someone in the kitchen. "Oh shit," she whispered, "they're here. Damn, Geoffrey, what size do you think I wear?" Rain snapped as her firm round ass engulfed the panties.

"Honey, I'm home!" Geoffrey sang.

She could hear the excitement in his voice. She hadn't heard it in a long time. It made her feel good; good enough to at least try and go through with it. "I'll be out in a minute!" she chimed. Rain rushed to her walk-in closet and pulled out her hand-dandy black wrap dress and threw it on. She applied a little gloss, primped her hair, and opened the bedroom door.

"Well, hey. I didn't think you'd be here so soon. I haven't even started dinner," Rain said gliding over to Geoffrey and giving him a quick peck on the lips.

"No need, I brought home take-out," Geoffrey smiled with lust filled eyes. He leaned over to her ear and whispered, "I've been thinking about this all fucking day." He pulled back and smiled. "This here, is Kevin, my friend from the gym."

Rain looked over at the tall, athletically built young man standing there and noticed he looked nothing like she imagined he would. He wasn't a short, round, balding man that she was sure Geoffrey would select to avoid any competition. Instead, Geoffrey had selected someone very similar in looks to his own. Someone who she'd date in a heartbeat. Actually, this Kevin guy reminded her of the guy she was dating right before she met Geoffrey. *Funny*, she thought. Rain approached Kevin and extended her hand. "Pleasure to meet you," she heard herself saying. The attraction was immediate. It scared her.

He grasped her soft hand and held it tightly. "Pleasure's all mine," he replied. The base in his voice traveled from his body to hers as they held onto each other.

Rain couldn't stop looking into his eyes as she pulled back. "You guys want to eat first and relax a bit," she said, breaking their gaze and turning to Geoffrey who was standing there with a slick grin on his face. As soon as she told him she'd fulfill his fantasy, he had set his plan in motion. And, within days, he had come home to tell her that he had found the perfect guy for her. At first, Rain couldn't believe her own fiancée was scouting fuck buddies for her, but seeing his face in this moment, she could see that he was loving every minute. She felt a wave of heat rush through her body and walked into the living room to pour herself a drink. "I think I need this more than food right now. Can I pour you guys a drink?"

The two men followed her like abandoned puppy dogs and sat side by side on the sofa. They watched Rain's chocolate skin glisten as the dimly lit recessed lighting casted a spotlight on her as she poured their drinks. By the third or fourth round, all inhibition had been suppressed and they began running through Geoffrey's 80's and 90's playlists on his ipod and taking turns dancing with Rain. It wasn't until Teddy's *Turn off the Lights* started blaring through the Bose speaker that things started to take a turn. Kevin tugged Rain by the arm and asked her to dance. Rain shot back the last swig of Absolute in her glass and stood up.

"I would love to," she slurred.

They danced in the small space in the center of the living room as Geoffrey leaned back on the sofa to let comfort set in. Kevin and Rain danced slowly and he pulled her in close so she could rest her head on his chest.

Feeling totally inebriated, Rain allowed her body to do what it felt and she placed her head on his chiseled chest as he wrapped his muscular arms around her waist and allowed his hands to move up and down on her backside, squeezing her butt every now and then.

Geoffrey watched Kevin take control over Rain and became slightly aroused. He rubbed his slacks to adjust his growing erection and tried to keep his composure.

Rain released the image of Kevin massaging her ass and replaced it with Geoffrey. She kept her eyes close as he began to kiss her neck softly with wet kisses before moving his hands to bow at the side of her dress. He tugged on it until it came undone and Rain's wrap dress opened up to her fuck me outfit.

"Damn! You look amazing," Kevin said before turning her around for Geoffrey's view. "You sure you want me to do this, man?"

Geoffrey looked up at Rain standing there with her outfit complimenting her smooth skin and accentuating all of her curves, and shook his head yes.

For a split second, Rain felt like a piece of property, but before she could act on it, Kevin was holding her from behind and nibbling on her neck. "I'm going to devour you," he whispered in her ear.

The thought of him doing things to her that only Geoffrey does, scared and excited her. She looked over at Geoffrey, seeking his approval.

Geoffrey had completely zoned out of their relationship and into his own little porno. He was at a point where he didn't see faces, just body parts. He rubbed on his pants until he was totally erect as he watched Kevin, now with almost his whole hand inside of Rain as she stood there with her eyes closed, enjoying every minute. That turned Geoffrey on the most. "Let's go to the bedroom," Geoffrey blurted out as he managed to get up from the sofa.

They followed him to the bedroom and Kevin walked Rain over to the bed and pushed her down. He knelt to his knees and started to lick the sugar from her walls as Geoffrey made himself comfortable on the chaise in the corner of the room. He continued to pleasure himself as he watched Kevin and Rain fuck like they knew each other. Geoffrey was even a little surprised when Rain sucked Kevin's dick after he fucked her in the ass: Something she'd never let Geoffrey do before. Geoffrey's mind raced as he sat there thinking about what he was going to do to Rain after Kevin was through with her; especially now that he sees she really can be the freak he needs every now and then.

Wayne stood in front of Ever's door contemplating whether to knock on it or just go home. He knew he was dead ass wrong for bringing Toy to Ever's job the other day, but he wanted a reaction from Ever. Ever hadn't called or replied to Wayne since Ever chased him out of his place with a meat cleaver. Even worst his plan blew up in his face, Ever didn't curse him out or show his ass like he expected. Wayne knew there was a chance he may have lost Ever. As Wayne turned to walk away Ever emerged from the elevator.

"Honey, he was sopping these biscuits up getting every drop of this gravy," Ever bragged to Samara over the phone.

"So I guess I know now why you haven't been responding to me," Wayne snapped with jealousy.

"Girl, let me call you back," Ever calmly said hanging up his cell. "You know it's against the law to stalk people Wayne. Besides what the fuck are you doing here? Shouldn't you be playing perfect husband and father in the burbs?"

"Look, I came here to apologize but it's obvious you could care less."

"You mothafuckin right, I don't! So, why don't you just leave and come back… Never!" Ever demanded brushing pass Wayne to open his front door.

"I went too far and I guess I just always thought you would be here. I never thought you would leave me," Wayne said, dropping his head in disappointment.

"And that's where you niggas go wrong. You think you can shit all over a person because they love you. Then you expect that love to be good and strong enough for them to never go anywhere, with little to no change or effort to keep that person loving you. Well, hate to tell ya' but that buck stops here, Baby."

"For whatever it's worth I love you Ever and I apologize for all the hurt I put you through," Wayne sincerely said staring Ever in his eyes.

Ever had heard Wayne apologize so many times before and being blinded by love he always chose to believe him. This time his blinders were off and he could really see Wayne meant every word spilling from his lips with true sincerity. Ever stood there frozen with his door ajar. Wayne stepped into Ever's personal space and kissed him one last time.

Ever, caught off guard felt a surge of passion erupt inside of him. Ever gave into Wayne's kiss caught in between heartache and hormones. Ever stepped back allowing Wayne to kiss his way into his loft never once parting their lips. Wayne slipped Ever's jacket off, then unbuttoned his shirt, kissing his way down Ever's chest before unbuckling his belt pants.

One for the road, Ever thought as he allowed Wayne to slip his erection into his mouth. Ever moaned as Wayne's warm saliva coated his dick causing it to stiffen to capacity.

Ever looked down at Wayne in delight; watching him completely submissive on his knees bobbing on his master piece. Ever placed his hand behind Wayne's head guiding his shaft deeper down Wayne's throat causing him to gag. Wayne kept slobbing and sucking as if his life depended on it bringing Ever's load to the surface. Ever erupted down Wayne's throat relishing in the moment knowing this would be Wayne's final performance.

Wayne stood to his feet excited, thinking he had won Ever back once again. Wayne unzipped his jacket preparing for a moment of full reconciliation. Ever pulled his pants up and flipped on the light.

"What are you doing? Don't you want to take this to the bed," a puzzled Wayne inquired.

"No, this is where we part ways. Goodbye Wayne," Ever said, walking over to the door and opening it. "Oh, and lets not have a repeat of the last time I put you out."

Wayne stood there in disbelief, feeling humiliated. "So that's it? You just think it's going to end this way?"

"Oh, I don't think, I know," Ever snapped, holding the door wide open.

As Wayne exited Ever's apartment rage filled his body. He had never felt so used before in his life.

"You think you can bust down my throat and put me out like this. I am not –."

"Wayne?" a woman's voice shot from down the hallway.

Ever poked his head out into the hallway to see who it was.

"Isn't karma a bitch," Ever said with sarcasm lining his voice as he slammed his door in Wayne's face, leaving him to deal with a shell-shocked Toy.

Scene Twenty-eight

Rain sat at her kitchen table with her eyes fixated on the clock on the wall. She was lost in space thinking about how her emotions were getting the best of her. Three weeks had already passed since she fulfilled Geoffrey's voyeur fantasy, but it was still the only thing she couldn't stop thinking about. The feeling of guilt plagued her body from the moment the escapade ended that night; not because she had sex with another man; Hell, Geoffrey wanted that. She felt guilty because she loved it. She wasn't sure if it was the whole idea of being as naughty as one can be, or having sex with someone like Kevin, who obviously knew his way around a woman's body. The pleasure she felt that night outweighed any sex act performed with Geoffrey, or any other man for that matter. She watched the hands on the clock tick tock around its circumference while she waited for Geoffrey to walk through the door from his morning run. She expected that he would want to make love in the shower, again. She had to admit since that night, sex with Geoffrey alone was becoming a bit boring, and she finds herself thinking of her night with Kevin in order to become completely satisfied. Out of all of the expectations she had before delving into Geoffrey's sexual deviancy, she never expected that she would find herself catching feelings for Kevin. The way he handled her that night, with both aggression and tenderness made her realize that Geoffrey wasn't the only man who held the key to her orgasm chest. She wondered if he realized that too, especially since she found herself avoiding his request to have Kevin over again soon.

"What am I turning into," she said aloud as she sipped on her coffee.

Her mind raced as she reminisced, seeing Geoffrey's face as he masturbated while watching Kevin please her beyond ecstasy. Rain adjusted her butt in the chair as her muscles in her lower region began to contract. "Damn, I knew it was a bad idea," she whispered.

"You in here talking to yourself?" Geoffrey questioned as he approached her with sweat covering his body from head to toe.

"Huh," Rain huffed and turned to look at him. "Um, yeah. Just thinking out loud about a few of my cases. How was your run?" she asked, diverting the conversation.

"Great as usual. You really should come with me one morning. The fresh air clears the mind as well as the lungs. You do realize that the gym is not the only place to exercise, right?" he teased.

"You know I love the gym. I like thinking that others around me are trying to reach a similar goal," she said as she stood up to make him a cup of coffee.

Geoffrey sat down at the table and wiped his face with his hand towel. He watched Rain's ass move underneath her sheer bathrobe and felt like the luckiest man in the world. He smiled at her lovingly as she placed the coffee cup down in front of him.

"Thank you, Baby," he said as he picked up the cup and took a sip. "I am going to hop in the shower and then head out to the office for a few hours before meeting up with Kevin later at the sports bar to watch the game," Geoffrey stated as matter of fact. "That is unless you would rather we come back here to watch it," he hinted and waited for her response.

Rain sat back down at the table across from him and thought for a moment. The lower half of her body wanted to see Kevin again, but the upper half knew that she shouldn't. "I don't think so, Babe. You two can go to the bar." She frowned.

Geoffrey gazed at her with disappointing eyes. "What's up Rain? Every time I mention Kevin joining us again you seem to find a way to evade the subject. I thought you enjoyed the other night."

"It was alright," Rain said, trying to play down that incredible night. "Really, it was an experience I will never ever forget, but I am not so sure I want to do it again."

"Why not? You and Kevin seemed to hit it off. In more ways than one, I might add," Geoffrey chuckled. "And, I sincerely hope you don't think I am upset or jealous in any way. I know you Babe, and I know your love is only for me." He smiled confidently.

Rain stared at his gleaming white teeth and silently agreed with him. He was right, her love was only for him, but after having sex with Kevin she realized her lust was attaching itself to someone else. It scared her. "I don't know Babe, I just don't want us to make it a habit of bringing someone else into our bed."

Geoffrey frowned at her reply. She sounded like his ex-wife. He tried not to compare. "If I thought that fulfilling my needs would bring harm to you in any way, I would have never suggested it, but I believe our foundation is on solid ground and no one can come between us. It's just that I watched how pleased you were that night and I want that for you always." He grabbed her hands and held them gently. "I won't rush you Rain, but we've opened Pandora's Box together, and I am letting you know it's OK to explore; As long as we explore together."

He made it seem so simple, so easy. Yet, it bothered Rain that he didn't take her emotions and feelings into the equation. Especially, since he decided to bring a man just as handsome as himself into her bed. Rain pulled her hands from his grasp and stood up to place her empty cup in the sink. "Ok Geoffrey, but not tonight. I am just not ready, but I will let you know when I am, okay?"

"Fair enough. You didn't say no, so a brotha' can't ask for more than that," he said, sliding his chair away from the table to get up. "You wanna come?" he asked as he turned towards their bedroom.

"No, I'm good," Rain replied. "Go enjoy yourself."

Geoffrey disappeared into the bathroom while Rain washed the few dishes left in the sink from the night before. She found herself immersed in her thoughts as the sink faucet ran and the soap suds enveloped her hands. At first she couldn't hear the chime on Geoffrey's cell ringing, but as it kept ringing the sound grew louder.

"Hello," she said, wiping her hands dry with the dish rag.

"Oh, hey! I didn't expect you to answer the phone." A voice sang in her ear.

"Who is this?" she asked.

"Oh, sorry, it's Kevin. How are you?" he asked with a slight hint of seduction in his voice.

Rain froze where she was standing and for a split second felt like hanging up on him. "Oh, hi Kevin, I am fine. How are you?" She prayed he couldn't hear the nervousness penetrating her vocal chords.

"I'm good now that I hear your voice," he flirted. "Where's the big man?"

Her cheeks became flush at his flattery and an involuntary smile appeared across her face. "He's in the shower. Should I have him call you back?"

"No just tell him that I will be at the bar around three. But since I have you on the phone can I tell you something?"

Rain hesitated for a moment, scared of what he might say. "Sure."

"I can't stop thinking about you," Kevin confessed. "I swear I tried, but you really put it on me the other night. It's been awhile since I had a real woman. You were exceptional to say the least. I didn't expect it." An awkward silence hung in the air as he waited for Rain's reaction.

She looked over to her bedroom and could hear that Geoffrey was still in the shower. "Excuse me." She wanted to make sure she heard him right.

"You heard me Rain. I can't get that night out of my head. I know it's wrong, but I really want to see you again: without Geoffrey."

Rain stood still as his words flowed through her ear drum like the sound of sweet music. He was thinking about her just as much as she was thinking about him, but she quickly realized that wasn't a good thing. Geoffrey was right; Pandora's Box was now wide open.

The scent of sweat coupled with musk permeated the air in the gymnasium as the college professor basketball league practiced for their upcoming game against the school's team. All pushing forty and over, and most out of shape, the men trampled up and down the court like wounded buffalo. Professor Mack and his soon to be brother-in-law were among the few that remained in top shape and played like teenagers.

"Alright guys, tomorrow morning at eight and be on time!" Professor Wendell shouted to the other men like they were his students. "We have to kick ass Wednesday night."

The men gathered their water bottles and sweat soaked towels, and made their way to the locker room.

"Yo man, wait up!" Professor Warren shouted as he jogged to catch up to Professor Mack. "What's up? Everything alright with you and my sister?"

Professor Mack wiped his forehead with his damp towel and looked over his shoulder. "Oh hey man, what's up? We're good. I just got a lot on my mind right now. You know, correcting mid-terms, getting ready for the holidays. Speaking of which, are you planning on driving up to your parents' place with us for Thanksgiving?" he asked as they entered the locker room one behind the other.

"Not sure yet, I'll let you know," Professor Warren replied, shaking his head as he opened his locker.

"What?" Professor Mack asked. "Did I miss something?"

"Naw man. I'm just thinking about when we first started our tenure here. I would have never guessed that we'd be here today, friends and you dating my baby sister. Funny how life plays out sometimes."

Professor Mack looked over at Professor Warren and agreed with him. "And, no worries man. Fawn is in good hands. What you got planned today? You want to come over later to watch the game? Your sister is making her famous lasagna," Professor Mack tried to persuade Professor Warren.

"Naw man, can't do it, got plans. Plus, I'm meeting a student in a few for a tutoring session. She's a little hottie, too." Professor Warren smiled at the thought of Samara's round ass and soft lips. Unlike Professor Mack, he saw no harm in taking on extra-curricular activities with his students. They were all of age and he was single. He found himself always having at least three women in rotation. He couldn't help it. He loved women, and he loved pussy even more. It was only a matter of time that his path would cross with Samara's. He just didn't realize it would take her so long to need extra help in his economics class. It surprised him when she approached him after class the other day and asked for a private tutoring session. Before he could respond, his classroom door was locked and he had her pinned up against it. Something he wanted to do to her since the first day of class.

"Uh-oh," Professor Mack smiled. "You better behave yourself man. One day you gonna stick that in the wrong woman." He thought about how he wished he never met Samara that fateful summer night. Now he can't stop thinking about her.

"Naw this one seems a little different. Like she can handle a little action without the fatal attraction. You might know her. I think she's in one of your business classes."

Professor Mack froze for a split moment and immediately thought of his personal seductress. "Maybe, but I doubt it. I am teaching over ten classes this semester. Too many faces," he said, trying distance himself from his students.

"I think you'd remember her. She's a little cutie." Professor Warren winked.

"Maybe," Professor Mack shrugged, "what's her name?"

"Samara...Samara Washington."

A wave of emotions erupted inside his body as Professor Mack thought of the two of them doing things enraged him. He tried to conceal his true feelings and hoped Professor Warren hadn't noticed. *What would he do if he knew about me and Samara,* he thought as he tried to suppress his jealousy. Professor Mack looked up in the air to give the false impression of him being in deep thought and then said, "Name sounds familiar, but I can't place her face," he lied.

"Damn Larry, you really do love my sister if you haven't noticed that yet," Professor Warren chuckled.

"Shut up, Kevin. Wait, don't tell me, you two already…," he inquired, needing to know as a tinge of anger began to set in.

"Not yet, it got kind of hot and heavy the other day, but I had another class that was starting. Who knows where it could have gone," Professor Warren smiled. "And, I'm not so sure I have room for her at the moment: Dealing with a situation with a friend from the gym and his wife."

"I have something real special in mind for you tonight," Sinclair purred slapping a pair black handcuffs around Tyreek's wrists restraining him to the bed.

"Ayo, Ma don't go doing no funny shit, like tryin' to play in a nigga's ass. I'm not with that shit," Tyreek nervously said.

Sinclair let out a slight chuckle, then slapped him across the face, "SHUT UP! I don't remember saying you could speak. Did I?"

Tyreek stunned by her aggressive nature but also turned on, replied, "No."

Sinclair grabbed Tyreek's face, "No, what?"

Tyreek stared into Sinclair's eyes and didn't see the loving woman he knew. Instead, he saw a dominating, controlling sex kitten who was about to take him on a wild ride. "No…Mistress?"

Sinclair dug her nails into his cheeks causing him to squirm. "Be still! You do as I tell you, understand?"

"Yes Mistress."

"Good boy, don't let it happen again," she said through a seductive smirk, holding her robe closed. Sinclair's heels clicked across the room as she walked over to her dresser retrieving her cellphone. After seeing that she missed several calls from Trevor, she put it on airplane mode and scrolled through her playlist before placing it on the speaker dock. She turned to face an unsuspecting Tyreek, *He has no idea what he just got himself into.* She chuckled to herself as Rihanna's *Skin* began to pump through the Bose speakers.

Sinclair slowly walked over to the bed and ran the tips of her fingers down Tyreek's body causing his erection to jump. She stepped back to the foot of the bed and twirled while opening her robe. She gyrated her hips getting lost in the rhythm. Tyreek sat up as far as he could comfortably. His dick stiffened as he watched her perform in her black leather boy shorts, matching strappy top, and leather stilettos. Sinclair turned her back to him then let her hair fall out of her bun down her back. She picked up her leather crop whip slapping it in the palm of her hand as she made her way back to Tyreek. She straddled him, whip still in hand as she rolled her aching passion against his eagerness making him wish his hands were free to touch her body. Sinclair reached behind the pillow to retrieve the blind fold she hid there earlier, then quickly placed it over Tyreek's eyes.

"Ayo Sin, man, I am not playing. I am not with this funny style shit."

Sinclair slapped him across the chest with the whip then pinched his nipples tightly between her fingers. "I said to shut the fuck up! This is what you want, right? That's why you made such a fuss to get me way over here on the other side of the world, right. Like I don't have other artists to tend to. Like I really want to be over here in England when your ass only had another week to finish this tour, but no you gotta always come with some bullshit. Disobedience will not be tolerated from you anymore," she said through gritted teeth. "Time to teach you a lesson."

Tyreek laid there with his ass clenched tight as he slipped back into his role. Her demanding demeanor was making him weak. "I just needed to see you Ma. A nigga couldn't take it anymore. How the fuck was I supposed to know the whole suite would catch fire."

"I swear, one more word and I am going to gag you." She opened up her carry-on bag of goodies and pulled out a vibrating cock ring attached to a set of nipple clamps and a remote. As she slid down his body she could feel how tense he was. Sinclair relished in the moment; she was going to make him pay for all his wrong doing both past and present. He didn't realize him causing her to fly out there has created another punishment from Trevor. She wanted to smack and kiss Tyreek at the same time for his ignorance.

She kissed him softly then bit his bottom lip before moving down his body. She licked his nipples while working her way down his body until she was face to face with his erection. Sinclair chuckled to herself as she slipped the cock ring down his shaft. Tyreek squirmed unsure of what she was doing. She quickly sat up looking down at him with a devilish grin then clamped both of his nipples. Before Tyreek could object she turned the cock ring on causing him to whimper and moan from the pain and pleasure of her torture device. Sinclair pulled her shorts off then slid him inside of her. Sinclair rode him with conviction while thrashing him with the whip.

"Say you're sorry mothafucker!" she demanded.

"I am sorry Mistress. Ouch!"

"Louder, I can't hear you!"

'I AM SORRY MISTRESS!"

Sinclair turned up the speed on the cock ring and rode him harder. "You nasty son of a bitch, fuck this pussy back like you mean it," she barked pulling on the nipple clamps at the same time.

She was enjoying watching him whimper and squirm like a little bitch. She whipped him harder and rode him faster until he erupted, letting out a loud helpless growl.

"Damn Tyreek," she snapped with disappointment unlocking his wrists, "next time you don't cum unless I instruct you to."

"I am sorry but that shit felt crazy," Tyreek said rubbing his chest then wrists. "I don't know where you're getting this shit from, but this is a side of you I've never seen before." He sat up in the bed and stared at her. "I ain't so sure I like it," he confessed.

She looked over at Tyreek as she peeled out of her leather outfit to go take a shower. "Whatever Tyreek, this is me now. Take it or leave it. You decide."

Sinclair vanished behind the bathroom door, leaving a bruised and battered Tyreek with something to think about.

ACT II

Six months later...

Scene One

The rain clouds eclipsed the morning light that peeked through the curtains of the massive luxury suite, and shone down on Ever, causing him to awaken from his first peaceful slumber in months. Ever sat up greeted by a dull thumping in his head, courtesy of the fuzzy navels he continuously tossed back the night before. Ever stretched then looked down at Brian's naked body sprawled out across his side of the bed. "*Humph,*" he huffed at the thought of another down low brother sharing sheets with him.

"Guess you'll be scurrying off to your baby's mama or whatever female you're seeing; dismissing me and what happened last night into this morning," Ever mumbled.

Ever's mind began to race, replaying his sexual encounters since his high school days back in Mt. Vernon, New York. It seemed that even back then he was always the dirty little secret to a closeted gay man too afraid to come out. His first secret lover was Kareem, the high school's captain of the football team. Kareem was in danger of being kicked off the team for his failing trigonometry grades and was in need of a tutor, bad. A mutual classmate knew Ever was a wiz at math and pointed Kareem in his direction. Seeing the desperation in Kareem's eyes, Ever agreed to tutor him every Tuesday and Thursday after football practice. From their first time alone, Ever could sense Kareem might be gay, or at least curious, but was unsure because of Kareem's reputation at school. Kareem was definitely a ladies' man and always had a bunch of them fawning over him throughout the day. He gave off a cocky and secure aura from a distance. But when in a close intimate space with Ever, Kareem's vibe was confusing.

It wasn't until Kareem showed up unexpected to Ever's house on a Monday evening for an unscheduled tutoring session that Ever found out just how on target he was. Kareem claimed that he had a final exam coming up and begged Ever for some extra help. Suspicious and curious of Kareem's ulterior motive, Ever allowed him in. As they sat side by side at the dining room table, Kareem nervously asked Ever where was his mother. Ever explained she was working late and wouldn't be home until well after midnight. With a raised eyebrow, Ever questioned why he wanted to know and without warning, Kareem swooped in and kissed him. Caught off-guard, Ever pulled back breaking their kiss, and stared at Kareem searching for an explanation in his eyes. Kareem placed his hand on Ever's leg and slowly ran it up his thigh, until he was massaging Ever into an erection. No words had to be spoken, they both knew what Kareem wanted and Ever wanted to oblige him. Kareem leaned in once again and softly kissed him, this time with deep desire. Before Ever knew it, he and Kareem were both naked from the waist down and fully engaged in a lustful sex act right there on the dining room floor. Kareem handled Ever like he would any teenage girl, filling him up from behind. It wasn't until Kareem asked Ever to return the favor that Ever realized that Kareem was really down-low and not just bi-curious. When they were finished Kareem looked at Ever as if he'd done something wrong then quickly dressed and left Ever's house in a panic. Later that night, a confused Ever called Kareem to find out what exactly was going on. Kareem answered and uttered the words Ever would hear repeatedly over the years to come, "Keep what happened between me and you: Between me and you."

Ever sat up in the bed and shook Kareem's words out of his head. He glanced down at Brian and rolled his eyes. *Hell, if I am going to continue to give up my good stuff to these lame ass niggas, I might as well be giving it to someone who loves me,* Ever thought as he angrily snatched his cellphone off the nightstand. He pulled up Wayne's number, but hesitated texting because it was him who allowed Wayne to suck him off like a two dollar slut in a back alley and then dismissed Wayne that fateful night. Now, feeling used himself, Ever realized how sorry he was and how much he missed Wayne. He needed to know if Wayne felt the same way, too. As he slid out of the bed and made his way to the bathroom, he paused in mid-stride with a devilish grin spread across his face. He slipped back in the bed next to Brian, snuggling up to him. Brian reached around from behind and pulled Ever closer to him until he felt Ever's morning wood pressed against his ass. Ever slid his cell under the sheets, snapping a picture of his dick against Brian's ass, making sure Brian's uniquely shaped birthmark on his hip was visible. He then kissed

Brian lightly on the back of his neck, immortalizing the moment. Ever then quietly eased out of the bed while snapping a few more shots of Brian before tip-toeing to the bathroom, and locking the door behind him. Ever leaned against the edge of the sink and swiped through his photo gallery to examine the photos. He then selected Wayne's number and sent the photos to him, hoping to get some kind of a rise out of Wayne; he really missed him. Ever turned off his cell and turned to face the mirror. "I just want you to see what you've been missing Officer Sanders," Ever said to his reflection in the mirror before turning to open the door.

"You're up," he said, greeted by a groggy Brian, slipping into his jeans.

"Yeah, I gotta go," Brian said without looking up.

"What do you mean, it's not even seven o'clock in the morning," Ever questioned, feeling like a cheap date.

"Yo, I told you last night that this would not be an all-night thing. I gotta pick up my seed and his mother today to go shopping."

"You know what, Brian?" Ever snapped, walking up to him, "I am sick of you niggas always down for the ride as long as it's in the dark on a quiet road." Ever couldn't stop thinking about his past sexual encounters with so many other men like Brian and Wayne, and Kareem. "I am so tired of you fake straight punk ass muthafuckas trying to show the world you love women, knowing that you really love this," he said pointing to his firm, round ass.

Brian stepped back and grabbed his keys from the nightstand. "Look, I don't know where all of this is coming from, but you and I knew what was up from the beginning. You can't come at me now six months later, looking for something deeper than what this shit is," Brian said walking pass Ever to the door. "If you can't handle what we got going anymore, let a brotha' know, but I am not trying to change up now, or later." Brian stood at the door waiting for an answer.

Ever stood in the middle of the room and stared at Brian up and down, "So take it or leave it? Is that what you are saying?"

"What I am saying is, I don't know why you woke up on the wrong side of the bed this morning, but shake that shit off and call me later. What we got is a good thing; don't fuck it up by acting like an emotional woman." Brian opened the door to leave. "I'll holla at you later."

Ever's fury overwhelmed his body and Brian's dismissive attitude hurt his feelings to the core. Ever sat on the edge of the bed; shaking with anger. Sick of being the secret lover of every guy he encounters, Ever decided he had enough and this time he would be the one to get the last laugh at them all.

Scene Two

The steady flow of rain bouncing off of the windowpane caused Toy's body to relax a bit as she lay there watching Wayne sleep peacefully like their lives mirrored the Huxtables. *You motherfucker*, she thought, staring at his closed eyes.

She felt like slapping him awake but she promised him months ago that she would forgive him for cheating on her and would forget the "incident" ever happened. But the vagueness to Wayne's story never sat right with Toy. She always felt like he was leaving out important pieces of his infidelity puzzle and she couldn't help obsessing over it. The image of her husband begging for someone else's affection in the middle of the hallway in some half decent apartment in downtown Manhattan was debilitating her both physically and mentally.

She thought she was strong enough to endure the struggle of trusting Wayne again, but it felt like just yesterday when she decided to surprise her husband at work for a late night out since her mother was in town visiting and able to watch the twins. Vivid images of that night played in her head like a cinematic movie.

She had arranged for a car to bring her into the city. She felt alive with excitement and anticipation, especially since their recent fifth year anniversary weekend had went off without a hitch. They seemed to have sparked that dull flame that flickered in their bedroom and that night Toy wanted to keep the flame burning. She took in the scenery as she sipped on her vodka and cranberry while the driver raced down the West Side Highway.

It wasn't until the driver pulled up to the precinct and she noticed Wayne hopping into his F150 pick-up truck that her feeling of spontaneity and elation had quickly deflated. She looked at her watch and then back up at his taillights as he backed out of his parking space.

"He's not supposed to be off for another hour, she said aloud. "Driver, sorry can you follow that truck please?"

"Sure thing Ma'am," the driver replied as he pulled into the line of traffic.

Toy slid as close to the front of the limo as she could to get a better view.

"Where is he going? Don't get too close," she said softly to the driver, feeling like a private investigator that she now wondered if she needed.

The driver immediately obliged her command and slowed up to allow another car in front of him. They drove for what felt like twenty minutes or more until they reached a dark industrial area that looked like it was once abandoned.

So many emotions flooded Toy's body; she sat back and gulped down the rest of her drink. She truly didn't know what to think. Why was Wayne here, in this back alley with no back up? Was he undercover? Should I even be here? She questioned herself as she watched him hop out of his truck and walk with ease over to a warehouse that had been renovated into loft style apartments: Like he's been here before.

She watched him as he trotted up the steps to catch the lobby door as a couple and their child were leaving. His actions showed Toy he knew them. Her mental questions immediately grew darker as her stomach fell to the soles of her feet. "Is he cheating on me?" she said loud enough for the driver to hear.

"Let's not jump to conclusions Ma'am," he replied, trying to cover for his fellow man and keep Toy calm so that she didn't take anything out on the back of his limo. "We'll give him a few minutes, maybe he is dropping something off," he said reassuringly.

She listened to the rational stranger and tried to relax. She poured herself another drink before sliding out of the back of the limo and darting up to the passenger side and tapping on the window.

"Oh shit!" the startled driver looked over at Toy. "What the fuck lady? You scared the shit out of me," he said, unlocking the door to let her in.

"Sorry, but I have a better view from up here. I promise to go back when he comes out." Toy sipped her glass without waiting for his response; her eyes fixated on the door to the apartment building.

After the fifth time of the driver bouncing back and forth from the bar in the back of the limo to the front seat, making Toy her cocktail, neither of them had realized that an hour had passed by.

"This isn't as strong as the others." Toy frowned.

"I made it exactly the same way," the driver lied. He realized she had had enough after her third round.

"I don't think so, but if you say so," she slurred. "What in the hell is he doing in there?" she asked as agitation began to set in. "I can't sit here any longer. I really have to pee," she giggled as she opened the door and managed to get one leg out.

"Wait, wait, wait," the driver quipped as he hopped out of the car and ran to the passenger side to come to her aide. "Let me help you."

"I'm good Tony," she slurred, pushing his hand away. "I will be right back. You stay right here. I am sure whoever he is visiting has a bathroom," she chuckled and tried to walk straight.

Tony watched her as she made her way up the steps and leaned against the lobby door to wait for someone to come out. "Hope you ain't in there fucking up, man," he whispered.

Toy walked quietly and slowly through the lobby corridor not knowing where to go next. She couldn't imagine why Wayne would be here. It bothered her. She tip-toed around each floor like a little church mouse sniffing for cheese. She climbed the stairs instead of taking the elevator, thinking that Wayne would most likely take the steps because most cops do. As she reached each floor she sobered up a little more and by the time she got to the fourth floor she said fuck it and decided to take the elevator to cover the last few floors. As the elevator halted on the sixth floor, Toy was coming to the conclusion that she had lost Wayne and would just have to call her surprise night a fail. As the elevator doors began to open Toy could hear a male voice shouting and she caught him saying 'put me out like this. I am not'. It wasn't until her drunken eyes fixated on the tall man standing at someone's door that she realized it was her husband acting like a fool.

"Wayne!"

A shocked Wayne looked down the dim hallway and wondered not only why his wife was standing there but more, importantly, for how long. He quickly tried to regain his composure as the sound from Ever slamming the door pierced his eardrum.

"Toy? What the hell are you doing here?" he asked, quickly approaching her so that she didn't get close to Ever's door. "I could have been in here apprehending a suspect. You could've gotten hurt," he sternly stated as he grabbed her by the arm and led her back into the awaiting elevator.

"I'm sorry Wayne, but I was just trying to surprise you and when I got to your job I saw you leaving, so I followed you here. What are you doing here, Wayne?" she asked with tears in her eyes. "I know this is not work 'cause I heard what you said."

Wayne's heart stopped as he glanced over at her. "You heard me say what?"

"That someone was putting you out. You wouldn't allow a suspect to do that. Plus, wasn't that the gay guy from that shoe store? What's going on Wayne?" Toy's disappointment was turning into anger.

A wave of relief rushed over Wayne's body. He couldn't imagine what he would have done if she heard him saying he just sucked Ever off. "Toy, please calm down. Can we talk about it in the car?" he asked as the elevator stopped to allow another tenant on.

Toy fumed as the elevator shot down the shaft to the lobby floor.

"Wayne, you have a lot of fucking explaining to do," Toy snapped as they rushed out of the elevator and she pushed the lobby door opened. "Get the truck and meet me at that limo over there. I have to grab my stuff and pay Tony."

"Tony? You fucking know his name?" Wayne asked, trying to deflect.

"If your ass wasn't taking so damn long, I wouldn't know his name," Toy barked without looking back.

She grabbed her purse, paid Tony and climbed into the truck. She stared at Wayne as he pulled off. Beads of sweat trickled down his temple as he tried not to look over at her.

"Well," Toy said, snapping her seatbelt into place. "I'm listening. And tell me the truth Wayne, or I will come back to this place and find out for myself."

Wayne's palms began to sweat as much as his forehead while he tried to decide to tell Toy the truth or keep his secret closeted a bit longer. "It's true Toy. That was the apartment of someone I was seeing but that is dead now. I was just trying to get a few things I left over there."

"A few things? How long has this been going on Wayne, and why was that guy from the shoe store there?"

"Not long, I swear," he lied, "a few months, maybe. I never meant for it to happen. That guy is her friend and I didn't find that out until tonight. I swear, Baby. You got to believe me. I swear on everything I love. That shit is dead. And you being here is just proof that it should be over." He looked over at her with pleading eyes as he grabbed her hand and gently kissed it.

It never took much for him to make Toy melt like ice on a hot summer day. And that night was no different.

Toy closed her eyes tightly and tried to suppress the incident back into her sub-conscious as she had done many times before in order to get through her day. As the rainy sky began to brighten with a grey hue, she glared at Wayne as he slept in a calming peace before looking over at his chiming cell phone sitting on his nightstand. She had the urge to reach over him and pick it up, but she knew it was locked because he changed his password on a daily basis.

"What are you hiding Wayne Richard Sanders?" she whispered into the morning air as she stared at him. "Well, whatever it is, I'm going to find out."

Scene Three

Sinclair sat at her desk typing away on her computer when the ringing of her cellphone broke her concentration. She looked down at the display and sucked her teeth in aggravation. *Didn't I tell him to give me some space? Damn, I guess six months of silence isn't enough for him to get the hint,* she thought rejecting yet another one of Trevor's calls.

Sinclair was disgusted with Trevor ever since her last visit to his sex dungeon. And, the mere thought of him having his way with her, now made her extremely uncomfortable. The chime on her cell went off again and without looking over at it, Sinclair grabbed the device and threw it in her top desk drawer.

"Leave me alone!" she snapped as those words triggered the memory of their last encounter. *Trevor had invited her over for their usual weekly sex date, seemingly normal in tone and demeanor. Yet, Sinclair knew he was probably still upset with her for not calling to cancel their date when she had to take that last minute overseas flight to deal with Tyreek. She braced herself for her usual punishment of a serious dick down, which deep down she enjoyed immensely. When she arrived at his home, Trevor was standing in the center of his dimly lit study room, sipping on a glass of cognac as Sinclair eagerly approached him. He stopped her in her tracks as a devilish grin covered his face and anger coursed through his veins. He slowly walked over to Sinclair, swirling his drink around in a small goblet. "So nice of you to finally join me," he said sarcastically as he stood face to face with her.*

"I'm sor- .",

Trevor placed his finger over Sinclair's lips, stopping her in mid-apology. "You're what? Sorry Master; is that what you were about to say? Nah, you're not sorry, but you will be," he said, sending the glass flying to the corner of the room.

Sinclair flinched at the sound of the glass shattering against the wall. Her mind screamed "get the fuck out of there!" But she quickly dismissed it as new role play.

Trevor grabbed Sinclair by her arms and squeezed them tightly. "I'm getting tired of you not abiding by my rules. You promised to always be available for me," he reminded her before roughly forcing his tongue down her throat. His kiss was rough and aggressive, and before pulling away, he bit her lower lip, drawing blood. "I'm going to show you what happens to bitches who don't listen."

Sinclair's body tensed up at him calling her a bitch because that was something he had never done before, regardless of how rough their play was. Before she could open her mouth to speak, Trevor's mouth was smothering hers again. The shock from his rough, swift actions made Sinclair realize he wasn't role playing at all. Her gut reaction caused her to try to pull away but he dug his nails into her arms and tossed Sinclair onto the leather sofa. Trevor pinned her down and ripped away her clothing until her nude body was completely exposed. Without warning or foreplay, Trevor rammed himself into her; pounding hard and fast while pressing his body weight down on her.

Sinclair gasped for air and looked up at Trevor. She didn't recognize him anymore. She opened her mouth to protest but felt a surge of fear rush through her body once they locked eyes. Trevor's eyes were empty and black with fury, revealing to her that he was really trying to hurt her.

Sinclair struggled to break free from Trevor's grasp. "Stop Trevor, you're hurting me!" she cried.

But her cries fell on deaf ears as Trevor held her down in place as he continued to damage her insides until she mustered up all of her strength to push him off of her. She kicked him hard in the nuts before breaking free from his assault.

"Leave me alone!" Sinclair screamed and snatched up her scraps of clothes and hurried out the door without looking back.

"No way, fuck that and him," she said, shaking that awful memory out of her head then turning her attention back to her computer.

Scene Four

Trevor angrily paced back and forth as he dialed Sinclair's phone number over and over again, hoping that she would eventually pick up. He was hoping to apologize, but when the calls went straight to voice mail, he knew that Sinclair was still upset with him.

"Fuck! That shit was months ago and she still acting like it was yesterday," he said aloud, his voice bouncing off of his living room walls.

He tried to remember the last time they met and in his eyes, it wasn't so bad. Trevor didn't realize that night his controlling, possessive behavior had reared its ugly head, again. *You always do this shit, man,* he thought as he paced back and forth, hitting the redial button on his phone. "You always find it easy to rope them in, but then you lose your head," he told himself.

Trevor took a deep breath as he listened to the recording of Sinclair's phone and decided to leave a message. "Yeah, Sin listen, I thought giving you some space would bring you back to me. It's been long enough and this shit is getting crazy. I need to see you and remember, you promised to always be available for me. Call me back so we can talk." He pressed the end button on his cell phone and sat it down on the coffee table.

He tried to remain calm and willed himself not to pick the cell back up so soon to call her again, but the form fitting dress she wore to work earlier was imprinted in his head and he wanted her back - bad. He realized he fucked up, and, lately, there were several nights that turned to mornings where one would find him sitting vigil in his black convertible with black tinted windows, parked on the street where she either lived or worked. It didn't take long in his disturbed mind to convince himself that she was over their last round of rough play and would be willing to play again.

Trevor sat down on the sofa and fixated his trance on the phone, wondering if she listened to his message. Anger quickly started to set in and his eyes grew dark as his mind started to think psychotic thoughts. Trevor slammed his hand against his forehead a few times to shake away the demented scenes playing in his head – he couldn't. *So, you think you can just ignore my calls and I'll go away. You fucked with the wrong motherfucka. You belong to me!*

Scene Five

Rain watched as the dusk settled in and the sun made its exit behind the horizon for the day. Her oversized window in her new corner office had a pretty decent view of the skyline as well as the bustling city below. The office was her boss' token of appreciation for another job well done with her latest not guilty verdict on her high profile case. Rain twiddled the pen with her fingers as she daydreamed about her perfect performance in court. *You did good, girl,* she thought as she stared down at the people below.

The win wasn't an easy one and the research she had to endure took up so much of her time she was able to avoid fulfilling Geoffrey's constant request to invite Kevin back into their bedroom. Not to mention that the last time she spoke to Kevin she felt a connection that her gut told her she should keep her distance. But now the trial is over and Geoffrey's birthday is right around the corner. He hasn't asked her yet, but Rain could feel the request coming soon. She could hear him now saying that seeing her with Kevin would be the best gift ever.

Lost in her gaze, the pen slipped out of her hand and as she bent over to pick it up she heard a light tap on her door. "Come in!"

As she stood up and turned to the door, she was greeted by a beautiful array of springtime flowers that immediately brightened her room. "How nice," she said, walking over to the gentleman holding the vase, his face still hidden behind the bouquet. "I wonder who sent these?" she asked, scouting for a card.

"They're from me," a deep sensual, masculine voice rang into the air.

Rain stepped back and tried to peek around the vase. The voice was familiar. "What are you doing here? How do you know where I work?" she said in shock and awe as she looked up at Kevin's handsome face.

His infectious smile was brighter than the flowers, causing Rain to smile nervously as she walked back over to her desk to create a barrier between them. He closed her office door and then placed the vase down on the empty corner of the credenza that was next to the door and walked around to her side of the desk and leaned against the edge of it.

"First of all, if anyone didn't know where you worked before they know now. Your picture and details of your case was in every paper and streamed online like crazy. Not to mention, your proud husband talks about you often at the gym." His smile grew wider.

"So you mean to tell me you came way downtown in rush hour traffic to congratulate me personally?" Rain asked, genuinely confused. "How'd you get up here anyway?"

"Listen, you can't keep adding questions after I answer one," Kevin chuckled. "I happen to know one of the bailiffs at the door. He used to date my sister back in the day. I told him if he let me upstairs to see you, I would let my sister know that he got a job and put in a good word for him." He laughed.

"He could lose his job, so you better make sure you tell her," Rain giggled.

"Hell, I'm not telling her shit. She's engaged."

They shared a humorous moment that quickly reverted back to Rain's train of questions. "But seriously Kevin, why are you here?"

Kevin walked over to the window and peered down at the passersby rushing to their next destination. He looked over at Rain and took in her natural beauty before speaking. "Well, Geoffrey approached me the other day," Kevin huffed.

Rain closed her eyes slowly, already knowing the reason why but she wanted to hear from Kevin. "About?"

"About us getting together for his birthday. I think he said in a couple of weeks and I have to be honest: I have to know how you feel about it. It's been so long since our first encounter, I wanted to ask you myself. I want you to want it more than him," Kevin said, walking over to Rain and taking her hand as she lifted from her chair.

"Well, Kevin I have to be honest: Geoffrey hasn't mentioned this to me, yet. So, I really haven't had time to think about it," she lied.

"Really," Kevin replied, pulling her closer to him. "I am sure he is going to mention it soon, so what do you think you're going to say?" he asked softly in her ear before kissing her lobe.

A shiver ran up Rain's spine as she melted in Kevin's arms. She held onto his waist to prevent her knees from buckling. "What do you think I should say?" she heard herself asking.

Kevin slid his hands down her back to her firm ass and squeezed it as he placed his soft lips over hers. His kiss was intense like he'd been waiting forever to touch her and without letting her go, he sat her on her desk, slid her skirt up to her waist, opened her legs and maneuvered himself between them. He looked at her as she lay back on her desk returning the gaze. Their eyes spoke volumes as he freed her from her underwear and unzipped his zipper.

"Anyone else still here?" he asked before leaning in and kissing her neck as he unbuttoned her blouse.

"Just your bailiff friend and the cleaning people," she managed to say between moans.

Kevin took his chances and proceeded to devour Rain on her new desk.

"Good, that means we can be a little noisy," Kevin uttered as he sucked on each of Rain's breasts causing her nipples to stand at attention and creating a fire in her nether region that only he could put out.

Scene Six

The cool crisp night breeze gently brushed against Samara's face as she rushed across the athletic field. She was glad winter was finally over and spring was in the air. She looked down at her cellphone to check the time, realizing she was running late to meet Ever she quickened her pace.

Since the Toy incident with Wayne, Ever hadn't been himself. No matter how hard he tried to hide it, Samara could tell he was hurting. *I wish I could get away with shooting Wayne's trifling ass in the balls; No good dirty bastard,* she thought as she made her way down the steps to cut through the basketball court. Samara was deep in her mental rant when a shadowy figure and the sound of a basketball bouncing on the concrete caught her attention.

The player's chiseled back and rippling biceps began stirring a heat in her body. She slowed her pace diverting her steps in the ball player's direction. As the identity of the figure became clearer with each step, her sex began to pulsate between her legs, taking on a heartbeat of its own. Her good conscious told her to go the other way, but her inner sexpot Sasha, rapidly emerged, causing her to stop cold in her tracks. "Hey Professor Mack," she heard herself flirtatiously call out.

Professor Mack gripped the basketball tightly between his hands, while turning to see her standing there looking sexy as ever. Her thigh length, form fitting skirt clung to her thighs, hips, and ass perfectly. Her V neck sweater showed off her supple breasts. He had tried his best to avoid being around Samara and, for the past several months was successful. Yet, watching her saunter over to him, he could not control is conflicting feelings for her. He bit his bottom lip as his dick stiffened with each step she took towards him.

"Hello, Miss Washington. What brings you out tonight?"

"On my way to meet Ever to work on a project for our sociology class: Haven't seen you around since the fall semester ended, you been hiding from me?" Sasha teased, "I didn't know you had it like that," Sasha said visually tracing the beads of sweat trickling down his neck, landing on his chiseled chest and his rock hard abs. "You're just the man on and off the court, huh?"

Her statement brought Professor Mack back to their explicit encounters, causing his dick to rise.

"There's more where that came from," he said, not trying to conceal his lust for her. Sasha smirked, noticing his manhood had risen to greet her too. She gazed at him up and down, giving him the fuck me eyes, almost willing him to touch her. "Well, a girl can't tell 'cause you've been trying to hide from me."

Professor Mack knew he shouldn't entertain her come on, but he quickly realized resistance was futile. He stood silent, lost in her sexy eyes, not realizing he was face to face with Samara's alter-ego, Sasha once again.

"I don't know what it is about you Samara, but I can't shake you no matter how hard I try," he lustfully confessed caught deep Sasha's trance.

"So, then why keep fighting it?" she questioned, stepping closer into his space. "You know you miss this."

Professor Mack placed his hand under her chin then leaned in and kissed her. Sasha dropped her saddle bag and wrapped her arms around his neck pulling him deep into her longing kiss. He guided her backwards to an unlit area off the court, not parting lips, until she was trapped between him and the court fence. Sasha reached up and gripped the fence, lifting her feet off the ground and wrapping her legs around his waist. He gripped her thighs securing her position then stepped closer until he could feel the heat of her desire against his now full erection. As their kiss intensified, low soft moans began to escape their mouths every so often when they came up for air. Sasha began to grind her honeypot with eagerness against his manhood, becoming wetter by the second. Professor Mack reached under her skirt pleased to discover she wasn't wearing any panties. Unable to resist the excitement and danger of fucking his student out in the open, he reached down and eased himself into her awaiting waterfall. They both let out a satisfied moan in unison as they got lost in their own world of forbidden heat.

Professor Mack stroked with urgency as she bounced herself up and down on the fence to match his stride. Her nectar rained down on him, causing him to glide in and out of her tightness with more ease. Sasha released the fence and wrapped her arms around his neck, driving him deeper inside of her. Professor Mack bounced her up and down on his girth, feeling her inner muscles contract and release around him as he stroked in and out of her with conviction. The rush and satisfaction of being inside of her became overwhelming, causing him to lose control and release his lustful load deep inside of her. "Oh shit!" he growled as his body trembled with pure pleasure.

Realizing what just happened, Samara quickly suppressed Sasha and regained her composure as she unwrapped her legs from around his waist. They stood there staring at one another still breathing heavy while fixing themselves.

"Sorry," he said, apologizing for not being more cautious. "I don't know why I can't seem to control this side of me around you.

"No apologies Professor. Grown folks should never have to apologize for something they choose to do." Samara bent down to pick up her bag, angry at herself for allowing Samara to emerge again. She threw the Professor an awkward smile before scurrying off into the darkness. *Ever's going to kill me,* she thought as she made her way to the library.

Scene Seven

The ambience of *Serenity Health Spa* was calm and relaxing, just what Sinclair needed after a long day of hard work. She beamed from ear to ear, taking pride in having just signed the newest shining female rap artist, Karma to the Centry roster. Sinclair pulled out all stops to ensure hip hop's next sex kitten would feel secure in knowing she was in good and capable hands. Sinclair eased into the steamy whirlpool Jacuzzi one leg at a time and sat slowly into the bubbling water as her body's temperature adjusted to it.

"Mmmm," she moaned and closed her eyes. Despite having a good day, she couldn't stop thinking about Trevor. His behavior had gotten totally out of hand and his latest incident two weeks ago showed Sinclair that he was unravelling rapidly before her eyes.

She looked up at the wall clock and wondered where Rain was. It wasn't like her to ever be late to anything, especially knowing Sinclair had to tell her something. When Sinclair called Rain earlier she told her it was important, and although Rain did mention she had to rearrange a few afternoon appointments, Sinclair didn't think she'd be this late.

"Damn Rain, hurry up," Sinclair said as she watched the door that led to the locker room. She hadn't told Rain anything about Trevor's crazy erratic behavior for fear of Rain's motherly 'I told you so' lecture, but now Sinclair had to tell someone and, at least Rain is a listener.

The locker room door opened and Rain glided through the threshold barefoot and naked with a terry cloth robe loosely draped around her shoulders.

"So sorry girlfriend, I couldn't get out of my afternoon appointment after all, but I swear I got here as soon as I could," Rain apologized and slipped into the Jacuzzi next to Sinclair and kissed her on the cheek.

"I was wondering where you were. Why are you glowing?" Sinclair asked, giving Rain the side eye. "What's going on with you? You're pregnant?"

"Girl, shame the devil and you too for putting that out into the universe!" Rain nearly shouted before laughing. "I'm not glowing and, hell no, I'm not pregnant!"

"Then why do you look so fresh and well...," Sinclair glared into her best friend's eyes, "So, well-fucked! You nasty girl!" Sinclair splashed her hands into the water. "Give me the tea and I mean, all of it!"

"What are you talking about?" Rain asked, "You called me and invited me down here in the middle of the week because you said you had something to important to talk about. We're not here for me." Rain smiled.

"Uh-uh, don't even try it Rain Simone Preston. We are going to talk about me, but first you are going to tell me where you were. You and Geoffrey sneaking off to his parking lot again?"

Rain looked over at Sinclair and wondered if she should share her secret. "You promise not to judge me."

"Me? Judge? Who am I of all people to judge, plus Rain, it's you so how bad could it be. You never fall off of the beaten path."

"I'm having an affair," Rain blurted out before Sinclair could say anything else about her being so predictable.

"What!" Sinclair covered her mouth with her wet hand. "What are you talking about an affair? How could you be having an affair, since when?" she asked shocked and stunned.

Rain hesitated for a moment. "Just a couple weeks now. It wasn't supposed to continue, I mean, without Geoffrey around, but -."

"Wait a minute!" Sinclair interrupted Rain, "Geoffrey?"

"Yes well, remember a while back I did that voyeur thing with Geoffrey and his friend from the gym?"

"Yeah, I remember," Sinclair replied, waiting for Rain to continue.

"Well, after that first time Geoffrey kept harassing me to do it again, remember?"

Sinclair shook her head. "Go on, Rain get to the good part!"

"Ok, the trial started right after that and it took this long for that nightmare to be over, but during that time Geoffrey left me alone, so I tried to forget that night ever happened."

"Why?" Sinclair wanted to know.

"Because Sinclair, that motherfucker was fine as hell and I didn't want that kind of temptation around me and my fiancée. Anyway, fast forward. I win the trial, my time is once again freed up, and you know Geoffrey's birthday is coming up soon."

"Get to the good part, please!" Sinclair quipped in high anticipation.

"I am in my office late a couple of weeks ago and I get a knock on my door with a flower delivery, and guess who the delivery man was?"

"Clearly, not Geoffrey," Sinclair snapped with a giggle.

"No, it wasn't Geoffrey. It was his friend...from that night!"

"What! How did he know where you worked? These niggas are crazy?" Sinclair said, thinking of Trevor.

"I thought the same thing at first, but he doesn't seem like the crazy type, and he explained. Anyway, we end up fucking: right there on my desk!"

"On your desk in a State building. Rain, I am shocked at you," Sinclair smiled devilishly. "I must say, this guy certainly brings out the little sexpot in you."

"Oh my God Sin, you have no idea. He came that day because Geoffrey wants the three of us to get together for his birthday and he wanted to ask me himself because after the first time it never happened again. Well, for the past two weeks we've been making it happen like every other day."

"Rain! You have to stop. You can't keep sexing this man alone and then try to act like you two barely know each other in front of Geoffrey," Sinclair said with some rationale.

"I know, I know. I told him the same thing just today. I told him that we couldn't see each other again until Geoffrey's birthday," Rain sighed.

"You think you going to be able to control yourself?"

"Absolutely," Rain assured her, "it has to stop eventually. I will be fine, just having a little of my own fun. Now let's talk about you."

Suddenly the water felt cold to Sinclair and a shiver shot up her spine. "Let's get out of this water and get our facials. I will tell you all about it," Sinclair said, maneuvering her body to get out of the tub.

Rain followed suit and within minutes the terry cloth robed duo were laying side by side with dark green paste drying on their faces and cucumber slices over their closed eyelids.

"So, I am listening," Rain said through stiff lips.

"Well, you remember Trevor, the guy from the internet?"

"Yeah, your sex slave guy,"

"Mmm-hmm. Remember when Tyreek was in Europe doing that six week tour? Well, Trevor got mad, again. But this time, he went too far and really tried to hurt me, so I had to cut his ass off for a minute. And at first, I was considering giving him one last shot, but then he started calling and harassing me. And, the more he called, the farther I kept my distance."

"Good for you," Rain said calmly, "he sounds a little unstable. You're lucky you didn't have to call the cops."

"Well, let me finish the story," Sinclair stated.

Rain sat up and took the slices off her lids to look at Sinclair. "Don't tell me you had to call the cops!"

Sinclair sat up and allowed the slices to fall off her lids onto her lap. "Not the cops, but my building's security. A couple of weeks ago, while you were being a hot temptress, your girl was almost murdered," Sinclair playfully stated.

"Stop trying to make me feel guilty! What happened?" Rain asked with concern.

"Rain, that motherfucker came to my job! I didn't even know he knew where I worked. First, he kept calling me all day like he's been doing on a regular basis, so I turned my ringer off, hoping he'd leave me alone. Next thing I know, it's about seven, eight o'clock, and I am getting off the parking garage elevator and some asshole is sitting on my car!"

"Oh my God Sin, what happened?"

"You know me, at first I was like who the fuck is that sitting on the hood of my car!"

They both laughed.

"But then as I got closer, I realized it was him. I started to confront him and question how he found out where I worked. But, when we locked eyes I saw that same voided, cold look in his eyes I saw the last time we were together. So, in a calm, direct, even tone he said to me, "So did you think you could just run off and stay away from me forever, Sin?" It sent a shiver up my spine, so I turned around and started running back to the elevator. He jumped off the car and started to chase me. Girl, I was in my brand new Michael Kors pumps, sprinting like I was Flo Jo," Sinclair said, laughing at the event now. "I got to the elevator and pressed the emergency button. The next thing I know, Trevor grabbed me by my hair, spun me around, and wrapped his hands around my neck, screaming some shit like "you belong to me!" Sinclair shook her head, remembering how she thought her life was over. "Luckily, the security guard was already on my floor and as soon as Trevor seen his flashing lights, he ran off. I thought I was going to die." Sinclair began to shake nervously, reliving the event as a tear escaped from the corner of her eye.

Rain tried to console her friend, "It's okay, Sin. He's gone and you are fine. Did you get a restraining order on the bastard?"

"I thought about it but that paper don't mean shit. If somebody wants you dead, they won't care about a piece of paper. I think I should get a bodyguard," Sinclair suggested as she looked at her friend for confirmation.

"If it will make you feel better, maybe you should," Rain agreed.

"Samara lined up some interviews, but I will start off slow and maybe just have someone around when I am working. I don't think that nutcase knows where I live. I haven't heard from him at all since the parking lot nightmare," Sinclair said with a sigh of relief and laid back down to make herself comfortable again.

"Count your blessings and let's hope he's already surfing the internet to find someone else to sink his hooks into. No pun intended," Rain laughed as Sinclair joined in.

Scene Eight

Tyreek stood quietly as he listened to Sinclair try to explain away the violent exchange between her and the stranger in the parking garage: The sole reason for her interviewing bodyguards. From the moment he arrived from the airport and stepped foot in the *Centry Music* building, the rumor mill was frantic with wild tales and exaggerated stories of what happened.

He listened intently as she told him how some crazy man appeared out of the shadows and tried to kill her. Tyreek watched Sinclair as she recounted her terrifying ordeal and he tried to sympathize with her but something was amiss. "Wait, hold up," Tyreek interrupted Sinclair, "if that nigga was some crazy muthafucka off the street, why the fuck you need a bodyguard?" Tyreek sat down in the plush chair across from her desk.

Sinclair dropped her head quickly in an effort to think of another lie to cover up the one she just told. She wasn't ready to tell Tyreek about Trevor because she knew he'd never forgive her for being so sexually un-inhibited with another man. "Tyreek I am afraid for my life. That crazy asshole got away. How do I know he won't be back? What if he is a stalker?" She questioned, trying to deflect Tyreek's train of thought.

"I'm sorry, Baby. I didn't mean to come off like an insensitive dick, but I'm here now and you don't have to worry about that muthafucka or anyone else," Tyreek said, standing up and walking over to Sinclair who was now staring out of her office window. "I got you Sin," he said, wrapping his arms around her waist and pulling her into him. "I would never let anything or anyone hurt you," he said before kissing her neck softly.

The light tap on the door interrupted Tyreek's attempt at seduction and Samara bounced through the door. "Oh, excuse me, I didn't realize you were here Ty. But Sin, your three o'clock interview is here."

"If it's that bodyguard shit, she's good. Send him home," Tyreek spat with both arrogance and confidence.

"Wait!" Sinclair shouted before Samara could leave the room. "Tell him I will be with him in a moment, please."

Sinclair watched Samara leave and turned to Tyreek as he wrapped his arms around her waist again. "Listen, I have to do this, okay? I just want to have a peace of mind." She looked into his eyes for some understanding.

"Fuck that shit. I'm home and you don't need no other muthafucka doing what I am here to do," Tyreek stated, protecting his ego.

"Baby, you are not always here," Sinclair said softly, "You are leaving in a few weeks to kick off the Summer Jam Tour with Karma, so what do I do then? I don't think I will ever see that bastard again Tyreek, but for now I just want to have someone around just in case another psycho tries to come at me. This is my life we are talking about."

Sinclair was getting so caught up in her own story at times she had to mentally remind herself of which parts were a lie. She just hoped there was enough blend of truth in the conversation for him to believe it and not investigate it any further.

Tyreek suddenly felt his heart ache hearing the terror in her voice. "Okay, Baby I hear you, but this bodyguard shit is only when I am away. And, I know we ain't back together, but we together until you feel safe again, you feel me?" His rhetorical question didn't call for an answer and Sinclair knew not to; instead, she shook her head in affirmation, wrapped her arms around his neck and gave him a long lovingly kiss.

Scene Nine

The semi-annual sale week at *Shoephoria* was finally coming to an end and Ever couldn't have been happier. As he turned the lights off and headed out the store, all he wanted to do was go home run a hot bubble bath, sip on some red wine, and get lost in soothing melody of Sade. His back ached and his feet were pounding, it was times like this he wished he had someone waiting at home to take care of him. He sighed at the thought as he closed the steel gates over the windows and door. As he stepped off the curb to hail a cab home, a pick-up truck came barreling down the street before coming to a screeching halt in front of Ever, just missing him by a hair.

Ever stood frozen as his life flashed quickly before his eyes and he tried to make out who was trying to run him over. "What the fuck!" he shouted. "You can't just be flying up and down this busy ass street. I don't care what time it is!" he yelled at the shadowy figure behind the wheel before realizing it was Wayne. "Oh shit!" Ever covered his mouth and darted back onto the curb.

Ever knew Wayne had received his picture messages. One of the benefits of an iPhone was knowing when a person has seen a message. But when Wayne never replied, Ever was left unsure of his reaction, but Ever quickly figured it couldn't be good with this unexpected visit. The dark tinted window on the passenger side rolled down slowly, releasing Wayne's *Gucci Guilty* scent into the air. Wayne sat there staring at Ever with a look of love and pain in his eyes.

Ever wanted to jump in the car, kiss him and tell him how much he missed him, and that he wanted him back; but the image of a stunned Toy in his hallway and the disappearance of Wayne since that day brought Ever's anger and hurt bubbling back to the surface. "What do you want Wayne," Ever spat in a disinterested tone, crossing his arms across his chest.

"Is that all you have to say to me? After you sent me pictures of you and your little boy toy, I would assume you had more than that to say," Wayne said, adjusting in his seat to face Ever.

"Hell, I sent those shits weeks ago, so whatever I had to say is history. Look, shouldn't you be on your way to suburbia to play the loving husband and devoted father or something?"

"Maybe, but I wanted to see you. No, scratch that: I needed to see you."

"Wayne I don't have time for your bullshit and lies. I need to get home," Ever said, stepping off the curb again.

"Just let me give you a ride home Ever. We need to talk," Wayne pleaded.

"I have nothing to say to you. After all these months, it's clear that we are done, so keep pushing that way. You saw from the pictures that I'm good," Ever quipped, pointing in the direction of the Westside highway. "Now be gone!" Ever snapped his fingers.

"Ever please, it's just a ride and a conversation. Is that too much to ask?"

Ever knew getting in the truck with Wayne would open that door that they both knew should remain closed, but he hopped in the truck anyway curious to hear what Wayne had to say. "This is just a ride and conversation Wayne, don't pull no fast shit or I will bust your head to the white meat." Ever closed the door behind him.

Wayne chuckled at Ever's sassiness. He missed it. "No need for all that," Wayne said, pulling into the line of traffic going the opposite way of Ever's house.

"See, you already starting off wrong! My place is the other way, Wayne."

"I know but I just want us to go someplace quiet to talk. We ended things really fucked up," Wayne said, heading towards Central Park.

One of the benefits of being a New York City Officer was knowing all of the routes and secret access roads that laced the massive park. And there was one spot in particular that Wayne liked best. Not to mention, Toy had been acting weird lately and Wayne didn't know when and where she would pop up. The last thing he needed was a déjà vu moment.

"Where are you taking me Wayne? I see you haven't changed: still telling folks what they want to hear to get what you want. I tell you what, we can go wherever you like but nothing sexual is happening, you understand?" Ever snapped, staring at Wayne's handsome profile. He was still one sexy specimen to Ever and he knew he would have to remain strong.

Wayne ignored Ever, tuning him out as he concentrated on the dark, unlit tree-lined road ahead of him. He travelled through the park like it was second nature until they arrived at a secluded spot near the upper West Side. Wayne backed his truck up in a tight little area that was normally used for patrol cars. He turned the ignition off and turned the radio down low enough to allow the slow jams to act as background music.

"What was that all about Ever?" Wayne asked, unsnapping his seatbelt and turning to look into Ever's eyes. "Why the fuck would you send that shit to my phone like that? The last time we saw each other, you used the fuck out of me and told me to fuck off. So, I do as you ask and you wait all this time and send me that shit." The anger in Wayne's eyes burned Ever's forehead.

Ever looked at Wayne while internally searching for the best answer. Fact was: he didn't know why he sent the damn pictures. He was mad: at Brian, at Wayne, at Kareem. Hell, he was mad at all of the men who used and abused him. "I don't know why I sent it. I guess I was just missing you," Ever blurted out.

Wayne dropped his head as a wave of anxiety flushed through his body. He didn't know what to expect when he left work to confront Ever, but hearing those words immediately softened him. "It certainly didn't look like you were missing me," Wayne chuckled to show Ever he wasn't upset. "But if it helps, I miss you too."

Ever looked over at Wayne and wanted to tear his clothes off and fuck until the sun came up, but he had to be strong. "That's nice to hear, but we both know that us being apart is best, right?"

"Right," Wayne agreed, "actually that is why I came to see you. After seeing those pictures, I realized that we never ended things and I want to. We need to, so that you just don't pop up like this," Wayne said calmly, trying to soften the blow. Things weren't all roses and chocolate candy with Toy, but Wayne had decided after almost getting caught that he could no longer live a down low lifestyle and he wanted to keep his family. "You know what I mean, right?"

The lustful look Ever had for Wayne quickly turned to resentment as he tried to respond. "Pop-up? What do you mean pop-up? You know what Wayne? You are still a selfish son of a bitch. I sent you those pictures because I missed you and you just said you missed me too, but then in the same breath here you are again trying to cover your ass, literally!"

"Ever, I swear it's not like that. It's just that after that night I changed. I haven't been with another man since then. Hell, I barely even looked at one. That night, looking at you and then over at Toy, I realized that I had come to my crossroad and it was time to choose which road I would travel: straight or gay. I have to admit, the way you treated me, made my decision much easier, and that night I went home with my wife and promised to be a good husband."

Ever looked at Wayne with respect for being honest and finally making a decision, but the hurt Ever felt made him less empathic. The part of him that wanted to get even crept into Ever's consciousness. "Good for you Wayne," Ever clapped his hands together at a slow loud pace. "Let me be the first to say that I am so proud of you. But just let me get this right. You mean if I tried to seduce you like this," Ever said, tracing his French-tipped manicured fingers up and down Wayne's thigh, "you'd feel nothing?" Ever's hand rested on the crotch of Wayne's pants.

"What I am saying is that I no longer put myself in these kind of positions, so I can be a better husband," Wayne said softly, but never touching Ever's hand.

Ever squeezed Wayne's crotch until he could feel Wayne rising in his hand, "You know you miss my touch," Ever whispered, leaning into kiss Wayne's earlobe. "Don't you?"

Wayne shook his head yes unable to verbalize what he was feeling. He spread his legs further apart so Ever could have better access to his jewels. "Squeeze them for me," Wayne heard himself whispering. "Harder."

Ever did as he was told and then unzipped Wayne's pants to release his erection. Ever stared down at Wayne's dick and wanted to devour him whole, but decided not to. He wasn't doing this to feel good. That wasn't on his agenda. Ever stroked Wayne's shaft and squeezed his nuts at the same time, causing Wayne to lean back in his seat and close his eyes.

"Oh my God! Ever you stroke dick so good. I really missed this," Wayne huffed as he tried to not cum too soon. He kept his eyes shut and allowed Ever to jack his dick like he used to do.

Ever watched Wayne fall back into a sensual existence, releasing all of his guards and falling into a euphoric state. Ever smirked as he watched Wayne take in all of Ever's pleasure like so many men do. Ever tried to fight off his own erection as he watched Wayne fall deeper into ecstasy, and quickly noticed his opportunity. Ever slipped his iphone out of his back pocket and while one hand pleasured his ex, the other snapped pictures of himself nibbling Officer Sanders' earlobe while giving him an explosive hand job.

Scene Ten

Toy sat nervously on the sofa in the family room and tried to watch television to calm down. She held her cell phone tightly in her sweaty palm and looked down at it every so often. Art's text said he'd be calling soon and she hoped he would have some answers. Wayne had been acting distant and standoffish since receiving that early morning text, and when he couldn't keep an erection the other night, Toy felt that something terrible was happening.

She didn't know what to expect when she entered the front door of *Prestige Private Investigation Services* the other day but she knew that she needed help. As she sat down on the worn, brown tweed cloth covered chair in the waiting area, a part of her wanted to get up and run. It was the first time in a long time that she had done something without Wayne's knowledge or permission, but in order to have a peace of mind, and more importantly, find out the truth, it had to be done. Art, the sole owner and operator of PPIS, assured her he'd help her find out what her husband was doing, be it good, bad, or indifferent.

Now, unable to sit still, Toy popped up from the sofa with her cell still in hand and rushed over to the wine bottle sitting on the kitchen isle. She sat the phone down and poured what was left in the bottle into the wine glass and was able to squeeze out a sip. "Shit!" she said aloud.

The chiming of the phone startled her, causing the glass to crash onto the floor. "Fuck!" she shouted before covering her mouth in fear of waking the kids. She grabbed the phone to answer it. "Hello."

"Yeah, uh Hi, Miss Sanders?" a scratchy voice asked.

"Yeah, it's me. Is that you Art?" she asked, grabbing a handful of paper towels to wipe up the floor before sweeping up the glass.

"Yup. So listen, I was able to tail him after work and for the last few days he really didn't show any activity worth noting, but tonight,"

"Tonight, what?" Toy interrupted.

"Well, tonight he took another route to the highway, which I thought was odd. We ended up downtown in a trendy shopping area."

"Huh?" Toy huffed, "Why would he be downtown at this time of night?" she asked, looking up at the kitchen wall clock that read 10:18 pm.

"Don't know, but he did pull over and after a brief conversation a, um…a gentleman got in the passenger side."

"And then what? Where'd they go?" Toy wanted to know.

"I was able to tail them to Central Park but then he lost me," Art said sadly.

"You lost them! Art, you promised to get me answers!"

"Listen, I am on it and I did manage to get a few pictures. They're a little dark but let me go back to the office to see what I can do with them and I'll get back to you as soon as I can."

Toy was relieved that he got pictures but hated that she'd have to wait to see them. She reluctantly agreed to wait for Art's call and said her good-byes. Toy swept up the rest of the shattered glass and made her way upstairs to the master bedroom to wait for Wayne to question him, so he could spin another lie.

Scene Eleven

"So, are you really going to come to my family's cookout?" Kevin said, smiling at Samara as they lay snuggled together underneath the crisp hotel sheets.

The Hilton in Times Square was only about thirty minutes from the university and it had become Kevin and Samara's secret love den since the beginning of the spring semester. He tried to heed to Larry's warning about Samara, but it didn't take long for he and Samara to solidify their sexual relationship. And now, he was really starting to feel like they could possibly take it to the next level.

"I said I would come, but are you sure about this?" Samara asked, feeling apprehensive.

"Look, I know when we started out it was more of a hook up kind of thing, but during these past couple of months, I have to admit, you got a brother thinking about us being exclusive." He smiled as he leaned in to kiss the tip of her nose.

The seriousness of his conversation caused Samara to tense up and she fought the urge to not pull her hand away. Despite them having incredible chemistry and mind blowing sex, she was nowhere near feeling that strongly for Kevin. Not to mention, not too long ago she was dangling from a fence getting her back blown out by Professor Mack. She often wondered if they knew each other, and concluded they must with so few African American Professors at her school. But she also figured if they did know each other, the Professor would never divulge their dirty little secret because everyone knew he was engaged, which made it so much easier for Samara to give into Kevin.

"So you seeing me exclusively would mean what: we are boyfriend and girlfriend?" Samara teased.

"I consider you my lady." The directness of his tone turned Samara on.

"Well then, I am," Samara heard herself saying as she leaned in and kissed his soft lips. "But how will this affect us and school? After all, you are a professor."

"Look, you are of age and what we do off campus is our business. Trust me, we aren't the first to have a professor-student relationship, not to mention I can care less about the people on campus. That's why you have to come on Memorial Day. All of the important people in my life will be there."

"I wouldn't miss it for the world," Samara moaned as she allowed her bare body to give into his touch.

Kevin pulled Samara closer to him, running his hand down the side of her face while softly kissing her lips. Samara climbed on top of him, staring seductively into his eyes as she eased him inside of her slowly. They both moaned in unison as the warmth of her wetness welcomed him in. There was something about Kevin that made her relax. The way he caressed her ass as she rode him steadily created a tingling sensation in the soles of her feet that traveled throughout her body. Samara rocked and swayed her hips on his massive muscle as her juices trickled down his shaft, over his jewels and onto the bed, moistening the sheets beneath him. Samara tossed her head back and closed her eyes lost in the moment, and for the first time ever she felt in total control of her actions: Not Sasha.

She quickly found her rhythm as she clung to Kevin while he held her tightly by the ass and slid her off the bed to bend her over the dresser and have his way with her. Samara stared at Kevin through the mirror as she pounced on what she now considered to be all hers. Kevin gripped her hips pushing deeper inside, making her wetter with each stroke. Samara wasn't sure if it was her strong feelings for Kevin or not that kept Sasha locked in her subconscious, but whatever it was Samara was riding solo this time.

"Grab my hair," Samara commanded in a sexy tone. Kevin grabbed a fist full of her hair and pulled her head back until she was looking up at him. Kevin leaned in and kissed Samara never losing his stroke.

"This pussy is so wet, hmmmm. Is it mine?" Kevin asked, flipping Samara over and lifting her up as she wrapped her legs around his waist. He leaned her against the wall and her mind raced back to her being against the fence with Professor Mack.

Samara shook her head back and forth, trying to shake the image of Professor Mack out of her mind as Kevin drove himself deeper inside of her. She began bucking and bouncing wildly on Kevin, finding herself reliving the moment at the basketball court as she internally struggled with an awakening Sasha.

Kevin had never felt Samara so wet and so warm. Unable to hold back any longer, Kevin grunted and moaned as he came hard while still deep inside Samara's warmth.

"I think I love you, girl," Kevin whispered as he wiggled out of Samara's leg grip and stumbled back onto the bed.

Samara sashayed over to the bed and lay beside Kevin and rested her head in the crook of his shoulder and immediately realized that in order to be faithful to Kevin her alter-ego, Sasha could no longer enjoy any sexual trysts with Professor Mack, ever.

Kevin kissed her forehead lightly and quickly came to the conclusion that if he was going to take this relationship to the next level, both his affair with Rain as well as the freak show they put on for Geoffrey would have to come to an end.

Scene Twelve

The street lined with newly refaced brownstones looked like any other neighborhood in the Park Slope area of Brooklyn. The clean sidewalks and swept porches with wrought iron handrails gave the street a rich, upper class feel that seem to segregate itself from the grimy streets of the New York that surrounded it.

Trevor drove at snail's pace, trying to find a parking spot. His inconspicuous white company van managed to hit every pothole, causing his equipment and supplies to rattle and shift. "Shit!" he snapped, as he looked back to make sure nothing had fallen over. "Damn potholes. Parking always sucks in Brooklyn," Trevor muttered as he watched a petite woman and her child climb into a parked BMW up ahead. "But today might be my lucky day. Hurry up lady."

Within seconds the woman had slid out of the parking space and Trevor pulled up to parallel-park next to the curb. He checked himself out in the rearview mirror before hopping out to grab the set of tools that were stored in the back. As he locked up the van and started walking up the street he smiled at his achievements. It was less than a decade that he and his brother established their own security system company, selling and installing the most innovative high tech residential and commercial security systems to the elite and famous. And, after signing a few lucrative contracts with the government, Trevor and his brother hired a complete staff to handle sales and installation while they dealt solely with the operations of the business. It had been a few years since he had actually installed a security system himself but this was a special occasion.

He tapped on the door softly as he cleared his throat. He watched an attractive blonde through the stained glass door as she approached to open it.

"Hello," she said joyfully like she hadn't a care in world.

"Yes, hello Ma'am, I'm from ISS: Imperial Security Systems. I am here to install your security system," Trevor said, flashing his badge that hung around his neck.

"Right, come in," she said. "Your saleswoman did a great job the other day. The system we currently have doesn't do half of the things your system will do. The cameras with the ability to watch from your smartphone impressed my husband the most. I think that's what sold us. Would you like something to drink?" she asked as she walked Trevor through the beautifully furnished first floor of the brownstone. It was obvious that her job was to keep the house lovely.

"No, thank you. Stacey is one of our top salespeople. Glad you chose us, you won't be disappointed," Trevor replied rejecting her bottled water and walking over to her living room window. He made a mental note to give Stacey a little something extra in her check next week as he shifted the heavy drape slightly to look over at the porch next door.

"I hope not," she sighed, staring at his muscular back that bulged out of his work shirt. "You know there was a break-in around the block just the other day and my next door neighbor was attacked at her job not too long ago. This world has gone mad."

Trevor stared at the matching stone lion statues that sat stoically like bookends on either side of the wrought iron handrails of the brownstone next door. *Even if you were real you couldn't save her,* he thought before turning to look at the woman with a wicked grin on his face. "Then I better get started so we can make sure your family is safe, agreed?"

"Agreed. You go ahead and do whatever it is you security people do. I will be in the study on the second floor if you need me," she said softly, almost flirtatiously.

"Just point me to your attic. I think I will start there," Trevor replied, stepping away from the window as his thoughts grew darker.

Scene Thirteen

The limousine's tinted windows blocked the beams of light cascading down from the mega screens and video billboards plastered on the sides of the high rise buildings that lined Times Square. Rain looked up at the buildings and studied the ads as they flashed in her face while the driver pulled up in front of the Marriott Marquis.

"What are we doing here?" she asked Geoffrey but kept her gaze on the hotel's entrance.

Geoffrey shifted on the stiff leather car seat and tried to suppress his excitement. He had been counting down the days to his birthday and made all of the arrangements so that Rain could concentrate on one thing: pleasing him.

"Babe, I realize that what I am asking of you is a lot, and I can tell it's something you're really not into or it wouldn't have taken this long for us to do it again. So, I thought we'd meet Kevin here instead of home. We'll keep our bed for us," he said softly as he lifted her hand to kiss it.

Rain smiled nervously at Geoffrey and hoped he didn't realize how sweaty her palm was. Except for a few texts from Kevin, they hadn't seen each other in a while and Rain felt like Kevin was avoiding her, but she convinced herself that he was just saving up for tonight. She prayed that the feelings she now had for Kevin would not be noticed by either of them.

"How thoughtful of you, Honey," Rain replied as she allowed the driver to assist her out of the vehicle.

Geoffrey slid out behind her and followed her closely as she led the way to the reservation desk. Neither of them noticed Kevin sitting on the bench behind them. Kevin watched the couple check-in. His eyes followed Geoffrey's arm hug Rain securely around her waist just enough so it rested on her plump firm ass. Kevin had developed a fondness to Rain that exceeded their transparent sexual chemistry. Lately, however, aside from a few text messages, he managed to keep his distance. A wave of guilt flushed through his body and for a split second he considered slipping out before they turned around, but he promised Geoffrey he'd partake in his freaky fantasy. And, since confessing his love to Samara, he promised himself that he would tell them tonight would be the last time: it had to be.

Rain and Geoffrey spun around at the same time as though they we dancing and the relaxed look on their faces caused Kevin to breathe easier. Rain spotted him first but it was Geoffrey who approached him.

"Hey man, didn't realize you were here already. You been waiting long?"

"Not at all. Just got here, actually. But I can't stay long," Kevin said as Rain approached them. "Got to be someplace by midnight, hope I'm not messing things up for you, man."

"Not at all, man. I think I can handle anything that needs to happen after midnight," Geoffrey teased, giving Kevin dap.

Kevin looked at him awkwardly not fully understanding his fetish, but liking Rain enough to play along. "So, you want to grab a drink at the bar first?"

"Naw, why don't we head up to the room and order room service? I'm ready for my present," Geoffrey said slyly and gripped Rain's ass.

The threesome entered the room with Geoffrey leading the way and turning on lights as he walked over to the chair across the room. He sat down and started taking off his shoes to get comfortable. He could no longer contain his excitement and had been longing to see his lady being pleased since the last time, which for him had been too long. Geoffrey hoped that by bringing Rain to neutral territory, she'd feel more uninhibited and connect with Kevin so the three of them can have more nights like these.

Rain and Kevin stood by the bed both watching Geoffrey; both feeling guilty and lusting each other at the same time.

"I'm going to freshen up," Rain interrupted the silence.

"You need some help," Kevin teased, trying to lighten the mood and heat up the room at the same time. He grabbed her hand lightly and felt her smooth skin as she pulled away.

"No, I'm good. Give me a minute," she said, looking into his eyes and feeling the euphoric high he always seemed to give her when they were together.

Kevin broke their trance and quickly averted his attention to see if Geoffrey noticed their intimate moment. He did. Kevin smirked at Geoffrey to cover his affection for Rain. "She's something else, man."

"I know, that's why I am marrying her," Geoffrey said proudly. "Just remember that you're here to fuck her not fall in love with her."

The stone look on Geoffrey's face made it hard to figure out if he was joking or not, but Kevin didn't want to make any problems for Rain, so he chuckled at Geoffrey's statement. "Don't worry my man, I'm good. Why do you think I have to be outta here soon? Let's call room service. I could use a drink."

By the time Rain made her way out of the bathroom donned with just her lace panties and bra, the two men were half way done with their first round of scotch and half dressed: Kevin in just his boxers and Geoffrey completely shirtless but fully dressed from the waist down.

"You pouring me one of those?" she asked Geoffrey, trying to hide her nervousness.

"Of course my love. You look amazing! Doesn't she look good enough to eat, man?"

"Yes she does," Kevin agreed, eyeing Rain up and down like a dog in heat. He loved her tight, athletic body, and he knew firsthand how nimble she could be. He had to remind himself that Geoffrey was joining them tonight.

"Thank you both," Rain said, grabbing the glass from Geoffrey's hand and tipping it to her lips. "Another, please," she gasped, slamming the glass on the table.

The men laughed as Geoffrey poured her another round. And, after the fifth or sixth round they all were inebriated enough to let their sexual desires surface and take control. Geoffrey found his way back to his chair that sat in front of the oversized windows that opened up to the bustling street beneath them. The room lights were off but the glare from the television and the Broadway lights illuminated the room just enough to allow Geoffrey to perform his voyeuristic act. He focused in on the swaying coupling standing in front of him and waited for them to get started. He watched them as they stared into each other eyes, almost like lovers. As Kevin cupped her face in his hands and kissed her on the mouth, Geoffrey sensed their passion and shifted in his seat. He shook his head to wean off some of the high. He wanted to pay attention.

Rain relaxed into Kevin's arms and allowed herself to be taken. It was what she did whenever he held her. Tonight would be no different. She wrapped her arms around his neck, more for support than affection thanks to the scotch, and allowed his kiss to penetrate through her body. His tongue was electric shocking the inside of her mouth, causing her to make soft moaning sounds.

He moved her to the bed and lay her on her back as he hovered over her like a thick blanket. Kevin continued to kiss Rain with focus and intent, like he missed her. His hands glided up and down her smooth chocolate skin and over the lace nuisance that prevented him from touching her softest spots.

"These annoy me," he whispered, breaking their kiss and smiling down at her as he tugged at her panties. "You don't need these." He slowly pulled them off.

Rain didn't resist, and, instead, maneuvered her body to assist him. She stared up at him, almost lovingly but full of lust and licked her lips. She mouthed the words I Miss You as he gazed down on her nude silhouette.

Kevin smirked, flattered by her openness and went in for another kiss and he made his way into what had really been missing him. He released a loud sigh as though a weight had been lifted off him and began to stroke in a steady motion.

Rain wrapped her arms around his back and pulled him in close to her body. She ran her manicured tips up and down his back and then in circular motions, making him squirm in delight to her touch. Kevin lifted her left leg and tilted it forward as he drove deeper inside her.

Geoffrey stared at them with intensity as their bodies contoured to positions that Rain had never done with him. As he gazed at the live show five feet in front of his face, he realized that he wasn't becoming aroused like before. Geoffrey took another swig of his scotch and shook his shoulders to ease the unwanted tension; the unwanted feeling of jealousy that kept peeking through his conscious. The alcohol caused his vision to blur, making the images in front of him look as though they were moving in slow motion. He watched Rain as she knelt on the bed in front of Kevin who was standing on the bed and holding the wall up with one hand for balance. Geoffrey watched Rain as she grabbed onto Kevin's hard shaft and eased the tip of his head into her awaiting mouth and began to make love to it.

"Damn!" Kevin growled. "Suck that dick."

His demand turned Rain on more and her motions quickened and she could feel his knees buckling as he held onto the wall now with both hands. She looked over at Geoffrey as if to say "this is what you want, right?" but noticed his face wore more of a grimace than a grin. She quickly pulled back, ceasing all action.

"What's wrong?" Kevin asked with a dumbfounded look on his face.

"I don't know, ask him." Rain pointed her head towards Geoffrey.

"What? What'd I do?" Geoffrey slurred with bloodshot eyes. "I'm just sitting here enjoying the show."

"Really? You don't look like you're enjoying it," Rain snapped, jumping off the bed and grabbing her panties. She suddenly felt ashamed.

"Yo, Geoff you alright man?" Kevin asked climbing down from the bed and slipping back into his boxers.

"What are you talking about Rain?" Geoffrey asked, ignoring Kevin.

"When I looked over at you, you were looking at us like we were doing something wrong; like you were catching us, or something." Her own guilt began to surface.

"I was not," Geoffrey lied; mad at himself for not being able to hide it. He never had the best poker face. "I...I was just wondering why you don't do some of those moves with me," he confessed. "Almost seems like you two practiced some of that shit," he chuckled, unaware of the secret they shared.

An uneasy feeling clouded the air and stifled Rain. "What?" she coughed. "Geoffrey, I think you've had too much to drink. You're imagining things," she said, convincingly.

Kevin grabbed his jeans that were neatly folded on the other chair that sat across from Geoffrey and pulled them on one leg at a time. "Yeah, man I have to agree, you're buggin. I was just doing what I thought you wanted me to do." Kevin had a pretty good poker face.

"No, no, don't get offended man," Geoffrey stammered as he looked up at Kevin. "Look, I'm sorry. It's just that something feels different. Not sure if it's this place or this scotch," he said holding up his glass, "but something just doesn't feel right to me." Geoffrey glared over at Rain. He realized he was drunk, shit he felt that from head to toe, but his heart was sober and the feeling he felt wasn't good. "Come' ere," he demanded.

Rain frowned as she looked at her drunk husband to be and wondered if this is what her life would end up like: random nights in random hotels fucking random men to sexually satisfy her husband. She shuffled over to Geoffrey and sat on his lap.

"What's the matter Babe? It's your birthday, you should be happy not upset. You know I love you, right?" she asked looking Geoffrey directly in the eyes, ignoring her lover just steps away.

"Yes," Geoffrey sighed and nuzzled his head in her chest. "Yo, Kev I'm sorry I fucked tonight up. Really. We can do this another time, cool."

"No sweat, man. Actually it's almost time for me to get out of here anyway. And, I was going to mention this to you later, but this is it for me."

"What?" Geoffrey and Rain asked in unison. They both looked to Kevin for an answer.

"Yeah, well I met someone and I know this might sound crazy, especially with what just went down, but I think we're going to take it to the next level and see what happens," Kevin said, buttoning up his shirt.

"Well good for you, man. I hope she is as fine as my Rain," Geoffrey bragged.

Kevin looked at Geoffrey and then at Rain. He wished that Geoffrey wasn't there just for a moment so he could kiss her good-bye, but he smiled at her instead. "Yeah man, you got a real winner on your hands. Take care of her." He looked back at Geoffrey and winked.

"Don't worry I got her," Geoffrey slurred. "She ain't going anywhere."

Rain shifted on Geoffrey's knee but kept silent, not because she didn't have anything to say, but because she knew if she said good-bye it would be for good. In that moment she realized why Kevin had been so distant lately: he was off somewhere falling in love with someone else. A numb feeling replaced her scotch induced buzz and a part of her felt like a fool as she watched Kevin turn to leave.

"You two take care, and be safe." Kevin closed the door behind him.

Scene Fourteen

Sinclair smiled as she pulled into an open parking space directly across the street from her place. "Today hasn't turned out so bad after all." She scooped up her bag and laptop, and eased out of the car. It was rare that she could ever find a parking space on this block let alone this close to home. She darted across the street and noticed her next door neighbor Karen standing in front of her steps.

"Oh hey Karen, what's up?" Sinclair asked, moving her items to one hand to give Karen a hug.

"Nothing much, this came for you today," she said, handing Sinclair a Fed Ex envelope. "The Fed Ex guy said it had to be signed for. Must be from one of those music moguls," she laughed.

"I doubt it," Sinclair snickered, "they move too fast to wait for someone to receive something in the mail." They both laughed. "Thank you, Karen."

"No worries. That's what good neighbors are for. Oh, by the way, I am sure you've heard about the recent break-ins in the neighborhood and with what happened to you and all." Karen frowned. "I want you to be extra careful. We just got our security system updated the other day. I think about you sometimes over here alone," Karen said with a friendly grin.

"How sweet of you, but really I am okay and you know lately Tyreek stays more than he goes!"

"Okay, but if you change your mind let me know. I have the number to the security company and the installer was a real cutie: Eye candy." Karen smiled and gave Sinclair a wink before trotting off to her own stairway that led to her brownstone.

"Will do," Sinclair sang as she climbed the four steps that led to her front door and slid the key into its keyhole.

Once inside, Sinclair slid her feet out of her heels and left them in the middle of the floor. She made her way into the kitchen turning on lights as she passed through each section of her airy but comfortable home. She sat at her island in the kitchen and examined the envelope before opening it. No return address. Sinclair pulled out a sheet of paper that had a picture of a set of eyes staring back at her.

"What the fuck is this?" She squinted at the cold eyes returning the gaze and tried to solve the riddle. She couldn't. Not to mention, she was too tired to give it too much thought. Her day was long and equally exhausting. Between grooming Karma for her first nationwide tour with Tyreek coming up and trying to find a bodyguard before they leave, Sinclair was spent, drained, caput. Sinclair walked over to the open bottle of wine on the counter and pulled out the cork before filling her glass. She took a few long sips and closed her eyes. She tried to relax but kept feeling like those eyes on the piece of paper were staring at her again. She swiped it off the island and ripped it to shreds before throwing it away with the envelope it came in. Suddenly, she felt like she wasn't alone. She stared up at the ceiling and all of the walls and an eerie feeling crept up inside of her. She tried to shake it off, but the feeling had ignited her paranoia. She slowly shuffled around the house barefoot, allowing the coldness of the hard wood floors counteract the warm feeling the wine was giving her. As she approached the front door to double lock it, she could see a shadowy figure standing on the other side of the door and her heart stopped. As the door knob started to turn Sinclair stepped back slowly.

Tyreek made his way through the door, startled by Sinclair standing there. "Oh, hey what up? Why you standing there like a scared white girl in a horror movie?" he joked.

"Shut up Tyreek, you just scared the shit out of me!" Sinclair quipped before putting the glass to her lips.

"I don't know how, a nigga been staying here for almost a month and I got a key," he laughed, "How many niggas got a key?"

"So happy I am here to amuse you Ty. But seriously, I got something in the mail today and it freaked me out. I am better now that you are here. I have to admit." She smiled.

"Good, cause I ain't going nowhere," he said approaching her and wrapping his muscular arms around her waist, "At least for another week or so." He leaned in and kissed her softly on the lips.

"Listen, I've been thinking," Tyreek said pulling back to look Sinclair in the eyes. "I know you and Samara have been interviewing bodyguards like crazy, but I think I found someone."

Despite not hearing from or seeing Trevor since the attack, Sinclair still felt the need to be protected and Tyreek was adamant about not leaving without her being safe. During the past several days, she and Samara interviewed over twenty bodyguard prospects and only one was worth giving a second thought.

Sinclair's eyes lit up like the Manhattan skyline on a crisp clear night, "You did? Who? Not one of your thug friends, Tyreek."

"Naw, I wouldn't trust none of them muthufuckas around you," he replied, taking her by the hand and leading her into the living room. They sat on the sofa and Tyreek began untying his Timberlands. "I'm talking about Kingston."

"Who is Kingston?" Sinclair asked, starting to feel the warmth of the wine flowing through her veins.

"One of Karma's bodyguards. I hung out with my man a few times, you know when Karma and I rehearsed for the tour and I think homeboy would be perfect. He is about his business and I feel I can trust him around you," Tyreek said with seriousness in his eyes. "I actually talked with him and gave him a proposition to think about."

"Oh, yeah? And, what proposition was that?" Sinclair asked with a furrowed brow.

"I told him that if he stuck around here to keep an eye on you; in turn, I would make sure nothing happened to Karma. You know, he watch my girl, I watch his girl."

"Tyreek I am not your girl, remember? We haven't gotten back together, and Samara and I still have to interview this Kingston person. Just because you like him doesn't mean I will."

"You will like him, trust me. But you just remember, we will always be together. Not sure why you ain't understanding that," Tyreek said, pulling her closer to him and smothering her with soft wet kisses. "I just want to do this to you all night, Sin."

Sinclair melted into his arms and allowed him to ravish her face and neck with his soft lips. She smiled at the thought of their bodies intertwined all night long and allowed her body to fall limp with pleasure. Within minutes, their bodies were bare and Tyreek was sucking on Sinclair's inner thighs in the middle of the well-lit living room floor: Both totally unaware that they were performing under the watchful eyes of the hidden camera in the ceiling.

Scene Fifteen

Professor Mack stood at the large dry erase board at the bottom of his auditorium style classroom. He was focused on writing notes for the day's class when Samara walked in. She stood in the doorway at the top of the room staring down at him diligently working. She wrestled with her emotions, unsure of how to break the news to him that they would no longer see one another. Samara took a deep breath then cleared her throat loud enough to startle Professor Mack's. He wasn't expecting any students this early in the morning, let alone Samara. A wide smile spread across his face at the sight of her standing there looking sexier than ever. They hadn't seen each other since their last romp in the basketball court. He wondered why she had gone missing, but he knew she'd reappear at some point, she always did.

"Why hello Ms. Washington, what brings you to my neck of the woods?" he asked, placing the cap on his marker and his book on his desk.

"Hey Professor, I was wondering if you had a moment?" she asked, still standing in the same spot afraid to move.

"For you? Sure. Come down and have a seat," he said as he motioned to the row of empty seats in front of him. He walked from behind his desk than leaned back against the front of it, crossing his hands in his lap to conceal the semi erection growing in his pants.

Samara made sure the door closed behind her then made her down the steps that led to him.

He watched as her hips swayed from side to side with each step. Samara felt a heat beginning to surface between her legs, as if her sex knew he was close. Once face to face they hugged one another. He inhaled her Dolce & Gabbana perfume and almost became intoxicated by it.

She felt herself become weak from his touch almost melting in his arms, but quickly gained her composure and pulled away to sit down in the empty seat in front of him.

"So, what's up?" he asked, still taking in her presence. He couldn't help it.

"Well, there really isn't an easy way to say this," Samara said, trying to prevent the tears from forming in her eyes.

"Samara, what is it? Are you alright?" he asked, reaching for her hand.

"Sorry, I don't mean to get so emotional." Samara took a deep breath then continued, "I'm ok. It's just this thing we've been doing has to really stop. I know we always say this to one another but I have someone special in my life now. I really care for him and want to see where things go: Without any distractions."

Professor Mack stared at Samara and could see the sincerity in her eyes as a tear escaped her left eye onto her cheek. "Samara it's alright. Maybe it's something that's for the best; for both of us. I would be lying if I said I'm not disappointed, but I want to see you happy."

Samara looked up at him in his hazel eyes, "You say things like that and that it what makes this so hard." She stood up to face him.

"I told you a long time ago that you do something to me," he replied, cupping Samara's chin and pulling her face closer to his. Their kiss intensified causing them both to begin to breathe heavy from the rush of hormones flowing through their bodies.

Samara wrapped her arms around his neck as she felt Sasha begin to stir from her slumber. Samara wanted to break away from the professor and run home to Kevin, but as Sasha emerged, Samara found herself recoiling inside of herself. Plus, the fact that another teacher or student could come rushing through the classroom door only intensified Sasha's desire for him more.

Professor Mack slid his hands down Samara's waist pass the small of her back until his hands were firmly gripping her firm ass. Samara released his neck then slid her hand down his chest. She pulled his neatly tucked in button down Oxford from his slacks and rubbed her way up his chest. Soft moans escaped her mouth as his hands made their way between her legs. He could feel that she was ready and scooped Samara up with one arm and then pushed everything on his desk to the floor with the other. As the desk contents glided across the floor, Samara lay across Professor Mack's desk, awaiting his touch. He eased her ripped jeans down her hips releasing one leg as he knelt down and then spread them wide apart for him to devour her weakness. His warm wet tongue gently stroked her throbbing clit. Samara began to feel dizzy as she faded to the background and Sasha took full control over her body. Professor Mack slid two fingers into her dripping wet slit stroking her g spot with each lap of his tongue.

"Yes, that's it. Eat that pussy just like that 'til she cums," Sasha demanded, gripping the back of his head and grinding on his fingers.

Professor Mack moaned and did as he was told until her warm wet nectar rained down on his chin and finger. He stood up, sucking her juices off his fingers as she lay shaking uncontrollably. He unzipped his pants releasing his throbbing manhood then climbed eagerly on top of her, entering her body with ease and urgency. Sasha gripped his firm ass pushing him deeper inside of her aching melting pot. Professor slowed his pace grinding in a circular motion kissing her deeply, attempting to hold his release. Sasha wrapped her legs tightly around his waist, pumping harder as she erupted, spilling her wetness on his desk top. Professor Mack struggled to hold it in but as inner walls contracted, gripping his tool, he exploded deep inside of her, coating her insides with his juices. He hated that this would be the last time they would share together, but at the same time, he realized she was right, this couldn't go on forever. He stroked her hair back then softly kissed her forehead. "I'm always here if you need anything," he said, staring deeply into her eyes.

Samara nodded her head not wanting to say goodbye. They both pulled themselves together quickly and then kissed one last time.

Scene Sixteen

Sitting impatiently Ever poured himself another glass of Merlot as he sat by candle light waiting for Brian to arrive. He had phoned to say he would be late but as the minutes turned to hours, Ever's blood began to boil with anger while the steak dinner he prepared for them grew dry and cold.

"It doesn't take this damn long to drop off no fucking money," Ever mumbled, trying to stop his mind from racing with thoughts of Brian standing him up to roll in the sack with his baby mama, or worse, another man. And, with each sip the merry-go-round of imagination spun faster and faster, fueling rage deep inside him.

Frustrated, Ever growled as he pushed back from the table. He grabbed the bottle of wine and his phone off the table then stormed over to his computer and plopped down in his chair. He sat back contemplating a good way to seek his revenge on those who had wronged him as he surfed the net when a sinister smirk spread across his face.

"They will learn the hard way what fucking with a motherfucka named me will cost them," he callously said with squinted eyes as he finished the last of the few drops of wine in the bottom of his glass. He was lost in the details of his devious plan when Brian's ring tone chimed, breaking Ever from his trance.

Ever snatched the phone up and answered it bitterly and cold. "So nice of you to finally call, Brian. What happened, forgot the number?"

"I'm sorry Ever. I'm on my way, some things jumped off over here. But warm that food up and get ready for me," Brian said as if everything was cool, completely ignoring Ever's sarcasm.

"What was so urgent that it took you two hours Brian? I stood in this damn kitchen cooking like Betty fuckin' Crocker, setting the table, and getting everything sexy up in here for you, so you could just leave me twisting in the wind. And you think what? I'm not supposed to be in my feelings about that. Shit, I deserve more than a half ass explanation," Ever quickly snapped, causing Brian to pause at his outburst.

"Yo, slow your roll, I'll explain everything when I get there, I promise," Brian pleaded.

"Fine, but if I don't like what rolls off your tongue, you can prepare to make your exit earlier than expected," Ever said before disconnecting the call.   Ever had no intention of putting Brian out but had to make it sound good. Tonight would be more than just dinner and casual sex. Tonight Brian would un-expectantly play right into Evers hands. His evil grin returned and spread wider across his face as he sipped his wine while setting the stage for his plan.

****

Brian braced himself for a verbal tongue lashing as Ever opened the door. However, much to his surprise, Ever was calm, cool and collected.

Ever greeted Brian with a smile as he led Brian to the table and pulled out the chair for him. Brian sat at the table watching his every move while trying to figure out why Ever was now acting like everything was all good. It scared him. He watched Ever serve him dinner as he tried to push the feelings of caution to the back of his mind. Ever sat down beside him and began to cut into his steak like their night was starting on time.

"Ever, listen …," Brian found himself trying to still explain his tardiness.

"Shhhh," Ever stopped him by placing his manicured finger over Brian's lips and looking directly into his deep brown eyes. "Relax, there's no need to explain anything. We're good."

"There isn't? We are?" Brian questioned, clearly confused.

"All that matters is you're here now. Why ruin or waste our time on arguing the rest of the night away and hurting feelings. Let's just enjoy the night the way we planned," Ever said sweetly as he leaned in to kiss and nibble Brian's earlobe.

Brian moaned softly to Ever's touch. Ever did that to him. Brian relaxed a little but remained skeptic. As Ever pulled back and began to refocus on his plate, Brian looked down at his and tried to erase the thought of Ever trying to poison him. Brian pushed his food around on the plate then smelled the wine, inspecting for traces of some sort of arsenic.

"Is something wrong with the food or wine?" Ever questioned, still suppressing his anger.

"Listen, I know you were pissed off earlier and now you acting as if nothing happened: Licking my ear and shit. Hell yeah, something's wrong. Did you poison the food?"

Ever laughed so hard, tears began to stream out of the corners of his eyes. "So, because I'm not acting like a damn fool, something has to be wrong with the food or me?" Ever asked, laughing even harder.

"Yell, scream, break something, or cuss me out. But damn, do something. Let me know what's coming because I know you Ever. Shit just don't die with you," Brian said scared to move from his seat.

"The only thing that's coming in this warm mouth, is your long, thick dick, and this hot tight ass all over you, every way we can think of," Ever seductively purred in Brian's ear. "So eat up Baby, cuz you're gonna need your strength."

Ever could see Brian was still hesitant, so he picked a piece of steak up off Brian's plate and ate it. He then sipped Brian's wine to reassure him nothing was in his food. Once Brian saw Ever was still standing, he allowed his stomach to take control and devoured the plate of food within minutes.

After clearing the table, Ever made his way to the bed and got comfortable, giving Brian a come hither finger. "I've been waiting for this all night," Ever said in a sexy tone.

"I have too," Brian replied, slipping out of his clothes to join Ever on the bed. Brian kissed Ever softly while running his hand down the side of his face.

Ever eased his hands down Brian's chest until they were full of Brian's rock hard dick and he squeezed gently causing Brian to moan.

"Mmm hmm, I can tell." Ever smiled, maneuvering so Brian lay on his back as he kissed his way down Brian's chest and taking Brian's dick deep into his throat. Ever sucked and bobbed up and down on Brian's massive tool as Brian gripped the back of his head pumping in and out of Ever's warm mouth.

Brian loved how Ever's touch was soft like a woman's, but his jaw was strong like a man's should be. Brian moaned Ever's name softly almost as if whispering, encouraging Ever to never stop.

Ever continued to devour Brian's manhood until he erupted in Ever's mouth. Brian watched Ever as he swallowed every drop of his nectar before bending over the edge of the bed for Brian to mount him.

"Why don't you come this way," Brian motioned towards the middle of the bed.

"Because if I do, I can't do this," Ever replied, placing his hands on the floor, leaving his warm awaiting ass in the air.

Brian looked at this new found position and all he could think of was the easy access this one would give him and he entered Ever's anus slowly. They both let out satisfied sighs and moans in unison as Brian caught his rhythm. Within minutes, Ever began throwing his ass back at Brian demanding him to call out his name. And, Brian obliged, making Ever so horny, he began to stroke his own dick, so they could cum together. As Brian's strokes became more focused and frequent, Ever jerked himself harder and as planned, they exploded together before collapsing; Brian on top of a half off the bed Ever.

"Why don't you relax and let me grab you a wash cloth and something to drink," Ever suggested in between breaths as he climbed from under Brian and made his way to his feet.

Brian didn't respond, and instead, lay back resting his head on the pillow. By the time Ever returned with a warm wash cloth in one hand and an ice cold beer in the other, Brian was snoring, lost in la la land.

Ever smiled at his ability to knock a man out with his sex game and walked over to his computer. He quietly moved the mouse around, waking the screen from its hibernation then logged on to make sure the web cam caught every twist and turn of the night's secret romp. Knowing revenge was now at his fingertips, Ever smiled wide and devious thoughts invaded his mind.

"He who laughs last," he whispered, shutting down the computer and making his way back to the bed to get a good night's rest with an unsuspecting Brian.

Rain sat behind her desk, staring at the beads of rain cascading in different directions against the smooth tempered glass as the sun shone through the clouds. She loved sun showers. A slight surge of guilt rushed through her body as she sat reminiscing about the steamy secret affair she shared with Kevin. She realized that he had awakened something deep within her that not even Geoffrey was able to do. And, even though she loves Geoffrey, she now found herself torn and questioned whether or not she was still *in love* with him. Not to mention, that ever since their last little voyeur escapade that turned out to be a complete bust, not only did Rain find herself avoiding Geoffrey like the plague, but Kevin was avoiding her just the same. She tried to suppress her feelings for Kevin and erase both him and that night from her mind but her efforts were fruitless and as she replayed that night in her head over and over again she could sense that Geoffrey knew something. The ringtone on her desk phone interrupted her thoughts as she lifted the receiver to answer it.

"Attorney Preston speaking," she said solemnly. The dullness in her tone gave away her depressed mood.

"Hey pretty lady, just thought I'd call to let you know that I am over here thinking about you." Geoffrey's baritone voice echoed in her ear. "Can you cut out early and go to dinner with your soon to be husband tonight?"

His jolly nature made Rain's stomach turn. She didn't feel like eating. She didn't feel like doing anything except meeting Kevin somewhere to rekindle the explosive sexual relationship. *Damn you, Kevin*, she thought as she tried to come up with another excuse to ditch dinner. "Sorry Babe, can't tonight. I promised Amber that I would help her with her exhibits for her upcoming trial. I wish you would have asked me earlier," Rain lied.

"You know if I didn't know any better, I'd think that you were avoiding me," Geoffrey said half joking. "But you know I understand. It's the nature of this beast that we call law, right? So, I guess I will see you later tonight?"

"Hmm, mmm," Rain purred into the phone giving only half her attention to him as she watched Dexter peek into her office. "I won't be too late, but don't wait up for me, okay Babe." She tried to sound sincere.

"Don't overexert yourself Rain, you have been running like crazy lately. I want to you slow down, okay?"

"I'm good, but I hear you, Babe. I will call you when I am on my way home."

She hung up before she could hear his good-bye and gave Dexter her immediate attention. "Well, Counselor what brings you to my side of the building?" she asked with a wide grin on her face. Dexter was the cutest white guy she knew and she was sure the crush she had on him was being conveyed through her bright smile.

"I must say Attorney Preston, I am impressed by your poker face. The way you just lied to whomever you were just speaking with showed me how you won that recent case. We both know Amber is on vacation for the next two weeks. Who are you avoiding, if you don't mind my asking?" Dexter made his way into her office and plopped down in the chair across from her desk.

Rain breathed a long sigh and debated on whether she should let this stranger into her personal life. Hell, it wasn't that long ago that she and Dexter formally introduced themselves to one another at Berg's Deli. She looked into his dreamy blue eyes and immediately felt like she could confide in him, a little bit. "That was Geoffrey, my fiancée. It feels like we are existing in alternating worlds right now, you know busy working, trying to plan a wedding, etc.," she huffed. "I think I am getting cold feet."

"You wouldn't be the first," Dexter said, adjusting his tailor made suited body in the chair. "It's only natural to have butterflies. But that should only last briefly, so if you have been feeling this way for a while, you may want to rethink it."

"That's what I've been saying to myself. I just don't know anymore. Some things have happened recently that has me thinking I should remain single."

Her comment intrigued him and Dexter leaned over and placed his elbows on her desk. "If you are thinking like that then you definitely have to slow things down a bit. You don't want to go into something so committed if in your heart you still want to shop around. That is why I am still single, makes mingling stress free." His smile brightened the room.

"Thanks Dex, I think I needed to hear a man's perspective. So, why are you here, in my office, after hours," she said, with slight flirtation. She couldn't help it – that's what crushes do.

"Actually, I stopped by to see if you have a file on an old case you may have worked on. But, by the looks of this office, you wouldn't be able to tell me right away." Dexter surveyed the small office that had files piled up in every corner.

"Hush Dexter, my paralegal just said that she is coming in next weekend to clean up for me," Rain chuckled. "Why don't you shoot her an email with the file name and number and she can look for it. How soon do you need it by?"

"I got time. I will send her an email in the morning. But now that you are off the hook with your man, feel like going down stairs to Murphy's and having a drink with me?"

His blue eyes drew her in and she heard herself saying "Sure, let me wrap things up here and I'll meet you downstairs in the lobby in ten minutes."

"Cool," Dexter replied, standing up to leave. "See you in ten."

She turned around in her chair and reached for her cellphone, debating whether or not to text Kevin: something she had done many times since their last encounter with Geoffrey, but like all the other times, she put the phone in her pocketbook and turned off her computer.

As she waited for the elevator, she kept hearing Kevin's last words saying he had found someone. Rain wondered what she looked like, if she was young and pretty. She wondered what this chick had that Rain didn't. Rain got on the elevator and pressed the L button and leaned against the wall focused on suppressing both the memories and the strong feelings she held for Kevin, but she couldn't. They had unfinished business to tend to and him darting off into his own world leaving her restless and behind wasn't going to be enough. She wanted a full explanation and was determined to get it. *Damn it Kevin, you owe me at least that*, she thought as the elevator door opened to the lobby floor and she found Dexter standing there waiting for her.

Scene Eighteen

"Miss. Hatorri your next interview is here," Samara's voice chimed through the phone's intercom.

"Thank you, send him in," Sinclair replied then stood up, smoothing her black pencil skirt out. His *YSL* cologne greeted Sinclair before he reached the chair across from her desk. Sinclair inhaled deeply becoming intoxicated by his scent as she sized him up. She could tell that he was a health nut because he didn't have an ounce of fat on him, even his lips were thin. He looked refined, like he had lived a few lives, even though he could have been much older than she. He oozed charm and charisma. And, despite his muscles bulging against his tailored suit, she could see the gentlemanly quality. She found herself looking up at him. *He must be at least 6'4",* she thought as her eyes met his. An involuntary smile formed on her face as she extended her hand. "So nice to meet you face to face, and thank you for coming on such short notice. Tyreek has said nothing but good things about you," she said, reluctantly releasing her grasp.

"The pleasure is all mine, Ms. Hatorri. Although I must admit, Tyreek caught me off guard when he suggested I stay here to secure your wellbeing." The seriousness in his tone immediately made Sinclair feel safe.

"I was even a bit more confused when I received a call stating you were requesting to interview me. Tyreek made it seem like it would be light duty," Kingston said unbuttoning his suit jacket. "May I?" he asked before sitting down.

"Oh, yes of course, have a seat, and please call me Sinclair. Miss Hatorri makes me sound old," she chuckled before sitting back down in her plush leather executive chair. "In case you haven't heard, and I'd find it impossible for you to not have, but I was attacked in the parking garage by some random lunatic. So now I need to be protected for a little while until I feel safe again," Sinclair said shifting in her seat feeling like the interview had turned tables. "So, Mr. Kingston, I'm sorry Tyreek didn't tell me your last name."

"James, Kingston James," he replied with a slight smirk.

"So, Mr. James the reason I wanted you to come in today is because it is important for me to feel comfortable. I trust Tyreek's judgment but that was pretty traumatic for me," Sinclair said calmly, taking back control of the interview.

"I apologize if I seemed rude and inconsiderate. Now that I know the situation I want you to ask me whatever you need to feel totally comfortable," he said sincerely and sat back comfortably in the chair.

Sinclair smiled at his ability to be genuine and delved into her slew of questions that she and Samara came up with. Some had nothing to do with the position, but Sinclair needed someone who would be available for her 24/7. He answered them all with direct straight answers. She was impressed.

"Would you be willing to do overnight shifts? Wait, before you answer, I should tell you I live in Brooklyn," she said with a girly grin.

"Ms. Hattori, I mean Sinclair." He smiled. "If you want me to protect you then that means you become my sole priority. Your life will be safe with me I can guarantee it," he said bluntly with a serious glare in his eye.

Sinclair sat stuck for a moment unsure of what to say but her mind had been made up: Kingston would be her bodyguard.

"Kingston, I must say, I'm impressed. I clearly see what Tyreek was talking about. I see you take your job seriously. And that is someone I need. I will have to ask you sign a confidentiality agreement being that you will have access to everything personal pertaining to me and my life outside Centry. Will that be a problem for you?" Sinclair asked with a slight hint of flirtation lacing her tone.

"That won't be a problem at all. I just have three questions for you: How much is this detail paying? Who's going to replace me as head of Karma's security," he paused, waiting for the answers to his first two questions.

Sinclair jotted down the salary on a slip of paper and slid it across the smooth mahogany desk.

"As for Karma's new head of security. I already have someone in mind for her. Trust me, she will be well taken of and in capable hands. Not to mention Tyreek already gave his word that he will keep his eye on her. I wouldn't have my pretty little artist protected any other way. And, what was your third question?

"I wasn't going to ask unless I wasn't satisfied with the first two but I am. So, the third is: when do you want me to start?" Kingston asked looking down at the seven figure number on the piece of paper in his hand.

"Tyreek and Karma leave for their tour next week, so let's start this weekend to give everyone time to adjust."

"Sounds good to me and I just have one request of you," he said, standing up to leave.

"What's that?"

"I am going to need to see the video footage of the attack. I just parked in the garage and this is not the easiest building to get into. I am going to need to know who I'm protecting you from. If there is something you need to tell me, and you want it held in confidence, we can do that when Tyreek isn't around," he said through a serious expression and stern tone.

Sinclair nodded her head in agreement then thanked him before escorting him to the door.

She never considered coming clean about Trevor to anyone at Centry, not even Samara knew all the details. But somehow she felt at ease with Kingston, and seeing that he already senses she knows her attacker, she couldn't help but feel completely safe in his presence.

Scene Nineteen

Toy nervously sat in the parking lot of Prestige Private Investigators with her stomach in knots and her palms sweaty. She knew whatever information Art had was going to bring her closer to the truth and possibly rip her family apart. Something inside of her screamed at her to turn the car around and go home and act as though none of this ever happened, but her curiosity got the best of her. She tapped her manicured fingers on the steering wheel, gazing around the parking lot, willing Art to drive up. "Come on Art, you made me wait long enough," she whispered.

Toy prayed Wayne truly had ended his affair, she couldn't bear the thought of the only man she had ever loved since high school, had been devoted to, stood by and supported, could not only betray her but continue lie to her. Toy found herself often asking what she had done wrong for him to seek comfort in the arms of another woman. The feeling of inadequacy crept into her psyche and her need for answers rushed to the surface as she watched Art pull his black classic Mercedes into his marked parking space. "About time," she huffed as she turned the ignition off and made her way across the semi empty parking lot.

Toy paused at the glass door for a moment, trying to suppress the nauseating feeling swirling around in her gut. She took a long, deep breath and walked through the front door. The spunky receptionist greeted Toy and informed her Art would be right with her. Toy thanked her then took a seat on the worn brown chair in the waiting room and attempted to appear calm and collected.

"Mrs. Sanders, come on in," Art said calmly, holding his office door open for her.

Toy's heart sank to her stomach as her nerves became on edge. She hoped Art was able to clean up the photos enough for her to be able to piece some parts of this puzzle together. It was not only consuming her, it was destroying her. She smoothed her skirt as she sat in front of Arts cluttered desk and braced herself for the worse.

Art sat down in his tattered chair and opened the manila folder that sat in front of him. "As I told you over the phone, the photos I took came out kind of grainy, but I was able to reach out to a friend of mine who's an expert in photo enhancement. This is as clear as he could get them," he said, sliding a large yellow envelope across the desk to her.

Toy reached for the envelope with a shaky hand. She took a deep breath then swallowed hard as she removed the pictures. Instantly, she recognized Ever and the stunned expression on his face. She flipped to the next photo that seemed to capture them in an argument, or at the least, that is what it looked like. The last two photos showed Ever getting into Wayne's pick-up truck and them pulling off. Toy lay the photos across the desk and spread them side by side.

"Do you know who this man is," Art asked pointing to Ever.

"I don't know him personally, but he works in a shoe store where Wayne took me once, and that's the same man who was at Wayne's mistress's place where I caught Wayne."

"What else do you know about him because I have a gut feeling he has the answers to all of your questions," Art said, lighting his Marlboro light cigarette and taking a long drag.

"I don't remember the address to the apartment building but I certainly know where that shoe store is," Toy said, looking down at the photos still trying to examine the pictures for more information, but found none. If anything the photos only raised more questions.

"Get me the name of the shoe store and if you can try to remember the address of the mistress that would be very helpful. Let me and my people do a little more investigating, but you have to promise me you will remain calm and not give your husband any indication that we are onto him, no matter what we find, no matter what you may see. If you want the truth you can't blow my cover. Understood," Art asked through a stern and serious tone.

"I understand," Toy said scooping the pictures up and putting them back in the envelope. "May I take these with me?"

"Yeah those are your copies. I already have mine for the file," Art said exhaling his cigarette smoke through his nostrils, making him look like a bull about to pounce on a matador.

"Thank you, Art," Toy said standing to make her exit.

"Don't thank me yet, I am not done. I should have more answers, and maybe even a few extra pictures for you soon."

"Sooner rather than later, please Art. I have to find out what's really going on with my husband. It's killing me," Toy replied with pleading eyes.

Art empathized with her pain. Hell, he knew exactly how she felt. After all that is how he got into this business, following his cheating wife once upon a time. "I will have something for you soon, promise. You have my word Mrs. Sanders."

"That works for me. Thank you, Art," Toy said opening his office door to leave.

"Ok I'll call you soon." Art smiled. He liked Toy and decided to make it his priority to find out what her philandering husband was up to.

Toy's confusion turned to anger as she headed home. In her mind, Wayne was still seeing that woman, and now she had proof. Why else would he be picking up that shoe guy? She was determined to find out the truth now more than ever. "Ok Wayne, you want to play games? Well, it's game on now, Bitch!" Toy said aloud through clenched teeth as she sped down the freeway.

Scene Twenty

"Well, this is different," Samara chimed as she perused the swanky Indian restaurant decorated in bright orange, red and yellow hues and neatly tucked in the corner of a semi-bustling block in lower Manhattan. The pungent aroma of curry penetrated her nostrils as she slid out of her shoes to take a seat on top of the oversized pillow on the floor next to a large round table.

"It sure ain't Berg's," Ever chuckled as he followed suit and slid out of his Michael Kors flats and squatted down next to her. "And, where in the hell is Sinclair and Rain? Those bitches are always bringing up the rear!"

"I just texted Sin, they will be here soon, be patient," Samara said calmly.

"Look Bitch, it feels like I haven't seen y'all heffers in a month of Sundays, we have lots to catch up on. Excuse me, waiter, can a diva get a cocktail please? Vodka and cranberry," Ever snapped.

"I'll take one of those too," Samara echoed.

"You guys couldn't wait for us," Rain sang as she and Sinclair swept pass the hostess and made their way to the table. "This is nice Sin, good selection," Rain said, opting not to come out of her shoes and taking a seat across from Ever.

"Who is that?" Ever asked looking over Rain's head and pointing to the tall caramel soaked specimen standing outside the front door of the restaurant.

"Oh, that's Kingston, my new bodyguard." Sinclair smiled. "I feel like Whitney Houston," she chuckled.

"Well, that damn sure ain't no Kevin Costner!" Ever squealed as the ladies laughed.

"No he is certainly not," Rain chimed in. "He is a nice guy. I must say, I felt overprotected on our way here. I might have to find me a Kingston."

"Girl, Geoffrey is about his size, your good," Samara replied.

Rain frowned at the sound of Geoffrey's name. Their relationship had taken a true turn for the worse since his birthday debacle. And, she knew it was more because of her than him. She couldn't shake Kevin even though she was doing a good job of leaving him alone. She still missed him. "Let's not talk about Geoffrey tonight, okay?"

The tone in her voice told everyone she meant it and everyone shook their heads in agreement as the waiter returned with Ever and Samara's drinks. Sinclair and Rain quickly ordered their drinks and told the waiter to bring out the restaurants most popular dishes for them to try, but nothing too spicy, Ever added.

"So, Sinclair are you going to tell us about this hunk of a man hovering over you, or am I going to have to go out there and have a conversation with him myself?" Ever asked, never taking his eye off Kingston.

"There really isn't anything to tell," Sinclair replied with a smile. "You all know about Trevor's crazy ass attacking me, and now that Tyreek left for his tour, he talked Kingston, who is really Karma's security, into sticking around here with me to make sure nothing else happens to me."

"Tyreek? I can't believe he would allow someone as sexy as that to stick to you like glue in his absence. Did he bump his head?" Ever asked jokingly.

"I said the same thing when I first seen him," Samara said. "But Sin can tell you that brother is all about his business. No time for fraternizing with his employers."

"That's why I hired him. I am in no mood for dealing with another man at this point. I had enough with Trevor. Not to mention, I can't get rid of Tyreek even if I tried." Sinclair laughed.

"I don't know girlfriend, if I had that around me 24/7 he would have to get it!" Ever quipped, snapping his fingers.

"Shut up, Ever! Aren't you already giving it to somebody?" Samara teased, still slightly jealous that Brian chose Ever over her.

"Please, I am about to kick Brian's down-low ass to the curb. But first, I am going to make an example out of him. A bitch is sick and tired of niggas taking advantage of this good stuff," he said, smacking his rear end.

"What do you mean?" Rain asked with curiosity.

"Should I tell'em Samara?" Ever asked, looking into his confidant's eyes.

"You might as well, cause if you don't you know my ass will," Samara replied.

"Tell us what?" Sinclair and Rain sang in unison.

"I've decided to put these down low imposters on full blast. And what better way than the internet." Ever smiled a devilish grin.

"Please don't talk about that damn internet!" Sinclair exclaimed. "I am still kicking myself for allowing Samara to put my profile on those damn dating sites. I mean, I admit at the time meeting Trevor seemed like harmless play, but mother Rain was right." Sinclair glared over at Rain. "That internet houses some crazy ass people."

They all laughed.

"Well, now you know another crazy ass because my blog site is almost ready. I just need a few more unsuspecting assholes to add in order to get my following rolling, and it's on!" Ever nearly screamed.

"You just be careful, Ever. You know that bitch karma does not discriminate when it comes to what goes around comes around," Sinclair reminded him.

"I got this," Ever assured her. "No one will ever be able to connect me with the site, except for those brothers who will be on there with their asses in the air. But I already know they won't approach me, and well, if they do, I will be ready."

"I hope so," Sinclair said with concern. "I would hate to have to kill somebody."

"I agree," Rain added. "Be careful, Ever."

"So, Samara," Sinclair turned her attention to her office assistant. "Earlier today you said you had to tell us something, what's up?"

Everyone looked at Samara waiting for her to spill her tea.

"What!" she said, placing her hand on the base of her neck like she was clutching her pearls. "I just wanted to let you all know that I am officially off the market."

"You? Off the market? Do I dare ask who had the capability to make that happen," Rain asked.

"Well, you know me. I like to get around so being single has been a benefit, but I met someone and he's pretty special." The glow on Samara's face lit up their table.

"He's a cutie too," Ever added.

"You know him, Ever? How does Ever know him and we don't?" Sinclair asked feeling left out.

"I don't know him, know him," Ever said, "but he is a professor at our school, so I've seen his fine ass around."

"It's not that same professor is it, Samara?" Sinclair asked.

"No, but they know each other: very well as a matter of fact," Samara said, allowing her mind to race back to the recent cookout she attended.

"What do you mean?" Sinclair asked.

"Remember I told you that I had a cookout to go to? Well, it was at my boyfriend's parents' house up in Connecticut. During the entire ride, something in my gut kept telling me to be prepared: For what, I didn't know. That was until we pulled into the driveway and parked behind a BMW that looked identical to Professor Mack's. But I brushed it off, telling myself we are in Connecticut, who the fuck doesn't have a BMW or a Mercedes, right?"

"Right," the gang chimed in.

"So we walk through his parent's place, which was magnificent. He showed me his old bedroom and then we made our way to the massive backyard. The crowd was already pretty thick, so for me all of their faces blended together. But then I looked over by the in-ground pool and there he was staring back at me with a disapproving look on his face."

"Oh no," Rain gasped, "What happened?"

"Next thing I know," Samara continued, "he's walking over to us and Kevin introduces him to me as his sister's fiancée!" Samara shook her head in disgust, glad she ended with the Professor when she did.

"Wait, fiancée?" Sinclair blurted out. "That motherfucker! What a bastard." Sinclair shook her head in disappointment.

Rain's eyes bulged but not because Professor Mack has a fiancée. "Wait a minute, did you also say your boo's name is Kevin?" she asked, suddenly feeling sick to her stomach. She looked over at Sinclair, who returned a questioning stare.

"Can't be," Sinclair said softly.

"Yeah, why?" Samara asked.

Rain sat frozen, quietly questioning herself, wondering if her Kevin is in fact Samara's Kevin. Rain wanted to kick herself for never asking Kevin what his last name was, but what would be the odds, there must be at least fifty thousand Kevins in New York City alone. Yet, something told her it was him. "Excuse me, I have to go to the ladies room. I think this spicy shit is getting to me," Rain said, lifting her body up from the floor and making a beeline exit to the back of the restaurant.

"What's her problem?" Ever asked, watching Rain dart off.

"I have to let her tell you guys," Sinclair said, keeping Rain's infidelity secret. "But she will be fine, Samara finish the story. It was getting good."

Rain stared down at her watered down drink and debated whether or not she wanted a refresher.

"Just go ahead and text him." Dex's voice broke her trance.

"Huh?"

"You heard me," he said, taking another sip of his beer, "Text him. That is the only way you are going to find out if its him or not."

Even though bloodshot, his piercing blue eyes still was able to penetrate through her skin. Dex had become a comfort for Rain and, since her dinner the other night with the girls, a shoulder to lean on. She told Dex everything about Kevin, even how they met, and although she expected Dex to look at her differently, he didn't. Instead, he became more intrigued and more supportive. It was clear that he felt Geoffrey had sealed his own fate by allowing another man to make love to his woman, especially one as fine as Rain. He made it clear to Rain that Geoffrey was a fool and deserved whatever backlash he receives.

"But, what should I say?"

"Just tell him that you need to see him. What you two need to discuss should be face to face," Dex advised in his attorney tone.

"You're right. I have to see him. I can't put it off any longer. I have to know if he and Samara are seeing one another," Rain said as a nauseating feeling mixed in with her bay breeze. She pulled her cell out of her bag and looked over at Dex. "Here's to nothing."

"Or everything." Dex shot back the last swig of his semi warm beer.

******

Rain beamed as she pulled her keys out of her bag to open her door. She was happy she took Dex's advice and texted Kevin. And she was happier that Kevin agreed to meet her. As she slid the key into its keyhole, she played back the conversation in her mind:

Rain: Hi, long time no talk to. Hope you are well.

Kevin: Hi yourself, all is well and you?

Rain: Not so good. I have to see you

Kevin: Kind of busy but I need to see you as well.
Rain: When is a good time for you? Soon I hope.
Kevin: Let me move a few things around, but I am sure I can make it happen soon, and text you in the morning, ok?
Rain: Yes, I will be waiting.

As Rain entered the apartment she was greeted by the inviting aroma of garlic and marinara sauce. It wasn't until that moment that she realized she was hungry and allowed her nose to lead her into the kitchen.

"Here she is! My beautiful future wife to be!" Geoffrey nearly shouted.

"What's the occasion?" Rain asked, looking at the bouquet of flowers sitting in the middle of dining room table.

"I wanted to surprise you with your favorite: my spaghetti, and a night of pampering. I just want you to remember how special I think you are," Geoffrey said, walking over to Rain and gripping her by the waist to lift her up.

"I know," Rain said somberly, wrapping her arms around his neck and looking into his eyes, trying to find that spark she used to see.

"Do you?" he whispered. "Do you really know how much I love you and how I just want us to go back to it being about us."

Rain motioned for him to put her down and she sat down at the table. Her excited mood and her anticipation to see Kevin had been dashed by Geoffrey's need to rekindle a flame that she feared had fizzled out for good. She watched Geoffrey as he poured her a glass of wine and handed it to her. She felt sorry for him: for their relationship.

"Here's to us. Here's to a long future together," he said, clinking her glass and taking a sip from his.

Rain tried to smile and share his moment, but she sensed that he knew she wasn't feeling the same way. "That food smells so good," she said, diverting his attention.

"Ah yes, and its ready," Geoffrey chimed as he rushed over to the stove and made Rain a plate.

******

"You always could make a mean pot of spaghetti," Rain sighed as she lay on her stomach while Geoffrey massaged her bare back.

"I'm happy you enjoyed it. No one would ever guess how much you eat; you only weigh a hundred pounds wet," he teased.

Geoffrey kneaded and rubbed her back until he could hear the faint snoring sound beneath him. Making her fall asleep was not his intention. He slowly leaned in and placed soft kisses on the nape of her neck and down the spine of her back, causing Rain to rustle to his touch.

With her eyes still closed and the thought of Kevin still heavy on her mind, Rain allowed Geoffrey's hands to awaken her innards and she maneuvered her body to meet his tongue, imagining that she was sharing this explosive moment with Kevin instead.

Geoffrey smothered each cheek of her ass with wet kisses before nuzzling his nose deep between her legs and licking her inner thighs as he firmly held on to her hips. He nibbled on her clit from behind with urgency and desperation. He wanted his woman back.

Rain's moans grew louder as her eyes remained closed and she got on her knees to allow him more access to her love.

Geoffrey welcomed the doggy style position and continued to make love to her with his tongue as her moans grew with pleasure.

"Oh my God!" Rain cried, placing her face into the pillow.

Geoffrey became aroused at her praise and furiously devoured her lower region with his mouth. He swallowed her sweet nectar as though his life depended on it.

Rain tried to control herself as the euphoric feeling enveloped her body and she gripped the bed sheets with her sweaty palms. "You make me feel so good, Kevin."

The sound of his name penetrated the room as though it came out of a boom box, causing everything in the room to become still.

"What did you say?" Geoffrey said, coming up for air and wiping his mouth with the back of his hand.

"What do you mean?" Rain asked, trying to sound clueless.

"Don't fucking answer my question with a question; who's name did you just say?" The anger in Geoffrey's eyes seared her skin.

"I...I don't know what I just said. I was in the moment," Rain lied.

"Don't fucking play with me Rain. You just said Kevin's name. You still seeing Kevin?"

"What? No, I haven't seen him since," she paused and they both looked at each other. "Since your birthday," she said, slipping back into her blouse and shuffling to the bathroom.

"Then why the fuck you still saying his name. What's up, Rain?" Geoffrey asked, stomping behind her.

"You started this Geoffrey. I told you from the start that it wouldn't be a good idea to bring someone else into our bedroom, but you just had to see another man fuck me!" Rain shouted as she sat on the toilet. "Now, here you are accusing me of something I said that I am not even sure I said."

"Rain I know what I heard and that is why I find it more unbelievable that nothing more is going on because you only seen that man twice," Geoffrey said, leaning against the sink, looking down at her. "What in the fuck is going on, Rain?"

"I don't know what you are talking about, are you sure you heard right?" she asked, trying to plant the diversion seed.

"Don't try that lawyer shit on me. I'm a master at diversion," Geoffrey said, disgusted with Rain's evasiveness.

Rain looked at Geoffrey as she stood to wash her hands. He moved to the side to give her some space and watched her move along as though nothing ever happened. Geoffrey shook his head and walked over to their bedroom closet and pulled out his duffle bag. He had almost packed it full by the time Rain entered the room.

"What are you doing?" Rain asked, totally confused. "You're leaving because you think I said another man's name?"

"I don't think shit. I know what I heard, and I am no fool. I didn't become one of New York's top criminal attorneys for nothing. My best quality is the ability to tell if someone is lying to me. One thing I know for sure is my intuition, and right now it's screaming at me that you are not telling me the truth. I don't know about what, but until you decide to fess up, I will be Raymond's."

Rain stood motionless as Geoffrey flung the bag strap over his shoulder and headed for the front door. A part of her wanted to stop him, tell him about the short lived affair, and how sorry she was; yet the other part of her wanted him to leave, to avoid her having to tell him to, it was a relief almost.

"Look, I know whatever is going on here started because of me," Geoffrey said as he opened the door. "But somehow I can't believe that it's all because of me, so when you are ready to share, call me."

He allowed the door to slam hard behind him, causing Rain to jump.

Scene Twenty-Two

Samara sat nervously next to Ever in the dark living space of his loft. The glow of his computer monitor shined brightly on their faces as they pieced together the photos and video of Brian and Wayne.

"What do you think Mara? I think it's a good start," Ever asked still moving the images around on the page.

"I think it's good. I just can't believe you're actually going through with this."

"You damn right I am. I think I need some more victims though. Why stop with just these two when there's a world of other men just like them that need this kind of exposure."

"Ever, you know I have your back but are you sure you want to do this," Samara asked concern lacing her tone.

"Yas hunty. It is time for someone to expose all these down low boy pussy hunters and put them on full blast."

Samara stood and walked over to the couch rubbing her stomach as it turned threatening to send her lunch back up to the surface. She plopped down and lay her head back on the soft cushion, still watching Ever work at his masterpiece. He looked like Dr. Frankenstein working on his project.

"I still can't believe you got crystal clear video of Brian busting it wide open, Ever."

"I know," Ever squealed with excitement. Ever pressed play on the video and began doing a celebratory twerk in his seat. "Yasss bitch yassss," Ever chanted. As he turned his chair to face Samara and found her lunch greeting him.

"Oh hell no! Don't get it on my carpet," Ever yelled, trying to avoid getting any on him.

Samara emptied the contents of her stomach onto Ever's hardwood floor and then stretched her body across the couch

"Bitch, no you didn't just blow chunks over watching my video."

"Ever," Samara sighed, "I think I'm pregnant."

"PREGNANT, You?" Ever cupped his mouth and rushed over to her, avoiding the mess all over the floor. "I'll get that up in a minute. Bitch, did I just hear your ass right?"

"Yeah me. This is the second month I missed my period. Its just...," Samara paused not sure of her next sentence.

"Just what bitch? You're about to have a baby. I'm gonna be a god diva!" Ever sang as he rushed to his utility closet and grabbed the mop and bucket. "Bitch you lucky you carrying our baby, or else I would make you clean this smelly shit up!" Ever chuckled as he looked over at Samara and noticed a look of gloom masking her face.

"Why you over there looking like that? Girl, be happy you have Kevin, you two are having a baby. Why look so sad? Don't worry about the throw up, I know you didn't mean to," Ever said holding his nose and wiping up Samara's lunch

Samara rubbed her stomach as tears began streaming down her face.

Oblivious, Ever kept cleaning and talking, "If it's a girl she has to have a fierce name like Milan, London, Paris, or Madison," Ever paused and placed the mop down. "What's wrong Samara? You're scaring me. I've never seen you cry, so spill the T girl," Ever said, sitting on the floor next to her and rubbing her hair back away from her face.

"Ever, I want nothing more than to have Kevin's baby. And I know once I tell him, he's going to be excited too. He's such a good man but, I'm not so sure this is his baby."

Hearing her words out loud caused Samara to cry harder at the thought that her new happy life may become a memory once she tells Kevin the truth.

"So if Kevin isn't the father who is because you haven't been with anyone else besides him, right?" Ever stopped and looked into Samara's eyes. "Don't tell that it could be Professor Mack's baby," Ever said holding his breath for the answer.

"Well, remember not too long ago when I was late meeting you to finish up that project? And, I told you I ran into the Professor at the basketball court? It was more like he ran up in me at the court. And then there was that quickie on his desk when we parted ways. So, yes, it could be his," Samara replied in a soft whisper. She began sobbing uncontrollably as Ever sat her up on the couch and she collapsed in his arms.

"The shade of life, that chemistry between you two is going to get somebody hurt! It's gonna be alright Mara. Whatever you decide to do, I'm here for you and you know Sinclair and Rain will be too. We have your back." Ever held Samara tightly wishing he could take her pain away. He knew how she felt, facing the happiest moment of her life that could possibly be snatched away from her. Samara wept, unsure of how to handle this situation and mad at herself for allowing her alter ego, Sasha to put her in it. For as long as she could remember Sasha had always been the bane of Samara's existence: the side of her that causes trouble and then leaves Samara to pick up the pieces, or suffer the consequences.

Samara took a deep calming breath then wiped her tears.

"Thank you Ever for always being there for me," she said giving him a hug. "Oh, and sorry about making a mess. I can't seem to keep anything down; doesn't matter what time of the day it is. They should call it all day sickness not morning sickness."

They laughed and Ever felt good that his girl was coming around. "It's ok, you're my girl. But next time you feel a little woozy do me a favor: Run your ass to the bathroom," Ever teased, hugging her back.

"It's getting late, I'm going to head home before Kevin sends a search party out for me."

"You gonna be alright," Ever asked with a look of concern.

"I'll be fine. I'm just going home and taking a long bath. I have to decide what I'm going to do and when I'm going to tell Kevin."

"Tell Kevin what?" Ever asked, stopping Samara in her tracks. "Not about the professor."

"Hell no, about the baby. I don't think I can ever tell him about the Professor. That would not only hurt Kevin but his sister Fawn, too. I have to admit, after meeting her at the cookout and seeing how much she loves Professor Mack's cheating, freaky ass, I'm not trying to break any hearts. I can't do that," Samara replied slipping into her jacket.

"Oh okay, a bitch had to make sure now. Call me when you get up in the morning."

"I will love you Ev."

"Love you too, preggo."

Ever sat back down at his computer desk to go over his website one more time. "I can't wait 'til this baby goes live!" he said to himself, before shutting the computer off and settling in for the night.

Scene Twenty-Three

Sinclair stood patiently on the front steps to her brownstone as Kingston made his way through her apartment to make sure all was clear: An act he'd been doing since his detail began. At first Sinclair thought it was overkill, but not hearing from Trevor still had her slightly paranoid, so she welcomed Kingston's over protective attitude.

Sinclair watched the cars pass by and hummed to herself to help the time go by faster, not to mention she had to pee.

"Hey Sinclair," Karen her neighbor shouted from her porch. "I see you have your own personal security system, and he looks way better than these cameras," she chuckled, pointing to the small camera tucked in the upper right hand corner of her front door frame.

Sinclair joined in her humor and nodded her head. "Yes he certainly is."

"That's funny because I thought you had called my security guy because I saw him in the area the other day."

"No, I didn't call him," Sinclair said, slightly puzzled, "Maybe Ms. Goldstein a few doors down called. You know she loves to keep up with the Joneses."

The women both laughed as Kingston approached the front door. "All clear," he said, opening the screen door to allow Sinclair access. "But this was on the floor in the kitchen. Looks like someone slid it under the back door." He handed a large manila envelope to Sinclair.

Sinclair reluctantly took the envelope from his hand and immediately began to think of the other envelope she had recently received. Her heart pounded as she made her way to the living room and sat down on the sofa to open it.

Kingston followed her and sat down next to her. "You okay?"

"I don't want to open it. You do it," she demanded.

Kingston took the envelope from her fragile hands and tore it open with urgency. He pulled out one sheet of paper with a picture with those same set of eyes, the irises colored in with black marker and the letters I.C.U. written underneath. Kingston examined the paper and the envelope and noticed there was no return address or even a postage stamp. It had been hand delivered. "You know what this is about?" he asked Sinclair calmly.

"Huh? Um…no, I mean a few weeks ago I got the same thing, but thought nothing of it," she confessed.

"So you don't have a clue as to who would send this to you? A jilted musician, or lover, even?"

Sinclair tried to suppress the thought of Trevor deep in her subconscious and motioned her head no.

"Are you sure Sinclair? I ask because and I hope you don't mind my frankness, but the other day I reviewed the garage footage from the night of your attack. And, I have to be honest, from what I saw he wasn't a random stranger," Kingston peered over at Sinclair for a reaction. Nothing. "Sinclair it looked personal: Your actions and body language in the footage made it kind of clear that you knew exactly who your attacker was."

Sinclair kept her gaze on the set of eyes on the paper and realized that it must be Trevor sending these cryptic mailings. She contemplated whether or not to let Kingston know the whole truth, but she did trust him.

Kingston sensed her reluctance "Listen Sinclair, if you want me to protect you, you have to be completely honest with me so I know exactly who and what I'm protecting you from. Most importantly, how to protect you. I need to know what I'm up against." The calmness in his voice spoke volumes about his strong character.

Sinclair sighed deeply and stood up to walk over to her bar. "You're going to need one too," she said grabbing two glasses and pouring double shots of Hennessy in each. "And, don't give me that you're on duty crap. If I am going to tell you who he is, I need you to be relaxed and non-judgmental," she said, walking back over to him and handing him a glass.

"I don't judge," Kingston replied, taking the glass and then a sip.

"You haven't heard my story yet." Sinclair sat down next to him to begin her explicit tale of woes.

******

"Wow, damn," Kingston said in shock and awe. He didn't realize that Sinclair was such a freak.

"I know, like I said: Don't judge me," Sinclair blurted out as the Hennessy kicked in causing her head to lean back on the sofa cushion.

"No judgment here, I promise," Kingston said standing up to place his empty glass on the bar. "That was just a lot to take in, that's all. But I'm glad you told me everything. Well, everything but this Trevor guy's last name," he said, pacing the floor back and forth.

Sinclair sat there watching him as if he was a pendulum swinging back and forth to hypnotise her. "I don't know," she said softly, almost dreamlike.

"You don't know his last name," Kingston stopped in his tracks. "You were that sexually involved with that man and you never got his last name,"

"See this is why I didn't want to say anything!" Sinclair stammered and stood up to leave the room.

"No wait!" Kingston grabbed her by the arm and spun her around to face him. "I'm sorry, really. No judgment. I just need to know everything about this guy, so I can make sure he never bothers you again."

They were so close, Sinclair could smell the Hennessy remnants on his breath. "Sorry, I never got his name." She pulled away from his grasped, feeling embarrassed and filled with shame. "I'm going to take a hot shower."

"Sinclair, don't worry. I will find out who this Trevor character is. It will just take some investigating. I'm sorry your upset but it will be okay, I promise." Kingston stood in the middle of the living room floor, watching Sinclair as she disappeared upstairs to her bedroom. He walked over to the coffee table and picked up the piece of paper and stared at the black eyes looking back at him. "What's behind this picture you sick son of a bitch," he whispered into the air.

Scene Twenty-Four

Trevor sat stoically at his mahogany wood desk in his study and sipped on his cognac as he watched Sinclair shuffle over to the bar. He was curious to know who the tall, dark stranger was but came to the revelation quickly that he must be her bodyguard because he'd been spending the night for the past few weeks and not once did they sleep together. "Nothing can keep us apart," Trevor whispered into the drafty room. He was impressed by his newest, more advanced security system he rigged in Sinclair's home the same day he installed her annoying neighbor's. The capability it had to allow him to view in real time impressed him and he loved that he could print still shots in five second intervals. His only regret was that he didn't utilize the audio option. He would have loved to hear what the two of them were talking about right at the moment because it looked juicy. The way the guy grabbed Sinclair by the arm when she tried to walk away was almost theatrical and for a quick moment had Trevor thinking he was watching an old silent movie. And, it intrigued him more when he watched the bodyguard stare at the mail he left for Sinclair. "You'll never figure it out," he said slyly into air of the drafty room.

He diverted his attention back to Sinclair as he watched her make her way up to her bedroom where she disrobed quickly and sauntered her naked body into her adjoining bathroom and turned on the jet shower heads. She slipped into the shower one leg at a time and Trevor started to become aroused at the sight of her sexy, well defined legs. He missed how they use to wrap around his back. Trevor sat back in his plush leather desk chair and unzipped his slacks to release his growing member.

He admired her as she lathered her body up with soap and began to stroke himself slowly. The tiny camera embedded in a tiny hole he created through her attic floor was in the perfect position and allowed him to see her amazing body from every angle. He squeezed his dick harder and stroked himself faster as the beads of water washed the suds away from her body. "Damn, I miss you Baby," he whispered, closing his eyes to imagine being deep inside of her. He continued to make love to his hand as Sinclair cleansed her body.

Trevor was so deep in his self sex session, jacking himself off to the point of eruption, he didn't notice Sinclair staring up at the little hole in the ceiling. A hole that she knew wasn't there before.

Scene Twenty-Five

Samara's mind raced as she pulled her motorcycle into her parking space then made her way to her apartment building's entrance. She wasn't sure how much longer she would be able to hide her pregnancy from Kevin, especially since she decided to keep it. And, even though she was already starting to show, just a smidgen, she still wasn't ready to spill the beans just yet. She walked in the front door and began undressing, leaving a trail of clothes to the bedroom. Kevin was sound asleep with the TV blaring the stats on ESPN. Samara tip toed into the master bathroom and started the shower. She didn't feel up to a long bath after a hard day at work, and weaving in and out of traffic during the drive home. She just wanted to lay down and fall asleep in Kevin's arms. Something she had begun to grow accustom to since he had practically moved in. They had to admit that her place was closer to the campus, but they also knew they couldn't stay away from each other for more than a few hours.

She welcomed the hot water cascading all over her body and she stood still as she allowed the aqua massage to relax her tense muscles. She couldn't help rubbing her growing belly with the loofa sponge in circular motions and smiling from ear to ear. She couldn't believe she was going to be someone's mother. She continued to shower as her spirits began to lift. After slipping into her white lace nightie that felt a little snug, she climbed into bed and nuzzled her small frame under Kevin.

"Hey Baby, did Ever get in touch with you? He called the house not too long ago," a half groggy Kevin asked. "What's up with him? Seems like you two have been hanging out almost every night lately."

"Yeah, I finally texted him. Work was brutal, but I don't want to talk about Ever or work. I just want to enjoy this moment right now," Samara cooed as Kevin wrapped his arm around her and pulled her in close.

"What's this," he asked rubbing the small pouch beginning to form in Samara's lower belly, noticing her once tight and flat tummy wasn't so flat anymore.

"Looks like these late nights hanging with Ever and snacking on God knows what is starting to show," Kevin joked as he sat up and looked down at Samara.

Samara tried to laugh but realized that this was the moment to come clean. She hoped he wouldn't run in the opposite direction, like her daddy did. "I wish it was because of that," she said somberly, killing his jovial mood.

"What do you mean?" Kevin asked completely oblivious. He rubbed her belly again and looked into Samara's eyes. "Is this what I think it is?" he whispered, staring at her belly.

"Depends on what you think it may be," Samara said nervously feeling vulnerable to his touch.

"Are you? Are we having a baby?" excitement filled Kevin's voice.

His overjoyed reaction to the possibility caused Samara to smile. "If I said yes would you be okay with that?"

"Baby, I'd be more than okay with that," Kevin replied, bending over and kissing her belly.

"Then yes: We're having a baby," she said softly as she gently rubbed his head as he continued to kiss her stomach.

"Why didn't you tell me? This is the second best news of the day," he said, lifting his head and leaning in to kiss Samara.

"I wanted to make sure I was so I took a home pregnancy test at Ever's earlier. Well, he made me take two to be sure. And, I am pretty sure." She smiled. "But you said this was the second best news. What was the first bit of good news you got?"

"I'm going to be an uncle. My sister and Larry are pregnant too!"

Samara's smile quickly turned to a frown as she sat up against the headboard and damn near choked on her own spit hearing that news. "That's wonderful. I'm so happy for them," she lied while trying to hide the feeling a dread.

"I'm going to be a daddy and an uncle. Thank you Baby, you truly are making me the happiest and luckiest man alive." He kissed her on the mouth and jumped out of bed. "Maybe, we can meet up with Larry and Fawn to celebrate." Kevin darted over to the bathroom to pee, leaving the door open.

The last thing Samara wanted to do was sit and eat with Professor Mack and his pregnant fiancée, especially since she didn't know if he was in fact the father of her baby too. A nauseating feeling filled her gut. "That sounds good," she belted out.

"Good," Kevin said stepping back into her tiny bedroom. "I will ask him at school tomorrow. And, before I forget, can you go by the dry cleaners for me tomorrow before you go to work. They called and I have some suits that have been there for a minute. I would go but I have a meeting I have to attend."

"Sure Baby, everything okay?"

"Everything is fine, Baby. I just have to wrap up some loose ends," Kevin said, kissing Samara's belly, hoping Rain will allow what they briefly had to end amicably. "I can't believe I'm going to be a daddy and an uncle." He gazed at her belly and then into Samara's eyes with a wide grin on his face.

Samara returned a loving smile and as the feeling of guilt rushed through her veins she thought, *yeah, or maybe just an uncle.*

The Starbucks on the corner of West 71st Street was bustling with patrons getting their morning fix to get their day started. Rain sat as patiently as she could as she stared at the front door anxiously waiting for Kevin to come through it. She was able to find a table for two in the back corner: a place where the two of them can go undisturbed. She wasn't used to seeing him so early in the day. Their rendezvous normally took place in the evening or night hours, although there was a time or two that they had each other for lunch. Their short lived affair was cemented in her mind. And now with her world quickly unravelling, she hoped that this meeting with Kevin would be at least uplifting. Rain sipped on her Chai latte as she watched customers come and go; it wasn't until Kevin approached her that she even noticed he had arrived.

"Oh, hi," she said, slightly taken aback by his handsomeness. She missed him.

"Hi yourself," he replied before leaning down to peck her cheek and then taking the seat across from her.

"You want something to drink, to eat?" Rain asked, staring into his eyes, still feeling that spark.

"No, actually I only have a few minutes. I have to get to work," he stated. "So, what's up?"

Rain tried to maintain her composure. She didn't know where to start and she certainly didn't want what the two of them had to end. She gazed at his face before speaking. She tried to read him but the glow bouncing off his face told her that this man was happy and content on how he left things the night he walked out of that hotel room door. Rain tried to form a smile to fight back the tears.

"Well, first I guess I should tell you that Geoffrey moved out the other day."

"What, moved out? I'm sorry to hear that Rain, really. I hope it wasn't because of what went on between the three of us."

"Sort of," she confessed. "It was more my fault than anyone else's. I guess I am still not over you: what we had, just the two of us."

Kevin sighed deeply and leaned back in his chair. He felt bad for Rain and felt worse that he contributed to the demise of her relationship with Geoffrey. He should have seen that coming when Geoffrey approached him in the gym with such an awkward request. He was mad at himself for allowing his dick to speak for him that day. "I'm sorry Rain," he said sorrowfully.

"You don't have to apologize. I just wanted to know where we were. You and me." She sat patiently waiting for an answer.

"You and me?"

"Yeah. When you left that night, I knew then that the three of us would never see each other again, but you kinda left the door open with us."

"Actually Rain," he paused but could not hide the smile that was forming on his face. The thought of him becoming a father filled him with elation. Nothing could stifle his happiness. "I am exclusive with someone right now."

The deflated look on her face caused him to reach out to her and place his hand over hers. "I'm sorry."

Rain pulled her hand back, unsure of how to react: should she be happy for him, should she be angry at him for starting a hot and steamy affair with her. "Really? Well, if you are so involved, why did you come to my office that day with the flowers? Why did you make me feel like you wanted me?"

"Because I did want you and at that time I was only dating, but since then things between me and my lady has gotten pretty serious. I'm sorry Rain, I didn't know I was going to fall in love with her."

His words made it clear that what they shared wasn't love and although she realized the two of them could never become an actual couple, Rain began to feel used. "You're in love?" The feeling of hurt came through her voice. She resented him for having something that she no longer did. "Can I ask you her name?" She prayed his lips wouldn't form Samara's name.

"You don't need to know her name Rain. Just know that I love her. In fact, last night she told me that we are having a baby," he said joyfully as he watched Rain's grimaced face that conveyed both hurt and rejection. "Rain, I am truly sorry that things turned out the way they did with you and my man. That was never my intention: even when we started our own thing behind his back. I wasn't thinking. I'm sorry." He couldn't stop apologizing.

"I don't need your apologies Kevin," Rain said as the hurt began to form into anger from being rejected. "Pregnant?" she wanted to make sure she heard him correctly.

"Yes, I am going to be a father and that means all of my philandering ways must end, but I really want to make sure you and I can at least still be friends." He grabbed her hand again and this time held it tightly. "I really don't want any animosity between us Rain."

Rain allowed him to hold onto her, if only for a few moments more. A wave of relief rushed through her body as she rationalized in her head that this woman he is so in love with couldn't be Samara because Samara isn't pregnant. She surely would have told the posse that kind of news. Rain sighed deeply before speaking. "Look Kevin, the reality is I knew that eventually what we had going on would have to end because it was wrong from the start, but it still makes me sad. We had chemistry, you know?" She looked into his eyes and tried to form a smile. "But I want you to be happy and you look happy. A girl can't ask for more than that, right?"

"Thank you, Rain, but it makes me sad that you are no longer with Geoffrey. I can't help but to think the break-up is because of me," Kevin confessed.

"Stop it!" she snapped, "Geoffrey and I are over because of us. I'm okay and you and I are good."

"You mean it?" he asked unsure of her genuineness.

"Absolutely, promise," she replied, trying to muster up a sincere smile as her heart sank to the soles of her feet.

"I wish you only the best Rain, and to be honest, you deserve better. Any man willing to allow you to do the things you did with me, in front of him no less, doesn't deserve such a good woman."

Kevin smiled before standing up from his seat and leaning down to kiss her forehead. "You take care of yourself."

Rain softened from the sensation his lips created and tried to smile despite the demise of their steamy affair. "You take care too," she mustered.

As she stared at Kevin making his departure not only from their quick morning meeting, but from her life, Rain didn't notice Geoffrey's partner Raymond watching the scenario play out before his very own eyes as he sipped on his morning cup of joe seated at a table for two in a little nook in the back corner of the coffee shop.

Toy's patience began to run thin as she sat in the bumper to bumper midtown lunch hour traffic. She was beginning to rethink her surprise visit to Wayne to take him out to lunch, and thought about making a beeline exit back home, when her cellphone blared through her car speakers interrupting her thoughts. She looked at the name on the display and quickly hit the talk button on her steering wheel to connect her blue tooth.

"Hi Art, how are you?"

"Hello Mrs. Saunders, I'm good. How are you?" Arts raspy voice questioned.

"I'm sorry I haven't gotten back to you. I've been really busy with the twins and needed to get my head together after the last time we met. I did get the address and name of the shoe store for you. If you can hold on a moment I can get them for you," she said reaching over to unlock her glove compartment and removing the slip of paper. Her hand shook slightly as she read the information to Art.

"Alright that should do it, and if I am not mistaken this is the same place where I spotted him picking up that young man you're familiar with. Oh, by the way, I'm still tailing him but he's been on the up and up, so we will fall back. In the meantime, I'm going to try tailing that fella from the pictures and see if I can find out what connection he has with the mystery women."

Toy sat silently for a moment, trying to make sense of Wayne picking up that gay man from the shoe store, but she quickly surmised that he was the link to Wayne's mistress and decided to let Art do his job. "Sounds good Art, and again, I apologize for my delay."

"No worries, I'm used to this. Wives and girlfriends often want to know what their spouse or significant other is up to, then once they start finding out they disappear. Sometimes it's to gather their thoughts, sometimes it's for good," Art said nonchalantly.

"Well, I need to know so you don't have to worry about me disappearing. I'm actually glad you called. It just convinced me to keep going with my plans to surprise Wayne for lunch. I will see if he's acting suspicious in any way."

"Whatever you do don't let on about any of this," Art said in an unsure tone.

"I won't. I just figured if I start acting as though I'm beginning to forgive him he may relax back into whatever he was doing. And with you saying he's been on the up and up that just makes me feel like he is still hiding something. I need him to slip up, Art," Toy said with an air of desperation.

"I agree with you. If he gets comfortable he may just give us something to work with. Make him as comfortable as you can without raising suspicion. Remember he's a cop and maybe a bit apprehensive at first. No matter what just keep your cool, understand," Art asked sternly.

"He may be a cop but he's my husband. I can handle him," Toy confidentiality said assuring Art she had it under control.

"Alright then Mrs. Saunders, we'll be in touch."

Toy hung up feeling more determined about her mission as she continued on her route towards Wayne's precinct. Wayne made mention that he had desk duty for the day when they spoke that morning. She just hoped after battling the traffic she would be able to catch him before he headed out on his own.

****

After parking and fixing her hair and makeup, Toy made her way into the busy precinct. She took a deep breath then put on a smile as she made her way inside. As she reached the top step that opened up to the lobby, she noticed Wayne coming to the front desk seemingly sharing a joke with the other officers.

"Hey honey," Toy said interrupting the guys' humorous moment.

"Hey Baby, what are you doing here," Wayne said in complete shock.

"I was in the area and decided to pop in. Want to grab a bit to eat? There's a little deli not too far from here that I hear makes a great sandwich."

Wayne looked up at the clock and realized it was lunch time. "You should've called me and told me you were coming. Fellas you remember my wife, Toy," Wayne said giving an informal greeting. They all greeted her then continued their conversation without Wayne.

"Let me grab my jacket. I'll be right back," Wayne said heading for the locker room.

As he slipped on his jacket suspicion crept into his psyche, *So, she just so happened to be in the area at lunch time, on the day I'm on desk duty? She's been giving me the cold shoulder lately, and now she's perky and acting normal. Either something is up or she has truly moved past the incident. I'm not sure which one so I'm just going to play it cool.* Wayne slipped into police officer mode: a place where he could wear his calm poker face while he tried to piece together Toy's hidden agenda.

Toy sat on the hard wooden bench waiting for Wayne to come out trying to act as normal as possible. She couldn't stop thinking about Wayne's connection to the shoe store guy.

"You ready," he asked leaning down and kissing her on the cheek.

"I'm starving lets go," she replied, standing to her feet and interlocking her arm with his. They hopped in her car and headed towards the deli. While in the car Wayne began to relax in the moment, as Toy put on her best performance of the forgiving wife. He was almost totally convinced they were on the path of reconciliation until Toy pulled into the parking lot of Bergs Kosher Deli. Wayne almost shit his paints. He knew this was where Ever and his friends met once a week. He silently prayed today wasn't that day.

"The sandwiches here aren't really all that great," Wayne lied trying to get Toy to change her mind.

"Maybe it was whatever sandwich you had, because I heard nothing but good things about this little spot right here. So come on," Toy said exiting the car and heading inside.

Wayne took a deep breath and prayed to the gods that Ever and his crew weren't inside. He slowly eased out of the car and reluctantly followed Toy inside praying like hell this wasn't some kind of set up.

"Thanks again girlfriend for letting me crash here for a while. I thought about staying at a hotel but with that nut case running about, I can't risk it," Sinclair huffed as she threw her suitcase on top of the bed in Rain's guest room.

"My pleasure," Rain sighed. "I can use the company. It's really quiet around here now that Geoffrey is gone." A frown formed on her face.

"I still can't believe that shit!" Sinclair snapped as they both made their way back into the kitchen. "You have to tell me what really happened Rain."

"To be honest, I really don't know. Well, that's not totally true," Rain huffed. "Ok, so Geoffrey's been staying at his partner Raymond's lately, you know, to give us some space. In the meantime, I met up with Kevin the other morning, just to finalize that affair face to face. And, although my heart melted as soon as he walked into Starbucks, I could see it in his beaming face that he was good with not seeing me anymore. You know, I could tell that he wasn't missing me," she said sadly.

"Rain, don't go there. You said yourself that the affair would have to end, right?"

"Yeah but you know me, I wanted to end on my terms. Anyway, he sits down and proceeds to tell me that he's in love and this woman is having his baby."

"What! A baby? Damn, he moves fast, but knowing that means he's not the same Kevin that Samara is seeing because she's not pregnant," Sinclair said before taking a long pause. "Is she?"

Sinclair glared over at Rain and sipped on the glass of wine that Rain had just poured her. "She would have told us, right?"

"She certainly would have told you. You're her boss, her confidant," Rain quipped with a slight air of jealousy.

"Well, since she and Ever started school the two of them have been like frick and frack. He'd know before me, and he is your boy. He didn't say anything to you?"

"Haven't spoken to him," Rain said, taking a sip. "But when we last seen Samara she didn't look preggers. I am sure he is seeing someone we don't know. There are just too many Kevins in the world for him to be the same damn one, right?"

Sinclair shook her head, "I damn sure hope so." She stood up to refill her glass and then sat back down next to Rain. "What happened next Rain, you take forever to tell a story." She chuckled.

"Well apparently, while Kevin was ending our extraordinary sex play, Geoffrey's partner Raymond had a morning meeting at the same Starbucks, what are the odds right? And, so Raymond watched the whole meeting play out. And, I guess from afar one would think we were being intimate. I don't know what he told Geoffrey, but I do know that by the time I got home from work that day Geoffrey had swung by and removed almost all of his shit, and left me this note," Rain said, handing Sinclair a small piece of paper.

Rain,

It's unfortunate that I had to find out about you and Kevin from Raymond, yes Raymond. He seen you two canoodling this morning. I felt it in my gut on my birthday and what he witnessed just confirmed my thoughts. I would not even have known it was him, but when Raymond described him, I immediately knew who it was. It doesn't bother me that he betrayed me, I expect that from any man, but I never thought you'd do this to me Rain. Yet, my mother once told me that you keep 'em how you get 'em, and the way I got you was wrong from the start. Karma really is real. I will come back for the rest of my things soon, but I want you to know that I love you and I will always love you. And, I know I opened Pandora's Box but I never thought you'd explore it without me. I guess I was wrong.

Geoffrey

Sinclair slowing sipped her wine as she read the letter word for word, soaking it all in. She never liked Geoffrey, but she never liked to see anyone with a broken heart. "Wow Rain. I can't believe this is the way he left. Don't you think you two should sit down and talk?"

"No, not really," Rain sighed. "Believe it or not, Sin, I am alright. To be totally honest, I haven't felt the same way for Geoffrey ever since we allowed Kevin into our bedroom the first time. And, now for him to walk away, which is something that I told him he would do. It just confirms that we weren't right for each other. I know we will have to talk at some point but right now, I'm good. Not to mention, I am still feeling Kevin."

Sinclair shot a look at her.

"I know, I know. I am not going to break up his little happy family, but now that I am single again, I have made a personal vow not to mess with men who are in any kind of relationship. Bad karma is a bitch," she stated.

"I hear you, but whatever you do, don't start that online dating shit. I have learned my lesson," Sinclair replied, shaking her head back and forth. "Trevor has made it impossible for any other online man to ever meet me, let alone date me!" she laughed.

"Yes, let's switch gears here. What did he do now? Did Kingston have to kill him?" Rain joked.

"Not yet!" Sinclair snapped. "But after finding a hidden camera in my shower, I think he will as soon as he finds out where Trevor is."

"Wait, camera? Sin, what in the hell are you talking about?"

"That is why I am here. The other night, my ass is in the shower minding my own damn business and I look up and there is was Rain: A little hole in my ceiling. A hole that was never there before. So I get out and I call Kingston to my bathroom. You know he's been sleeping on my couch. He comes up stairs and immediately tells me to get dressed. I do as I am told and within minutes he has me in the car driving me to the nearest hotel. It wasn't until we were in the hotel room that he explained to me what that hole was and that he had to comb through my place to see if there were anymore."

"Scary shit," Rain blurted out. "But how do you think the camera got there?"

"At first, I wasn't sure, but then it hit me. My next door neighbor told me she recently had a new security system installed. I think it was Trevor who installed it but her ass is away on a family vacation, so we have to wait for her to get back. Until then Kingston wanted me to be someplace where Trevor would not look for me."

"Are you sure he won't find you here?" Rain asked, now concerned for her own safety.

"I am not sure of anything that crazy mutherfucker would do, but Kingston is outside staking out the perimeters. Knowing him he will sleep in his car. I have to say he takes his job very seriously."

A wave of relief enveloped Rain's body and released a heavy sigh. "Oh, good. I am sorry Sin that you are going through this. Makes me give some thought to rekindling with Geoffrey," she teased.

"Yeah right, I know you Rain. When you are done with someone, you are done."

"This is true; onto the next chapter of my life. And, this time I just might look for someone who doesn't look like Geoffrey or Kevin," she said with a grin as the thought of Dex's face filled her mind.

Scene Twenty-Nine

Samara shifted in her sit, trying to keep her cool as Professor Mack and Fawn made their way across the crowed tiny restaurant to their table. They all agreed to meet at Amy Ruth's in Harlem to grab some soul food. Samara loved their *Ludicris* dinner; she could use some fried chicken, mac and cheese, and collard greens with a half lemonade half iced tea to wash it all down. But at this moment all she could think of was jumping up and hauling ass. Kevin and Samara stood to greet them as the waitress placed two more menus on the table. Fawn hugged Samara sending a surge of guilt and nausea through Samara's body. She didn't know if she could look Fawn in the face all night knowing she was carrying such a heavy secret. Yet, she tried to put on a happy face and avoided eye contract with the Professor. The two women complimented one another as the men greeted one another as they all sat down. When Professor Mack turned his attention to Samara, she could feel a wave of heat come over her. Even now, Professor Mack had the power to beckon Sasha with just a look.

"He smells so good," Sasha whispered to Samara, as she began to bubble to the surface. Samara fought mentally to suppress Sasha back into whatever dark corner she had been hiding in. *Not now, go away!* Samara demanded before excusing herself to the restroom.

Samara rushed through the door quickly locking it behind her. She stood there staring at herself in the mirror before dabbing water on her cheeks and forehead. "Get it together," Samara whispered to herself as she fixed her hair. As she stared at herself as she applied her lip gloss, her image changed in the mirror.

"Not going to happen!" the reflection shot back at her causing Samara to jump back in horror. Samara slowly looked at Samara up and down as Samara stood in shock, not believing her eyes.

"I won't be lying in wait much longer, Samara. I will come back out!" the image in the mirror disappeared as Samara's horrified expression looked back at her. Samara touched the mirror not sure what to believe as the knock on the door interrupted her.

"Is everything alright Samara," Fawn's voice snapped Samara out of her shock.

"I'm fine thanks. I'll be out in a moment," Samara replied, pulling herself together.

"Ok, we're waiting on you to order," Fawn said before her footsteps faded off as she headed back to the table.

Samara exited the restroom and walked back over to the table, the feeling of nausea becoming stronger with each step.

"I was getting a little worried about you, Baby. Everything alright," Kevin asked with concern as he pulled Samara's chair out for her.

"I'm fine, Baby," Samara said, looking up at Kevin lovingly and placing her hand on top of his.

Kevin leaned down and kiss Samara on the forehead before taking his seat next to hers. Professor Mack squirmed in his chair fighting back his jealously as he watched the two love birds. He caught himself shooting daggers across the table at Kevin as he watch Samara swoon over him. Part of him wished he had the nerve to leave Fawn and be with Samara when he had the chance. He missed how she made him feel alive. Being with Samara was like being with two different women. One moment they could be having an intelligent conversation, and the next, she was a sex vixen, full of passion and heat. He knew Kevin was getting the best of both worlds with Samara. He didn't realize how much he truly felt for her until he saw her with Kevin at that cook out, but by then it was too late. He knew that Kevin didn't bring a woman home to meet his parents unless he was really feeling her.

The waitress returned, placing drinks and cornbread baskets on the table. The waitress took everyone's order then left the couples to talk.

"So, Kevin what is the good news you wanted to share with us," professor Mack asked.

"Well Larry, I wanted to share our good news with you and my sister before anyone else. Being that we are now in the same position," Kevin beamed, wrapping his arm around Samara.

"OH MY GOD! You're getting married," Fawn blurted out in excitement.

"No we're not getting married. You want to tell them or shall I," Samara giggled.

"We're having a baby too!" Kevin's excitement and news caused Professor Mack to send his wine spewing across the table.

"You alright over there?" Kevin asked laughing as he handed the Professor more napkins.

Samara didn't find it funny, she knew there would be some kind of reaction. But wasn't expecting that.

"I just wasn't expecting that. Forgive me," Professor Mack said wiping him chin. "Congratulations you two. I'm truly happy for you both," he lied.

"This is so exciting," Fawn cooed, "Wait until we tell mom and dad. Just think, cousins being born around the same time. When are you due?" Fawn asked Samara.

"I'm not sure yet. I have to find a doctor and make an appointment. I just took two home pregnancy tests," Samara said taking a long sip of her drink wishing it had alcohol in it.

Fawn looked down in her purse and pulled out a card. "Here's the number to my ob/gyn. They will take great care of you."

Samara thanked her, taking the card a sliding it in her purse.

Professor Mack was still sitting in shock, his eyes diverting between the both of them like a disapproving father. Professor Mack excused himself and retreated to the restroom.

When he returned the food was being placed on the table. He managed to keep his composure through the rest of dinner. The conversations were light and because of Kevin and Fawn taking over the conversation of them becoming both parents and an aunt and an uncle at the same time, neither of them noticed the awkwardness happening on the other end of the table.

They finished dinner and exited the restaurant. Kevin and Samara walked the Professor and Fawn to their car. This time, Professor Mack hugged Samara and whispered in her ear, "We need to talk." He looked at her as they ended their embrace and the look in her eyes showed him she agreed.

Fawn hugged Samara tightly and welcomed her into the family before getting in the car and driving off.

Samara and Kevin walked arm and arm to his car, chatting about the night's events: Both of them holding secrets that could destroy the happiness they both felt.

Scene Thirty

Sully's Tavern was packed to the brim as a multitude of officers gathered to celebrate the retirement of one of their decorated brothers in blue. Wayne sat on his usual corner stool tossing back his sixth Corona enjoying the party and celebrating his own personal victory. With Toy and their family life getting back on the right path, he felt an ease and calm wash over him with each day that passed. As far as he was concerned, his secret was safe. He could now try to clean up the mess he made with Ever. He knew that he and Ever had to stay away from each other but the thought of their last encounter in Central Park caused his dick to stand a salute Ever's hand and oral skills.

"Hey Steve, how about another double shot of Jack Daniels," Wayne shouted above the crowd.

The bartender retuned with Wayne's drinks as Wayne pulled out his cellphone.

Wayne: Hey You

Wayne typed and held his breath, hoping for a warm response from Ever.

****

Not far from his apartment, Ever sat on the cushioned bar stool at *The Midnight Owl*, making subtle passes at the bartender who was serving him very strong Patron margaritas. He and Ever were sharing an unspoken conversation: one he would regret once Ever was done with him. Ever reached for a napkin with the intentions to jot his phone number down when the vibrating in his pocket interrupted him. He pulled the phone out and almost dropped it when he saw Wayne's text across his home screen.

"Damn, does the muthafucka have GPS tracking on my ass or something," he hissed under his breath before unlocking the phone. He sat and stared at it for a moment, unsure of whether or not to reply. Ever thought back to the photos he took of Wayne and thought, *why not get his ass on video, too.*

Ever: Hey back at you stranger

Wayne sat staring at his phone and was just about to give up when Ever's text popped up on his screen. Wayne slung his shot back before replying.

Wayne: It's been a minute since the park. Missing you. Meet for drinks or whatever.

Ever tapped his finger on the bar top, contemplating his next sentence then summoned the bartender over and asked for a pen. Ever jotted his phone number down and slid it to the bartender along with a tip. The bartender opened the napkin then looked at Ever, giving him a nod and a smirk. Ever held his glass up to toast then downed the rest of his margarita. He picked his phone back up then headed out the door. Ever stood curbside hailing a cab and replied to Wayne.

Ever: meet me at my place in about an hour.

Ever slipped into his cab, beaming from ear to ear knowing Wayne would soon have a feature video on his website. "Make a left three blocks up, I'm not far from here."

Wayne smiled as he read Ever's text and slid off his barstool. "I'm out everyone! Joe, best wishes with the retirement. Find something useful to do," he teased as he hugged his brethren before sliding out the front door. He walked with a slight lean over to his pick-up, hopped in and sped off into the distance, unaware of the extra set of eyes on him.

Art started his ignition and followed closely behind Wayne as he made his way downtown. "Give me something," Art said, lighting another of many cigarettes.

Scene Thirty-One

Sinclair walked through the front door of her brownstone with mixed emotions. Part of her was happy to be in the confines of her own home, but the other side felt naked and violated knowing her privacy had been invaded.

"We've combed through the whole house and found a total of twelve cameras. Had you not noticed the one in your bathroom ceiling, we would've never found the others," Kingston said as he closed the door behind him.

"I can't believe this shit. How the hell did he get in my house in the first place," Sinclair asked as shock and disbelief masked her face.

"We're still trying to figure that out. It's clear we aren't dealing with someone who's wrapped to tight. He's done this before."

"So were you able to find him," fear lacing Sinclair's tone.

"Unfortunately, the information you gave me lead us to a dead end. I don't think Trevor is his real name. But we will keep looking, don't worry he will be found. As soon as your neighbor returns we won't have any problems getting to him," Kingston confidently said, putting Sinclair's mind at ease.

"Thank God Tyreek is coming tonight. I really need him right now. Will you be staying too?"

"I think you'll be fine with Tyreek here. I have more research to do on this guy. In the meantime, I think you may want to come clean with Tyreek and let him know about this guy. I know you may not want to hear that, but unfortunately, it doesn't look like this guy is going to just go away."

The seriousness in Kingston's tone sent a chill up Sinclair's spine. She wasn't ready to tell Tyreek out of shame and fear of losing him. How could she explain that she met some random guy on the Internet and allowed him to do things with her and to her that she hadn't even allowed Tyreek to do to her. Her heart felt like it was breaking from the thought of what the outcome of her honesty could be.

Kingston place his hand on her shoulder, "It will be fine. Sure he'll be mad at first but that man loves you. I'm sure you two will work this out. And, if not, then you know what you have to do."

Sinclair looked up at Kingston with tears in her eyes, "I'm not ready to face that just yet. Please, I need you to find Trevor or whatever his name is."

"I will do my best," Kingston said, releasing her shoulder and sitting on the couch.

Sinclair pulled herself and her thoughts together before grabbing her bag to head up stairs to her bedroom. Before she could reach the first step, the front door opened and Tyreek was standing there. The look of disgust in his face caused Sinclair to freeze where she stood. She wasn't sure how long he was outside the front door, or how much he had heard. She looked over at Kingston, who had a look of complete shock across his face. It was clear he was thinking the same thing.

"Baby, your back," she said half excited.

"Yeah, and what a welcome back it is," he said, shaking his head in disgust.

"Baby I can explain," Sinclair said, dropping her bag and rushing over to Tyreek.

"Explain what. I already cursed Samara's ass out," Tyreek tossed his bags to the floor.

"It's not her fault either it's," Sinclair still tried to explain.

Tyreek stopped her in mid-sentence, placing his finger over her lips.

Kingston stood ready for whichever way this played out.

"I know that's your friend, so you don't have to cover for her. Besides isn't it her job to make sure the fucking car is at the airport on time. I mean, shit how many times has she done this before? How the fuck does she forget to confirm."

A wave of relief settled over the room once Kingston and Sinclair realized he hadn't heard any of their conversation.

"Fuck that. All that matters is that I'm here now," Tyreek said, kissing Sinclair's forehead and wrapping his arms around her.

"Kingston, my man, what's good. How was everything on the home front?"

"Everything was quiet for the most part," he lied looking at Sinclair.

Sinclair sunk into Tyreek's embrace trying to hide like a chastised child.

"Well, since you're here now," Kingston continued, "I'm going to head out. I have a pressing matter that just came up before I go heck on Karma," Kingston said, buttoning his sports jacket and heading for the door.

"Ayo man, thanks for looking after Sin for me. Drinks on me tomorrow night," Tyreek said, giving Kingston a pound.

Kingston nodded then headed out the door.

"Now, back to you beautiful," he said wiping a strand of hair out of Sinclair's face. "I missed the hell outta your ass," he said, palming her round supple backside.

"Oh yeah? Prove it," Sinclair said through lust filled eyes.

Tyreek scoop Sinclair up and headed towards the stairs when he noticed her bag.

"What's that doing out," he asked looking puzzled.

"I stayed at Rain's house for a few nights. She and Geoffrey broke up and she didn't want to be alone," Sinclair lied, leaning in and kissing him.

"Well, I don't want to be alone either. You gonna take care of me?" he said playfully as they reached the top of the staircase.

"Of course Daddy. You know mama always takes care of you."

Tyreek laid Sinclair down across the bed, slowly removing her clothes until she was completely naked. He kissed down her neck to her chest, stopping to take each breast one at a time in his mouth. He kissed and licked small circles down to her navel, as he eased two finger inside of her, until he felt her warm, wet juices seep from her forbidden fruit. Sinclair let out soft muffled moans as Tyreek's warm tongue massaged her clit. She gripped the back of his head slowly rolling on his face into her love. "Right there baby, don't stop," she whispered lost in the horizon of an orgasm.

Tyreek did as she commanded until she erupted her passion all over his chin and fingers. Tyreek stood and undressed himself while Sinclair laid there playing in her juices and licking it off her fingers.

"Come let me suck that for you," she beckoned.

"I want you to feel me inside of that warm pussy, first," Tyreek said as he crawled on top of Sinclair and entered her slowly.

Sinclair gasped as his girth stretched her flower open and pushed her walls back.

"Go slow Baby, make love to me," she said, nibbling on his ear.

Tyreek stroked her insides as she opened wider for him, pushing his ass down for him to go deeper inside of her. They both moaned in between kisses as they sunk deeper into the moment. The whispers of passion echoed through the air and into the ears of Trevor's watchful eye as he lurked behind Sinclair's designer dresses in her bedroom closet.

www.ingramcontent.com/pod-product-compliance
Lightning Source LLC
Chambersburg PA
CBHW071005280626
47160CB00015B/1400